Magic to Memphis

Magic to Memphis

What if your life is working from the inside out?

A NOVEL

JULIE STARR

RUFFDOGBOOKS
CHELTENHAM, UK

Published by Ruffdogbooks
Cheltenham, UK
ruffdogbooks.com

Published simultaneously in
The United States and United Kingdom.

This is a work of fiction. As in all fiction, literary
views and insights are based on experience; all names,
characters, places and incidents are either products of the
author's imagination, or are used fictitiously.

Paperback: 978-0-9930237-1-2
Ebook: 978-0-9930237-0-5

Text and Cover by Bookwrights.
Printed in The United States and Great Britain.
Cover background art © hitdelight / Dollar Photo Club

For Liam, definitely.

Part One: Escape from Dorma

One

The package sat on the kitchen counter where Jessie had dumped it three days ago. In the trailer's early morning gloom, DHL's yellow and red wrapper glowed faintly. Next to the package, dirty dishes sat alongside takeout cartons and empty dog food cans. Jessie scowled at the package once more and decided again not to open it. It had traveled across two states, but she figured it could stay where it was a while longer. If this was a battle of wills, she was still winning.

As Bear shuffled toward her, his claws tapped on the linoleum floor. The brown and white pit bull was wearing his permanent frown; one look fits all.

"Hey big fella," she said, and knelt to rub his cropped ears. Bear was fifty pounds of pure ugly, a fighting dog that was retired before his first bout. Jessie knew that living in a rented trailer next to a dumpster was just fine with Bear. On the floor, heaps of clothing stretched in different directions; she kicked through one pile and pulled out some combat pants. The pants got teamed with a bullet belt, a torn vest, and work boots that she'd sprayed purple. She spiked her short hair and applied heavy makeup she knew made her look older. At seventeen, she could do without the hassle of people asking her age.

Breakfast was cereal for two and Jessie chewed slowly, eyeing the package. She hadn't heard from her mom in almost a year but then again, her mom's drinking made her unpredictable sometimes. Whatever was in the package, it wasn't baked goods, a letter of forgiveness and an invite back to Kansas. Since it arrived, Jessie hadn't been able to pick up her guitar, and around her, half-finished song sheets lay waiting. *This thing's a jinx*, she thought. She needed to dump it or open it. *Maybe I'll open it and then dump it.*

A label with her mother's spidery scrawl was taped over the original, and Jessie wondered if her mom had gotten into recycling before remembering that to recycle you actually had to give a shit. She tore the wrapping off to reveal a cigar box, its surface faded and yellowed with age. Her mother had treasured this box; Jessie and her sister used to watch her with it. Not that she or Mary had ever been allowed near the box; anything to do with her father was off-limits, especially conversation. A hollow feeling crept into Jessie's stomach, but there was no way she'd let herself cry.

Inside the box she found photos, postcards, and yellowed newspaper clippings about her father and his band. She touched everything gently, hesitant to read anything properly. Maybe he'd gotten married and had another family, or maybe he'd died or something. However, everything dated back to when he'd been together with Jessie's mom. In the photos, her dad looked youthful and stocky, and his lopsided grin felt familiar. *He looks a bit like me*, she thought.

A child's bracelet lay under the photos, its marbled blue beads threaded with silver. There was also a heavy gold ring, with a vivid-green emerald and carved symbols at its edges. She rolled the ring around her palm and whistled softly. There must be something special about it to have stopped her mother pawning it for booze. The five postcards were from her father to her mother after he'd left. Jessie found the oldest, and traced her finger over her father's childish handwriting. She decided to read only one; that way they'd last longer. As she read his words Jessie held her breath. He sounded excited about being on the road with the band as they made their way to Memphis. Her heart skipped as she read it again: Memphis. *Maybe he's in Memphis,* she thought.

The news clippings covered the Braves' hometown gigs and the pieces used her father's nickname, Billy J. She'd heard it before, but didn't know what the "J" represented. *Who doesn't know their father's last name?* Her anger at her mother flared again; the postcards were years old and he could be anyplace by now. She slammed the box shut.

"Let's go Bear," she said, and as Bear stood up, he grumbled.

They left the trailer and headed out of the park. Jessie gave the hood of her shabby red pickup a slap on the way past; with no proper license, the bus was safer. They walked through the trailer park toward the bus stop, passing rows of temporary housing. Litter rolled around them like tumbleweeds. When she'd arrived in Dorma, Vera's Mobile Homes had seemed a good place to stay hidden. Jessie's trailer was at the back of the park near the dumpster, and the stench from rotting garbage grew foul in the heat. Vera, the stinking landlady, had offered two weeks free plus a promise that the smell would disappear in a few days. Jessie had been hard up and sleeping in the truck, so it had seemed like a good deal.

Jessie reminded herself that she'd got her way out, that the music contest in Memphis was her escape from this cage. As lead singer in a band herself, she'd be there soon and her father's postcards felt like a good omen. What if, years later, he was still in Memphis? *I'm setting myself up to get disappointed again*, she thought.

They got to town early and as usual, Bear spent the bus journey trying to hold the floor down and then jumped off the instant the doors folded open.

"What's up, fearless?" Jessie knelt down to give him a hug. "Still don't like the bus, eh buddy?"

Bear pulled away and then slowed to a shuffle. He reminded her of a bad-tempered old man, and his studded collar and neckerchief just added to the effect.

As they crossed the street, a sudden strong breeze whipped up the dust around them and instinctively she covered her eyes. Bear pulled back and barked at the wind, as if he could halt its advance. Jessie steeled herself against the force of it and walked on.

Heroes was Dorma's attempt at a contemporary coffee house, with pictures of TV and film stars covering the walls. The coffee was okay, plus no one minded Bear tagging along. Jessie ordered an Americano with an extra shot and chose a sofa by the window.

Back at the counter, the cashier's shrill protest drew her attention.

"Mister, I don't know what this is but it isn't US currency." The cashier held an oversized pink bill up to the light and frowned. The man in front of the cashier chuckled and dug inside his jeans pocket.

"I'm so sorry," he said. "I completely forgot where I was for a moment." The stranger smiled at Jessie and then back at the rest of the line. "I guess the last thing you need is me turning up from my travels with the wrong currency." He smiled at the cashier again. "I apologize; I've just arrived and I'm feeling a little disoriented...and you're being so reasonable about it."

The cashier stopped frowning and began to smile. "Oh hey, don't worry about it," the server beamed. "Have the coffee on me—why not?"

Jessie stared. *Unreal*, she thought.

The guy was a biker of some sort: long black hair, Harley boots, and a leather jacket— he could even be a Hell's Angel. As he stepped away from the counter, his movements seemed gentle and considered, as if the world moved more slowly for him.

He headed in Jessie's direction and as he saw her, he raised his eyebrows. Jessie grabbed a newspaper from a rack, opened it, and pretended to find something of interest. The biker chose the table next to hers, and as he watched her, his steel gray eyes glinted. People often stared. It was something that went with heavy make-up, black and brown spiked hair and mismatched clothes.

"What's great that's happening in the world today?" he said.

Perfect, she thought, *a weirdo.*

"Dunno," Jessie said, trying to concentrate on the headline in front of her: "Synchronicity: An everyday kind of magic?" The article went on to say that people could make things happen, like coincidences.

That's just dumb, thought Jessie.

"My name is Finch," the man said. He waited for her to look up and then smiled. "But my friends just call me Finch." With a slight beard and dark mane, he was a cross between Jesus and Jack Sparrow.

"Okay, great," she said. *Maybe he's dangerous*, she thought, *dangerous isn't always obvious.* Jessie turned back to the article. The journalist's name was under the headline: Finch. As she looked up, he met her stare like he hadn't looked away.

"You're reading my article," he said, looking pleased.

"So did you put this here?" Jessie looked back at the reading rack. *I picked the paper, didn't I?*

"Aaah, you're mistrustful of everyday magic. That usually happens." He sounded wistful. "I guess that's growing up for you."

"Mistrustful of what? Like maybe someone decided to put a newspaper in a rack then follow people around to see if they read it?"

"There's a simple logic that makes it pretty reasonable," he said.

"Try me."

"Well, I wrote the article, obviously," he said. "I'm walking around on the day it's published, which is today." He waited as she checked the date. "I'm bound to bump into at least one person reading it. That person just happens to be you." Jessie's eyes narrowed.

"You did know about everyday magic once..." he said. "And then you did that thing. So then you stopped noticing it."

"That thing?"

"Yes...you threw away the idea of any kind of magic at all."

Jessie opened her mouth to speak, but no words came. The moment slowed and his words hung in the air. *Did I do that?* she wondered. *When did I do that?*

In the kitchen, someone dropped a tray and dishes crashed down onto a tiled floor. Jessie turned as a man cursed in Italian and a girl's voice shouted back. Inside her head something pressed the 'pause' button and everything hung in space. *What's all this shouting?* she thought. When Jessie eventually looked back at Finch, he was already stepping out onto the busy street. He'd left a small card on the table. On one side was a gold feather, and on the other side a question:

What if your life is working from the inside out?

Two

orma was where Jessie happened to be when she decided she'd gotten far enough away from home. She'd been sixteen, flat broke, and living out of the truck. She'd kept going because to admit defeat and go home was always worse. Dorma wasn't exactly "happening-ville," but her fake ID worked, no one cared enough to ask many questions, and having a dangerous breed of dog was only occasionally an issue. So she kept to the usual places and routines, and for over a year things had been some kind of normal. She'd gotten a job in a record store by displaying musical knowledge far beyond her years—not that the store's owner had a clue how old Jessie was.

Ray's Records was at the end of Main Street, near the bus depot. The location wasn't a problem, but sales certainly were. These days most people downloaded music from the Internet.

Jessie and Bear walked into the air of doom, complete with a gloomy female vocalist moaning in the background. The record store was long and narrow, with racks down its length loaded with CDs and DVDs, plus some vinyl records at the end for collectors. Ray stood at the counter, bearing down on a box of CDs. He muttered something about Jessie cleaning out the back room. The fact that she'd been cleaning the room for five days straight was irrelevant to Ray.

In the back room, Jessie slumped down onto the sofa and picked up an issue of *Rolling Stone*. From the counter, she heard Ray shout, "Dude! It's a record store; you can't bring those in here."

She walked out to see a matted hobo of a man with a vast bunch of helium-filled balloons, each no bigger than a grapefruit. His weathered face was a mask of wrinkles, but his steel gray eyes were quick and bright. Ignoring Ray, he approached Jessie directly, speaking in an awkward accent, Russian maybe. Behind the counter Ray looked at her, then back at the man.

"Lady, I am look for place to leave my balloons. They are one hundred. I come back for them later. Five sharpish."

"Sure, why not? Bring them on through the back," Jessie said. *That'll teach Ray for making me clean again*, she thought. Ray dropped the CDs back in the box.

"I'm sorry...excuse me?" Ray said.

As the hobo followed Jessie into the storeroom, the bobbing cloud of bright colors danced its way through the music racks. Ray rushed around the counter to follow but knocked over a bargain basket filled with CDs and DVDs arranged in alphabetical order. Ray grabbed at the items and began re-stacking them, muttering letters as he did so. Moments later the man left, nodding at Ray on his way out.

When Ray got to the storeroom, Jessie and Bear were gazing up at the balloon ceiling.

"So what? It's ha-ha, make the boss look funny day?" Ray asked.

"Look, I'm not sure what happened here, but I think maybe we're going to have to clean the room another day," Jessie said and shrugged.

"Where the hell are you going?" he asked as she walked past him.

"To serve some customers, Ray."

At the counter, a line of people stood waiting to pay. Strangely, she hadn't heard them come in, and before she'd served the last person, more had arrived.

That afternoon at Ray's Records was close to mayhem. A heady mix of music lovers arrived but Jessie didn't know where from. Ray was soon nailed to the cash register and Jessie was dispatched to walk the aisles, while Bear lay low under the counter. People were browsing, ordering, and amazingly, buying. Their musical tastes varied, and Jessie sold a limited edition of *My Way* by the Sex Pistols to a Japanese collector who paid 300 dollars without blinking. Later, she had to separate two housewives fighting over the last copy of Eminem's greatest hits.

Just before five, the last customer drifted out with Michael Jackson's entire back catalog and the store went quiet. As Ray began to count the day's take, the door chimed once, and the balloon man returned.

"I am returned for my balloons. I know how many," he said, shaking a finger at Jessie.

"Yup, there's still a hundred," she smiled. Come on through the back," Jessie glanced at Ray but he didn't look up. The old man collected his hundred balloons and left, pausing only to wave at Jessie on the way out. His gray eyes looked familiar somehow.

"Strange guy," said Ray, still checking his sales. "You know, I figure we served around a hundred customers today... that's more like it."

Jessie stared at him, waiting for him to make the number connection. *No chance*, she thought. At the spot where the balloon man had paused, a long white feather lay on the floor. She picked it up.

"Jessie, you go. I'll finish up. Here's your pay and here, get yourself a beer or something."

Ray held out the bills without looking at her; eighty bucks and twenty dollars extra. Stunned, she folded the money into her pocket.

"Hey, thanks Ray. Good day, huh?"

Jessie walked out into sunshine on Main Street. She made it as far as a bench and then sat down, still holding the feather. Something wasn't right—or just not the same as it was. She pulled Finch's card from her pocket and stared at its message:

What if your life is working from the inside out?

"Bear, this is nuts," she said, tossed the feather, and then stuffed the card back into her pocket. Forget the hundred balloons and Ray's really random act of kindness. What was important was that she had money for beer at O'Neill's on the way home.

Far from Dorma, outside a Kansas pool hall, an Egyptian called Kabos parked the white Dodge pickup at the back of the lot. He killed the engine and as he checked his teeth in the interior mirror, he pushed at one of the front ones. On the dashboard sat a small statue of the Egyptian god Set, the god of chaos.

Kabos considered his options. He had searched for many years to unearth this thief, and he toyed with the different ways that he might deal with him. He liked gutting people, which could get noisy but that didn't bother him. Kabos thought about the band and how they'd robbed him of the knapsack. That night at the sports bar was still as sore and bright as a fresh tattoo. Maybe he would find the other members of the Braves soon, but tonight he was content to have found this man. First, he'd make Scuz tell him all he knew, and then he'd watch him spill much more.

For the next two hours, people arrived and left. No one noticed the white pickup at the rear or its driver, motionless and staring at the entrance. When the old station wagon finally arrived and Scuz got out, Kabos' smile was as cheerless as his dark eyes.

Three

'Neill's was an open-mike venue, a place people went to get noisy. Jessie and the band did sessions there, as warm-up to the main event. In front of an audience, Jessie felt alive in a way she couldn't describe; the rest of the time she felt like a star waiting to shine. Work, band practice, and living in the trailer were what happened in between.

Jessie's thoughts wandered to the Memphis Music Contest. She'd spent months practicing, writing songs, and saving money where she could. These days, just the thought of Memphis made her stomach lurch. *Maybe we can get lucky,* she thought. So far, the only really lucky break she'd ever had in her whole life was finding Bear, because as far as she could figure out, Bear was the one thing in this world that actually needed her.

Now, in early evening, she welcomed the quiet of the bar; just the usual guy cleaning up a little, polishing glasses and chatting to the regulars. That was cool—he'd serve her even though she was underage.

"If you're looking for credit, I ain't giving any," he called over to Jessie, only half joking.

"Hey, I got money," she said.

Jessie sat up onto a barstool. She put a ten dollar bill on the bar and waited for her beer. The voice from behind her was cheery.

"Jess, you finished at the shop already?" Danny was the bass guitarist in the band. They'd met in the music shop, and he'd invited her to try out for the band. "Hi Bear, hey fella..."

As unpaid manager, Danny did all the organizing between jobs and the posters he was carrying were for their next gig.

"Yeah, I guess. Christmas came early. We had a boom day and it really spooked Ray—so he closed up early."

"The guy's a regular Donald Trump, huh?" Danny's smile continued. *How can he just silently gaze without talking?* she thought, wondering again how he was such a hit with the girls. With floppy hair and cheesy good looks, he was like a shampoo ad. To Jessie, if you wanted to be a real rock star you needed real dirt.

"You not working?" she asked.

"Start in twenty minutes. All-night inventory— the constant pressure of the supermarket industry." He hesitated. "You get back okay the other night?" Jessie had refused his offer of a ride.

"Yup. Arrived back to a special delivery. A package from back home." She thought of the box and its questions.

"Yeah? Is it your birthday or something?"

Jessie shrugged. "Nah, my mom decided to dump some of Dad's old stuff on me. Newspaper clippings of his band, photos—that kind of thing."

"No Rolex, then?"

"I wish. There was an amazing ring of his, though, that's kinda weird—ancient looking." She remembered how it didn't fit with the postcards and clippings. "You still on for practice tomorrow?"

"Sure." He paused. "Jess, try not to be late, please?"

"Geez, what is it with you people?" Jessie put her beer down.

"Okay, okay, that's cool." He held a hand up. "I'll see you tomorrow."

He tossed the posters on the bar and signaled to the bartender, who gave him a dry smile. Danny took the stairs two at a time and didn't look back.

Jessie had another beer and then left. The exchange with Danny played on her mind; everyone in the band was older than her and she knew being late was a big deal. She decided to spend what remained of the twenty bucks on pizza to share with Bear. She'd heard the new place on Jefferson was all right.

As she approached the pizza house, Jessie was stalled by the lettering painted on the shop window: "*Piuma Dorata,*" and below that, "Pizza as light as a feather." The painted lettering encircled a huge golden feather. Inside, the feather theme went nuts: it was on T-shirts, pizza boxes, and the paper napkins. *What's with the feather thing?* she thought.

Back at the trailer, they ate the pizza from the box. She put Bear's in the lid, and smiled as he licked gingerly around the olives and then gulped everything down.

Rescuing Bear had been one theft Jessie didn't regret. She'd taken a terrified bundle from under a breeder's truck.

Nearby, a baying crowd was shouting at a dog fight. The young dog was there to be sold into the sport. As Jessie had approached, Bear had stepped backward, hesitated, and then padded toward her. Jessie had knelt in silence to receive him, knowing that he would be coming home with her. In the trailer she'd kept him warm, fed him and cuddled him for hours at a time, until he stopped shivering and started playing. These days, they stayed together. Bear had become Jessie's shadow, just as she had become his light.

With the pizza finished, she fetched the metal train, added this week's wages to the roll and counted it all out. A bank might have been safer, but she didn't have any idea what was involved. Lots of questions probably, and people who made her feel awkward. Besides, handling her money relaxed her. She had her share of the contest entry fee, plus enough to stay a while in Memphis if they did well.

The cigar box lurked on the couch amongst the debris. Jessie still didn't know why her mother would send it. The whole thing made zero sense. She remembered peeking around the door of her mother's room to see her crying over its contents. Her mom had been holding a picture of Jessie's father in one hand and her drink in the other. The memory of it still brought back a lurching feeling of despair.

Bear jumped up beside her to watch as she opened the box once again, but the contents weren't much. For a man who'd apparently had big plans, her father hadn't left much of a trail. She tossed the box on to the counter.

"Come on, Bear."

Before turning in, she walked Bear around the trailer park and around them the sounds of trailerdom rose and fell like waves. Men shouted at women and women shrieked back, while rap music boomed loud enough to make walls rattle. Televisions blasted a barrage of ads, talk shows, and so-called reality TV. Jessie was still bothered by Finch and his feather card that said that life worked from the inside out. Like a kind of magic. *My insides must be pretty messed around to conjure this scene up,* she thought.

Jessie passed the trailer where Vera lived with her creepy boyfriend Ralphie. A picket fence enclosed a pile of scrap metal and household remains. It was difficult to see what any of it was in the gloom. Inside, light from the TV flickered with flashing images of random violence.

She remembered what her mother had spat at her as she'd left: "You'll come crawling back when you hit rock bottom."

Her younger sister had sat on the bed and watched as Jessie packed quickly, stuffing her things into bags. At that moment she'd been angry and upset and she'd thought she was best off just leaving.

"I'll call, Mary. You'll see. I'll get a place, no problem. I'll call you." But Mary's gloomy silence was something she couldn't forget.

Jessie had called, but as the pretense of success wore thin, it became less regular. Now, she knew rock bottom was here in this trailer park, but the problem with pretending things were okay was that she couldn't go back.

As Jessie and Bear approached the trailer, the light over the door flickered on and off. If the power was out again, she'd be having another cold shower in the morning. Behind the trailer, the electric box buzzed, but its faint scorching smell was lost in the stench from the rotting garbage.

◎   ◎   ◎

In the Kansas pool hall, Kabos sat in the shadows and watched Scuz playing pool. The beer in his hand had gone warm, but then Kabos didn't drink beer. He felt his loathing rise like bile. It wouldn't be long now.

With his fast smile, and careless mouth, Scuz attracted glances from other players. As he circled the table he wavered. In one hand he held a bottle and in the other he held a pool cue. His opponent missed another shot. Scuz laughed, shouted "Loser!" and banged his boot down hard. With his greasy Stetson and checked shirt, he looked like he'd been working the ranches, but Kabos doubted this flake had seen hard work recently.

Kabos had watched Scuz defeat his last three opponents, once fairly and twice by deception. As Scuz boasted and joked around, he swaggered like a cockerel.

He wondered how he'd ever been fooled by such an obvious fraudster. Ten years before, Kabos had visited a sports bar with the intention of amusing himself and had watched as people partied around him. His father had never let him go out to parties or have friends; even his pets all seemed to die young. Maybe it was natural to be distracted, he reflected. Plus there had been TVs everywhere, with their bright colors and flashing images. It had been mesmerizing. He'd sat with his knapsack on his knees, and decided that the crowd around him was bovine and drunken, no danger to him. At the next table, all the three men seemed to do was argue. The one called Scuz had stolen someone's beer, and another one was telling him to return it.

In the nearby bus station, Kabos had fallen asleep with the knapsack tied to one arm. He'd woken to the chuckling of a nearby beggar who had seen the theft of his bag and its precious belongings. Worst of all, he'd had lost the ring and the temple dagger. He'd made the laughing beggar give a detailed account of the theft, and then killed him. Without a weapon, he'd had to gouge, bite and finally throttle the man to death. The idea that the priceless relics had been taken from him made his head want to explode with fury. It was a fury that had kept him going every day since.

Tonight, a flash on Scuz's belt told him what he already knew; the finest craftsmen in ancient Egypt had fashioned the dagger. He was disgusted that it was being soiled by an infidel, but Kabos also wanted the emerald ring, and he prayed that Scuz had it with him. Maybe here his quest had reached a turning point: Scuz had the dagger and so must know where the ring was. Kabos savored the moment and planned how to approach him. The pool tables around the hall looked fairly busy. There was no point attracting attention, he reasoned. He could wait.

At the tables, Scuz should have been enjoying himself but in the shadows, someone was watching him. He stared into the darkness but it was impossible to see the man's face. His clothing suggested rough work, or just rough living. Scuz smelled the putrid odor of decaying vegetation. It was an odor he'd smelt before, but he struggled to recall where. He tried not to be distracted, but something about this man was bad, rotten even. The clack of the cue ball interrupted his thoughts. His opponent had just sunk another striped ball into a corner pocket. Scuz turned back to the pool table.

It was time to finish this thing.

Four

Jessie awoke to the sound of Bear's low growl a heartbeat before the banging started. Outside, her landlady was 300 pounds and as mean as a cornered snake.

"Rent!" Vera blasted, her fist not missing a beat on the trailer door. "And it's two weeks late! C'mon, I know you're in there."

The walls of the trailer shook as the pounding continued. Resistance was futile.

The pit bull's growl became a snarl as Bear jumped off the bed and headed for the door.

"All right, wait, will ya?" Jessie tossed the thin sheet to one side. She hadn't bothered to undress last night, and her boots were the only thing she needed to put on. The sticky linoleum was something to avoid in bare feet. Pulling the trailer door open sucked the stench of Vera's sweat inward, and made Jessie want to gag.

"Two weeks," Vera repeated.

"I heard you." Jessie's stare was a match for Vera's. The woman held out a sweaty palm, and Jessie thrust the cash forward. "And there's something wrong with the hot water," she said. "It isn't heating up. I've been taking cold showers for a week now."

"Tell someone who gives a damn." Vera counted the cash. Bear edged closer, his growl soft and rumbling.

"That thing belongs in a cage," Vera snapped. *Could she have Bear taken away?* The thought shook Jessie.

"I think we're done here?" Jessie said.

Vera's fake smile turned her face from ugly to hideous.

"Oh, sure thing honey, I'll just see you guys the same time next week." Then she hawked loudly and spat to one side. Sneering at Bear, she said, "That's the devil's dog."

Jessie started forward and then stopped herself. *Think about Bear.*

"Bear, here," she said in a low tone. Bear waddled back inside and coils of frustration rose in Jessie's stomach; her landlady had the upper hand, and they both knew it.

Inside, the chaos of the trailer was undeniable. She reminded herself that the music contest was just three weeks away and the trailer would soon be someone else's problem.

Jessie bent to give Bear a quick back rub.

"Hey buddy, we're going to Memphis real soon." But she struggled to sound upbeat. Something felt odd again this morning, dark even. Maybe it was being woken up like that. The dream she'd had was trying hard to return. She remembered a strange man—or was it a scarecrow? It felt like he was both; he'd been trying to tell her something.

The cigar box sat loudly on the counter. Lifting the lid, she slid on the ring and found the second card. On one side was a picture of Elvis Boulevard, and on the other, her father's small writing:

September 10th

Corinne,

Things still tough, but me and the band have some great vibes, so hold on tight. Mitch and Scuz say hi! Mitch's uncle has contacts here— tell Jessie her old man's gonna be a big star real soon. Give her and Mary a kiss from me, and look out for the Braves!

Billy J.

xx

Jessie was seven when he left. Her mother moved them away from Colonna shortly after. By now, few real memories remained. She remembered his loudness and the way the house changed when he was home, as if he woke everything from a half sleep. She thought he called her mouse. *Did he call me mouse?* By now she couldn't really remember.

She guessed her dad's band had changed their name after they left. Maybe they altered their image to secure a contract or airplay. The other names, Scuz and Mitch, sounded like names people grow out of. Who knew what they might be called now? The newspaper clippings said the band was a four-piece and someone called Gabe was the fourth member.

So why wasn't he mentioned in the postcard?

She needed to get to work. Looking at the clock, she saw she was running late. It was already ten-thirty.

"Crap. Bear, c'mon." She shoved the stuff back in the box, grabbed her bag, and bolted out of the trailer. As she ran past her old truck, she gave the hood a thump.

"Come on, Bear, move!"

Jessie jogged toward the entrance to the trailer park, checking behind her for Bear. His short legs paddled and his body rocked with effort but still the distance between them grew. She slowed, and then stopped to wait for him. Looking around at the lines of laundry and plastic toys, she sighed. She thought of the package and wondered if it might trigger change, like when a domino is knocked over. Maybe all those things in her way would tumble and fall. Then Jessie reminded herself that today would be the same as any other: work, music, and then sleep. After all, what else was going to happen?

Five

As they reached the entrance to the trailer park, the bus was already at the stop, two blocks away, and Bear wouldn't be rushed. She thought about picking him up, but he hated that and besides, he was too heavy. The bus pulled away. One person had not boarded and was leaning against the bus stop: Finch.

As Jessie approached, he turned and smiled as if he had all the time in the world.

"Greetings." Finch held up a Styrofoam cup. "Want some coffee?"

"No, thanks." The coffee was tempting, but she reminded herself she didn't really know this guy. She looked around, *has he been waiting for me?*

His smile was eternal. "Notice anything unusual lately?" he asked. Behind him, the graffiti on the bus stop seemed to fade.

"You mean the trick with the balloons, or the stuff with the feathers?" she countered. "Was that you?" *Maybe he's an actor.*

"Balloons and feathers? Sounds interesting. What happened?" he asked.

Jessie watched him for a while; his eyes were certainly familiar. *It couldn't be him*, she thought. *I'll watch how he reacts to the story.*

"Okay, so some foreign guy came into where I work and left a hundred balloons. He was pretty memorable, had this kinda Rasputin thing." Jessie told him about the balloons, the flood of customers, and seeing feathers. It sounded even crazier the second time. Finch just stared off into the distance beyond her.

"Feathers keep appearing..." he rubbed his chin. As he strolled around the bus shelter, he tutted softly. She noticed he had a precise way of moving, like no energy was wasted. If it was him in the shop, she realized there was no way he would admit it.

"Look, forget it; this is stupid." She kicked her toe into the ground, trying to crush a small stone under her boot. "What are you doing here anyway?"

"Well, I guess I'm being a bit of a tourist today."

"In Dorma?"

"Well yes, although I have kind of run out of sights here." He smiled. "I'm thinking of moving on soon."

"You're travelling by bus?" she said.

"No, not today."

Jessie waited but he simply shrugged in response. She realized that while she was trying to stay hostile toward him, it was actually impossible. His features stayed soft, no matter how much she scowled at him.

"You still pushing that whole 'everyday magic' thing?" *That sounds rude,* she thought. *Maybe he's actually just nice.*

"It seems I am."

"You mean the Easter Bunny, the Tooth Fairy—all that?" she said.

"Well, almost, though actually...no, not really," he said. "It's different than that. It's like... okay—when you were a child, what was magical to you?"

Jessie paused. Having a drunken mother that adults frowned over and kids taunted her about wasn't very magical. Trying to stop her little sister from crying at the sight of mommy unconscious on the bathroom floor usually sucked. Or at school, being so poor that she got bullied for it—that wasn't enchanting either. She'd learned to trust no one, especially where it came to what happened at home. Getting herself and Mary taken into care was something to avoid most days. Then, as she looked at him, one nice idea came back to her, a stupid dumb idea, and remembering it made her sigh.

"Why would I tell you?" she said.

"Why wouldn't you tell me?"

What's the harm in telling him? she thought.

"What's the harm in telling me?" he said.

Weird. She stared at him. His expression reminded her of a baby, like he didn't know anything—but might just know everything. *It is fun talking to him, though.*

Jessie explained how she'd been crazy about dragons and always wanted to save one from an evil knight. She thought the whole fairy tale thing about dragons was back to front—that it was dragons that needed rescuing, not dumb princesses. At school, she'd drawn a dragon being saved. The picture had won a prize, and that felt like she was special. Now, she pouted at the memory.

"So you did believe in magic?" he said.

Jessie paused. "Kids don't *believe* in magic," she said. "It's just there, isn't it?" Finch raised his eyebrows and nodded.

She remembered how different the world felt when she was a child. In her mind, supernatural things had existed with everyday things, and she hadn't thought to separate them. Like on Christmas Eve: it was as if the whole world had magic dust on for a night. She'd been excited because it was really happening. Presents had appeared and in the morning her father had been there to watch her open them. Just the sight of her mom and dad laughing and kissing and clowning around seemed like magic now. In the silence that followed, Jessie realized she'd been staring at the floor.

"Anyway, you get older and realize that stuff doesn't exist." Her flat tone made her shrug. "But that's fine."

Finch didn't speak; he just looked at her for a while and then sighed. It was a perfect match for what she was feeling. Jessie tried to smile.

"What I don't get is why you want to drag up how kids believe in magic and everyone else knows it's garbage?"

He paused. "That's simple. I happen to know that there is another kind of magic."

She watched him. *Really?*

"Not a child's magic – another kind. An everyday kind." He tapped his nose.

"Man, you're just nuts." But she grinned just the same. A warm glow spread across her chest. There was something about him that was so open it was almost as if there was no one actually there. *Maybe he's got Native blood in him,* she thought. *People say there's something in that.*

He sat on the shelter bench and stretched his legs out in front of him. "You said that gradually, over time, you found out that some stuff you thought was true had been made up by adults, yes?"

"Right."

"And when you realized that stories like Santa Claus and the elves weren't true, you decided not to believe in any kind of magic?"

"It's the same thing... isn't it?"

He shook his head and his long hair swayed. "Maybe you threw a whole idea away instead of just part of it," he said.

She could suddenly smell home: her bedroom, comics, clothes, hot chocolate. Jessie looked at him. Something was slipping a little, but she didn't know what. She swayed and put one hand on the frame of the shelter. The bus appeared and she needed to get on it. She moved toward it and then turned back.

"Jessie, your coffee." Finch offered her the cup and she took it automatically. "Americano with an extra shot." He nodded. She wondered how he knew her name. *Did I tell him that?* Then he put a finger up and looked down for a moment. "There was something else I meant to say..." He paused. "Right, yes, it's...enjoy your journey," he said, smiling.

The bus pulled in and Finch gave a theatrical bow and waved her and Bear onto it before turning and walking away. Sitting down, she saw something in the corrugated holder around the cup. It was another card:

There is always an end before a beginning.

Jessie and Bear arrived at Ray's Records thirty minutes late. It wasn't the first time, but it was going to be the last.

Ray was at the shelves, looking over the stock from yesterday.

"Morning Ray," she called over. "Should I start on the back room again?" *That ought to do it,* she thought.

Ray didn't look up. "Nah, you can turn back on your heel and go back to wherever you just came from," he muttered, thumbing through the easy listening section. "And take beefcake with you."

"What?" Jessie stopped walking. "For a lousy thirty minutes?"

"That was thirty minutes for me to wonder why I should employ you, and so far, I haven't come up with many reasons. So I've decided you're done here," he said, and walked toward the back of the shop.

As he walked away, Jessie knew it was final. Slamming the door after she and Bear marched out didn't help. She'd tried to hide her scorn for Ray, but obviously not well enough. A heavy, lurching feeling opened up in her stomach. *I really messed up again,* she realized. Crossing Main Street, she decided to walk around town with Bear for a while. Maybe she could find another job, just for a couple of weeks...but after some futile calls to bars and stores, they ended up back at the trailer.

In bright sunlight the trailer was a disaster. She slumped down onto the couch and stared at a hole in the linoleum. The job was all part of the big plan: save what she could, and maybe add to it with a few dollars from playing at O'Neill's. A wave of hopelessness washed over her, and she swallowed her tears back down. She'd gotten used to being alone, mostly, but just sometimes not having anyone to talk to, someone who really knew her, made her stomach ache with gray despair. She called Bear up beside her and wrapped her arms around him.

Things could still work out, she reasoned. With her savings she could still make the contest. This was a setback, that's all. A small tear escaped, like a traitor breaking ranks. Bear leaned his weight in against her and made a sound that was half whine, half sigh.

Six

essie worked on some songs, practiced her guitar, and gradually felt better. One of the songs felt really strong. It was soulful, had real heart and just working on it lightened her mood. It was a rock ballad, a change in direction from the stuff the band usually played. She was still a little apprehensive at the thought of showing it to them—to Danny mostly. Tonight was a practice night for the band and she decided to take it along. Maybe they'd use it as one of the songs they needed for the contest.

She chose an outfit from the floor. The fishnet tights were already torn, and a frayed denim mini plus unlaced Doc Martens pressed the message: stay away—you won't like me.

Jessie and Bear walked back into town. She needed to stop using the buses now to save her cash. The trouble was, walking took longer, and Jessie realized they'd be late again for practice. At the highway, she tried thumbing a ride but had no luck, just horn blasts from truck drivers as they speeded past.

The band practiced in an old warehouse a mile out of Dorma. Its location was remote, and with no one to complain about the noise, it was ideal. It stank from the paint and chemicals that were stored there but a friend of Danny's let them use it for nothing. When she finally arrived, she saw Danny's beloved '69 Camaro parked near the entrance. *Hope he doesn't go at me for being late.* Next to it, Nico and Sophie's van had a new custom paint job: a rock band made up of skeletons, with a cemetery behind. Jessie guessed that the artwork was Nico's latest idea, paid for by Sophie's latest allowance check. For a moment she hoped that Ed was late too, and then realized he would probably have traveled in with Sophie and Nico.

Inside, the group had set up against a backdrop of racks filled with cartons.

"Wassup, guys... you started without me?"

Danny looked up from twisting the pegs on the bass guitar and shook his head. Behind him, Nico scowled from over his drum kit. To one side Sophie chewed gum, while Ed appeared to be editing a program on his keyboards. A microphone and stand stood front and center, intended for Jessie.

"Hardly. We're short of a vocalist and lead, aren't we?" said Nico. Danny held his hand up.

"Jessie, we've all been here an hour and you're acting like that's no big deal."

Danny's remark hurt, not because she wasn't ready for a hassle, but because it came from Danny.

Nico's scowl made Jessie hesitate. She knew Nico thought Sophie should get a shot at lead, and he'd be happy to see Jessie take a fall if that's what it took. One glance at Sophie was enough; her smile was an apology. *Try stalling,* she thought.

"Okay. So I'm late but look, I'm here now. Let's just start, okay?" she said.

"Let's not," muttered Nico.

"Now what?" she sighed. "Let's get to it, can we? There's a Memphis newcomer contest to be won, or did you all forget?" She held up a folded piece of paper and tossed it onto a speaker. "Anyway, I've got a new song for us. It's okay, I think." The song was about her father; the lyrics were about a search, a search for truth and maybe resolution. She'd planned just to show Danny it in private but hoped it might buy her some time now. *What if they laugh at it?* she thought. *Too late now.*

Ed, Sophie, and Nico were motionless. Jessie guessed they'd been vocal enough before she arrived, but it was up to Danny now.

"Jessie, it's just that…well, you keep letting us down with this. It's great when you're here, but you've got to admit…"

"Admit what? That I couldn't get a ride?" she said. It felt just like a fight with her mother; Jessie was the big disappointment. "Look, I've got no cash for the bus and I couldn't get a ride, sorry—how's that for you?"

"Great," drawled Nico, picking at the end of a drumstick. "Just peachy."

"What's the matter, Nico? You been stuck for something to play?"

"Nope, I'm just waiting for someone worth playing for," he said, "and we've all decided that you're not it."

Danny frowned at him and then shook his head. Nico stared back. Sophie had been tugging at her blonde curls since Jessie had arrived, and now seemed annoyed with her French manicure. On keyboards, Ed suppressed a cough and looked downward. Jessie knew the final decision was Danny's.

"I'm sorry, Jess," he said.

"Fine. Screw you. Bear, here."

She strode out of the warehouse, giving them the finger as she did. In reply, Nico played a drum roll followed by a cymbal crash and laughed.

Jessie got as far as the main road and then lost her momentum. The bus stop had a low wall, and she slumped down against it. The facts of her situation advanced like dread. If she wasn't a lead singer in a struggling rock band, what hope did she have now?

She wondered about going back, of making some protest. Nico was like the head of a pack of wolves, and the thought of facing him again was ugly. She remembered being mocked at school by a group of older girls, of being surrounded by people who seemed to hate her. The first time Jessie had been taunted she'd cried and regretted it. The girl's sing-song chant had followed her down the corridors as she ran: '*Loser, loser, poor little loser...*'

She looked back at the warehouse door. *No way.*

Jessie put her hands over her face. After years of staying away from people, she'd recently begun to wonder if the band could actually become her friends. With Danny especially, she'd felt like maybe she could trust him and even wondered about telling him why she'd left Colonna. Sophie had seemed mostly OK too, for a rich kid with whom she had exactly zero in common. She pulled Bear in close.

Behind her, in the warehouse, the band began a cover of "Because the Night." It had been Jessie's suggestion the week before. Sophie was having a go at singing, but the low intro wasn't right for her voice and the effect was pitchy.

She jumped up. "Come on, Bear."

Kabos was so frustrated by the irate woman's attitude in Kansas he'd nearly killed her just to shut her up. If she hadn't been standing on her front porch in broad daylight he might have done just that. Under the influence of a hallucinogen Kabos had sprayed into her face as she opened the door, she spoke freely. Unfortunately, her ranting and foul language drew attention from passersby until a young girl appeared behind her and hushed at her to keep the noise down. What calmed Kabos was that the woman was not only willing to tell him all about the ring but also encouraged him to go and get it back from her runaway daughter personally. Apparently the adolescent was blamed for putting the woman through almost two years of sheer hell and she'd finally had enough of it.

Searching the map, he finally found Dorma: bigger than a village but hardly a town. The teenager shouldn't be too hard to find, he decided. All he needed to do now was find a trailer park in what looked like Hicksville, and the Pharaohs' ring would be his again.

Back at the trailer Jessie changed her clothes while Bear followed her around more than usual. Making food seemed like something to do while the world finished crumbling. She attempted to clean a pan and dumped a can of beans into it. Scraping the mold off some cheese, she dropped that in, too. She and Bear shared the mess, both eating from plates on the kitchen table. The food tasted abnormal in her mouth as her stomach stopped responding.

Her father's black Gibson guitar stood in the corner, mocking her. Jessie pushed her half-full plate toward Bear and put her head on the table. For the first time she wondered if maybe he didn't make big in Memphis after all.

From the cupboard, she lifted down the cigar box. As she slid the ring on her finger, it felt warm and its surface was slippery. *Maybe it has some kind of coating on it*, she thought. Around the emerald the symbols looked like hieroglyphics: a bird, a feather, and the sun with rays coming from it. Even in the gloom of the trailer, it glinted. From the box, she picked out the third postcard. Her father's tone was more formal this time.

September 27th

Corinne,

We're still making progress. How are things with you and the kids? Hope they're both behaving for you and being good. I'll call you when I get more settled.

Billy J.

x

Jessie wondered how many more times her father had called home. She remembered her own experience of leaving: the relief of escape, the thrill of the adventure, and the shrinking contrast of reality. The trailer was suddenly a cage to her, its dark shadows threatening doom. She packed the box away and thought of her little sister. Checking the pockets of her combats for coins, she started to leave. Bear hopped off the sofa after her.

"No Bear, stay here. I'll only be gone a while."

For once, she just wanted to be on her own. Bear stalled, his eyes big with confusion. He started forward again, but she stopped him.

"Look, just stay there," she snapped.

Bear watched her leave him. Fleetingly, she realized she had never done that before. She'd never left him alone in the trailer, but he was a dog, wasn't he? Wasn't it about time she treated him like one? Anger brought tears close again. Locking the door, she headed toward the park entrance. She heard Bear's anxious barking and almost stopped, but her thoughts were tangled. She remembered him limping behind, slowing her down. *Stupid dog, you made me miss the bus.*

Later, she'd try and retrace her thoughts—was that the impulse she needed to catch? Why hadn't she taken him with her? Still, Jessie kept walking, through the debris of the trailer park and toward the exit.

Seven

Jessie walked down the dirt path out of the park. It was late and somewhere someone was playing an Adele song; her soulful voice flowed like liquid sorrow.

At the phone booth, a middle-aged woman was installed for the evening. Jessie paced around for a while. An image of Bear alone in the trailer returned, and her stomach turned over.

"Come on, will ya?" She banged on the side of the booth. "I'm in a real hurry."

The woman finished and walked out, muttering. Under the bright light, Jessie dialed the familiar number.

"Hello?" Her mother answered within two rings. Damn. She'd expected it would be Mary. This must mean her mother was close to sober.

"Hi, it's me," said Jessie. *Maybe I should mention the package,* she thought.

"Oh, right. Wassup?" Her mother said.

"Nothing, I just wondered if Mary was in?" Jessie tried to sound casual.

"No, she ain't here, Jessica."

"Okay, well, maybe some other time."

"Yeah, okay, another time…" Her mother seemed to pause.

"You okay?" Jessie asked.

"Well, aside from a pile of bills, no job, and a car that won't start, I'm just dandy. My prince is on his way."

"Right." Jessie gave up. *What did I expect?*

"That all?"

"Yeah, just tell Mary I called, will ya?"

"Oh sure."

Jessie took a breath. "Mom?"

"Yup."

"The stuff in the box…about the Braves…"

"What about it?"

"Can I ask what his last name was?" her voice suddenly faded.

Her mother sighed, "You know I don't say his name, Jessica."

"Fine. Whatever."

She put the phone down, rested her head on the telephone, and breathed out. *Mary isn't there.*

The stale smell on the handset brought her back around. Leaving the glare of the phone booth, she returned to the trailer park. Her mother had sounded casual, almost flippant. *Is it that easy for her?* Jessie hadn't expected a warm reception, but her mother's indifference was somehow worse than her anger.

Entering the park, something wasn't right. Several people were shouting, and their voices sounded full of panic.

Jessie knew it was her trailer long before she reached it.

"Fire!" someone bellowed. "Fire!"

The smoke was already high. Clouds of gray and black billowed up into the night sky. She began to run, too slowly. *I left Bear.* It took her time to find speed, a single thought like the beginning of an end: *I left him in the trailer and the trailer is on fire.*

From three hundred yards away, she saw flames flash at a back window. *The bedroom's burning.* How long had she been gone? Surely not that long? Trailer fires took hold in minutes; too much flammable material and with everything so close together, no space. *I need to get in and find him.*

Two hundred yards. Her arms and legs pumped as she sprinted. She pulled at the snagged keys in her pocket. She could see people gathered. *Why aren't they doing anything?*

Still one hundred yards away. The acrid stench smelt like tires burning. She ran harder toward the dark shadow. Flames danced on the roof and jumped down its length. The keys came loose from her pocket. *Please don't drop them.*

Only fifty yards to go. She pushed people aside. "Move, just move!"

Almost at the trailer, she stumbled. Arms grabbed at her. Someone tried to restrain her, but Jessie was like a train.

"My dog!" she screamed. "My dog is in there! Get the door open!"

Only blank eyes stared back. As the adrenaline surged around her body, everyone appeared sluggish. It felt like a slow-motion nightmare.

Someone called for a hose. An old man stood with a broom, trying to break the living room window. Was Bear barking? The blood rushed into her ears and she struggled to take in the information. Only the occasional flash of flame lit the inside.

"Please," she pleaded to herself. "Oh God, somebody please."

She blasted though the line of onlookers. *Too long*, she thought, *it's taking too long*. She took the trailer steps in an instant and grabbed the door handle. It was fiery hot, burning her hand but fear had her numb. The acrid smell of molten plastic engulfed her. She slowed her fingers as she handled the key, *keep calm hold it steady*.

The key rattled into the lock. It turned. She pulled the door open. Toxic smoke billowed out. The full force of the heat hit her face as the glass door panes cracked like gun shots. Her breath was taken by its sucking, roaring gasp. It was then that she knew all was lost. She could not get in there. She stumbled forward, but something solid was at her feet. There, he was there by the door. She dropped to him, and shielded him from the heat with her body.

"Bear!"

Jessie lifted him as fast as she could, not knowing what direction he was in, she got her arms underneath. She dragged him away from the furnace. *I've got him.*

Bear was heavy. She was used to that, but now he was limp, lifeless. He didn't struggle from not wanting to be carried; he wasn't grumbling at the closeness, a shifting, kicking bundle. He was completely still, a dead weight.

Jessie stumbled back down the steps, away from the blaze. She staggered a few yards with his bulk and slumped down on the hot grass.

She laid him down; his body was fiery to the touch and his fur was dry like straw. As she struggled for breath, she tried to coax him awake.

"Come on, Bear. Come on, fella. Come on! It's me, Bear, it's me."

She heaved and coughed fumes out of her lungs. Her legs shook as the shock set in. On the grass at her knees, Bear was still. Behind her, a woman's voice was sad.

"Poor little thing..."

Jessie hugged Bear, and then realized that might make it worse. Clearing the grass from around his nose and mouth, she stroked his parched fur. Frantically, she searched around her, but the cluster of people just watched her, their faces blank.

Her thoughts felt like prayers. *Please don't take Bear from me.* Gently, she lifted his head with one hand and pushed his body with the other. He felt limp and hot. *I need him to keep going.* A sob escaped. Jessie held the next one down with its bitter taste but still the tears came and she coughed them away.

He twitched.

"That's it, Bear, c'mon buddy!"

She began to cry properly. Her breath was jagged. Her nose and eyes streamed as she wiped the snot and tears away with her hands and sleeves.

"Please Bear, you can do it, for me, Bear, *please*."

She stroked him softly; his coat was singed and brittle. *Please breathe please breathe please breathe.* Just for a moment, he opened his eyes, but for Jessie it was enough. *He's alive.*

A few yards behind her, the trailer burned. Everything she owned—all her money, her precious things: the cigar box, her guitar—was consumed in the hunger of the fire. Jessie felt the radiating heat on her back as she watched Bear for more signs of life.

Bear coughed. He sounded weirdly human, like a smoker in old age. Opening his eyes, he saw Jessie and reached toward her. His tongue tried a faint lick.

"Ssssh…S'okay, lie still."

From her heart, hope rose like a phoenix. Jessie watched him. *Maybe he's going to be all right.*

To one side, the small group of onlookers edged closer, interested in the dog's movements.

One of them called over, "Honey do you need a place to stay?" Not exactly offering, just asking.

"No, thanks, I have my truck," said Jessie, not looking up.

"You might want to get a vet to take a look at him in the morning," the old man said. Jessie nodded. The others turned and shuffled away.

"Strange how Vera's not here."

"Did anyone call the fire department?"

But Jessie didn't care about Vera, the trailer, or her stuff. Bear started to cough again and suck in air, his body still limp. The old man fetched a metal bowl of water. She took it from him and dipping her fingers, she smoothed some across his mouth. "Water, Bear. Come on, drink the water."

The dog's tongue escaped with a faint lick. *That's a good sign.* She looked back at the man.

"Thanks...really," she said. His face looked gray in the half-light, gaunt and emaciated; he wore suspenders over his vest. His wife stood by his side, a blanket in one hand.

"For the truck," the woman offered.

"Okay, thanks, I mean really." Jessie put it to one side, and then turned back to Bear. The couple watched, motionless, then after a while they wandered away.

In the background, the trailer cracked as it burned. Two men with hoses were putting out the flames. Jessie recognized Ralphie, Vera's boyfriend, spraying down the outside of the trailer as the bedroom roof collapsed. He was paying particular attention to the cables in the back. Jessie wondered how lethal the problem with the electricity had actually been.

Gradually, Bear came around. After watching him struggle for a while, Jessie gave in and helped him to stand. He lapped some of the water, then half laid, half collapsed as he started to shiver. Jessie wrapped him in the blanket and carried him to the truck, cradling his weight on one leg as she unlocked the cab.

"That's it, let's get you comfortable, fella," she said, and laid him carefully down onto the passenger seat, then went to retrieve the water. She kept talking. "It's okay; here I am, not going anywhere. See? Here I am."

Jessie put the water on the floor mat and sat on the truck step, at eye level with Bear. She stroked his head; as he watched her, he frowned.

"Thought you were a goner there, little man."

Her voice choked at the thought. Bear shivered but still felt hot. Behind her, the drama of the fire settled to a close.

Just Ralphie and his buddy remained, washing down the smoking remains. The fire had started at one end: the sleeping and bathroom areas were now completely destroyed. The living room was still recognizable, but blackened and charred.

"Okay Frank, we're done here," said Ralphie. "I've got a beer going warm."

They checked over the wreckage before they left. Neither man spoke to Jessie, which was fine by her. She watched the debris smolder and fume, and thought of how suddenly everything had changed. The black mass of the trailer loomed in the darkness. A dragon's breath had taken its toll, and in the morning the loss would be counted. Jessie remembered Finch's card, '*There is always an end before a beginning*', but she still didn't understand it. What sort of magic was this?

Eight

essie spent the night in the cab curled around Bear. She woke early, gradually recognizing the dusty dashboard, the vague smell of burning and the hardness of the seat under her. Again, she'd dreamt of a strange place, but her dream drifted away like mist. Bear had coughed a lot, which kept both of them awake. Sleeping in the truck reminded her of before, of being on the road, living on her wits, working out ways of getting money or food, but that was a life before Bear.

Next to her, Bear stirred, and then she remembered: the fire and running and her panic, then desperation. *What if Mary had picked up the phone?* she thought. The fear of losing Bear returned, and made her feel shaky, like she wanted to cry again.

She smoothed his head, not wanting to wake him, just wanting to touch him. "Look, I can't do all of this without you," she whispered. His fur smelled singed and foul; it was worse up close.

Outside, the burned-out trailer smoked in the morning light. In its final death throes, its looming presence drew her toward it. From the alloy steps, she tested the floor and then headed toward the remains of the kitchen. The harsh stench of cremated furnishings tasted bitter and foul. The bedroom area was hardly there, its flimsy structure now exposed. Everything else had been consumed by the flames. The linoleum was melted and patches of filthy water sat on its surface. Beside the blackened fridge, in fragments of charred wood, she found the toy train, dark and buckled by the heat. *The cash is gone,* she thought.

Jessie pried it open, and the ash of the money roll emerged. As she pulled out the disintegrated notes, her fingers turned black with soot. Brushing off the outside layers, she worked her fingers toward the middle and saw that some notes at the center might still be usable. There were three twenties and a ten, just a fraction of the $890 that she'd saved. The money was her stake for the contest, somewhere to stay, and maybe a slot of studio time. Jessie had known last night the cash was ruined, but seeing the black ash made her stomach lurch.

Most of the trailer roof was gone, and she could see down the full length of it. In bright daylight, it looked bigger. At the far end the roof still partially covered the lounge area and the small cupboard above the sofa bench was blackened and blistered. She stepped over roof segments, burned clothes, an old lamp, patches of wet and filth. The buckled figure of the guitar lay on its back, its stickers all melted, its strings now charred wire.

The painted surface of the cupboard door was black and oily to touch and its plastic handle pulled free and fell to the floor. Jessie levered the door open, dreading the sight of the cigar box. However, on the shelf it looked virtually untouched—a little darker maybe, but still okay.

"You beauty," said Jessie, and her words escaped into the morning air.

Jessie picked her way out of the trailer feeling a few shades lighter. She had her father's cards and clippings back and the bracelet and the ring. Most importantly, she still had Bear and as she approached the pickup, she made her decision. Dorma felt as rotten as the taste of bitter ash in her mouth. They needed to leave, and they must go today. The image of Memphis was still clear in her mind and Jessie decided to leave while she still had wings.

She used the laundry area to get clean. Using some soap she found in one of the sinks, she washed herself as much as she could. The smell of smoke was still in her clothes, but at least she'd gotten it out of her hair. Bear's fur was filthy and in the oversized sink, he struggled feebly then stood still while she gently soaped him. He kept sitting down, which made the process awkward. With cool water, she rinsed him carefully and examined his skin for burns.

As they walked back Bear's tongue lolled out, and even a slow pace made him pant and wheeze. His eyes were bloodshot, probably from all the coughing. Jessie wanted to carry him but knew he wouldn't like it, so she kept stopping to let him rest. *He's still sick,* she thought.

As she started the truck its engine roared into life. At the nearest gas station, she filled the tank, and then bought essentials: toothbrush, soap, bagels, and coffee. She tried to share the bagels with Bear, but he wouldn't eat.

Jessie checked the truck's oil and fuel levels and tried to calculate how long they'd be on the road. It was probably seven hundred miles to Memphis. She knew in the old truck that would take at least two days, probably more, and that was if the engine held up. She pumped the tires, checked the oil and then wiped her hands on the paper towel left by the pumps.

"Jessie, wait," said a voice behind her. Danny's hair hid his eyes, and it took her a while to see the concern in his face.

"I went to the trailer—it's totaled," he said.

"No shit, Einstein." Jessie didn't look at him.

"What happened? The place is a disaster..." Danny checked the cab and visibly relaxed when he saw Bear.

"Turns out my landlady's electricity is more messed up than she is." Jessie glanced back at him. He was doing that staring thing again, but all Jessie could think about was the fight in the warehouse, and she hoped that he didn't see how humiliated she felt.

"So what now?" Danny followed her as she slammed down the hood and started to leave.

"Time to move on, I guess. Thought I might look in on Memphis." Her smile felt like a grimace. "My dad's probably there. He'll sort stuff out."

"Will you enter the contest?"

"Yes, I might just do that." She stared at him. *Is he mocking me?* The urge to get away from him was all she could think about. Get away, run away, now.

"Jess, about last night..."

"Yeah, your new vocalist sounds amazing. Too bad she can't sing."

"Sophie's all right, she just needs a chance." But Danny sounded doubtful.

"Whatever. Well, you're giving her a chance now." Jessie moved toward the cab. *Not like me.*

"Jess, here, take this." Danny held out his hand.

"What?" she said, and took the folded paper he was offering.

"It's the ballad you were working on," he said, watching her face. "I think it's great. I made a couple of suggestions."

It was the song about her father; Jessie felt sick. *Why didn't I pick it up when I left?*

"I like the tone too, it's a different style."

"Yeah well, it's just some dumb ideas."

"Jess, it's good. You know what you feel. That's what counts."

She gave him the hardest stare she could muster, but the thought of him reading the ballad felt awful. "Look, shouldn't you be at work or something? Isn't there some old lady needing her groceries bagged or something?"

"Geez, Jess, you just don't quit, do you?" Danny held up a hand. "Good luck, just… ah, whatever." He turned and walked away. As he reached the sidewalk, he stalled but then carried on.

Jessie watched him cross the street. He had a loping, moody kind of a walk. With one hand he cleared the hair off his face and it immediately it fell back where it was. *I should go after him,* she thought, but her stubbornness rooted her to the floor. She reasoned that Danny could have talked the band around last night if he'd cared enough. *Which means he just didn't care enough.*

Jessie got back in the truck, fired it up and kicked down hard on the gas pedal. She headed out east onto the highway. On the steering wheel, her knuckles were white with tension. She cut off two cars before she realized that she needed to calm down. She wasn't exactly road legal, so the last thing she needed was to attract attention with bad driving. Maybe she should try and find Finch before she left...*He said there'd be an end and a beginning...* The thought chewed at her, but she dismissed it.

"Just you and me, Bear," she muttered. "We'll do all right."

◎ ◎ ◎

At the trailer park, someone was picking over the charred remains of the fire: a bony, taut-looking man carrying a sheathed knife. He'd dragged some things out of the trailer and was sorting through them on the grass. Vera wandered over, stopped a short distance away and then moved closer. The man's clothes were shabby and mud stained and his hair fell lank with grease. He worked through the debris methodically and had a pile of stuff to one side waiting to be sorted. Crouched over, he hadn't seen Vera.

"Find somethin' of interest here?" Vera said, watching him lift up a scorched jumper.

Kabos stared at her, and then turned back to the pile of clothing.

Vera moved nearer and as she drew close, leaned over.

"Fella you'd have to be pretty desperate to..."

"Where's the girl?" he asked. His fingers were quick as he checked the pockets of a jacket.

"That little nobody?" Vera sneered. "Gone to the shelter maybe; how the hell would I know?" Vera now stood over him. "What I'm asking you, fella, is..."

Kabos whipped his hand sideways and seized her ankle; his grip was rigid and strong. Beneath his fingers, Vera's flesh gave way and her bones creaked then cracked. He let go as quickly as he had grabbed her. Vera stumbled backward, gasping. The sound of her screams followed her back to her trailer. When Ralphie had finally gotten her coherent enough to explain what had happened, Kabos was gone.

Nine

Jessie drove through the day, out into the wilderness. Even with the windows down, the searing heat in the cab was relentless. Bear lay motionless on the floor while around her, the sun washed the color from the landscape. Fields merged with endless roads and Memphis felt like a far-off land that wasn't actually getting any closer.

Toward nightfall, she pulled over into a truck stop; the gas station close by carried groceries and provisions and would be somewhere to get some food in the morning. She watched Bear for a while and hoped that in the cool he'd be able to rest.

Under the interior light she read one of the postcards, the fourth one, almost the last. She put the ring on and pushed it around with her thumb as she read.

October 10th

Corinne,

Things getting a bit tough to handle here— no big deal, just the usual hot-headed stuff with the guys. Sorry to be mean on the phone last night; it's just not the right place for you and the girls right now. You know I'd have you all here if I could. Keep Jessie practicing her music and tell her she can have the Gibson one day soon.

Billy J
xxx

The picture on the back was a night shot of the famous Beale Street in Memphis, with its neon-lit music bars, clubs, and shops. Her ideas about Memphis were based on musical myth and legend. The city was home of the blues and birthplace of rock 'n' roll. So many artists had started their careers here—B.B. King, Howling Wolf, Carl Perkins, and Johnny Cash. She wanted to see it all: to see where Elvis lived, where Martin Luther King was shot, and to see Beale Street, of course. Jessie realized that she'd be walking down that street very soon and the anxious feeling in her chest returned.

That night, Jessie dreamed again, only this time she knew she was dreaming.

The scarecrow watched her as she struggled up the hill. The ginger earth was uneven so she sighed, and then because she sighed it became a truly unruly and ever so muddy plowed field. Above her, on the brow of the hill the scarecrow tilted in the sunshine, tutting softly and shaking his head. Then the tutting noise got louder inside her head and made her ears all fuzzy and buzzy. Jessie scowled at all this and so her boots got bigger. *Is this Kansas?* The scarecrow seemed to be saying something but his mouth was all sewn up.

"What?" Jessie shouted and as her frustration turned to anger, her legs felt even heavier. *Is this hill getting steeper?*

"Why make it so hard?" His words danced around her head like a playful echo. *Is he singing?* His sing-song tune rose and fell like a playground taunt as the scarecrow faded into the distance. *I'm not getting anywhere,* she realized.

Jessie woke in the truck. Beside her, Bear sighed and shifted as the strangeness of the dream floated away. The acrid smell of the fire lingered around her and on Bear, even though she'd washed him. As he blinked awake his bloodshot eyes were alien and his breath came in wheezes. Jessie stroked his head but couldn't speak.

Outside, the traffic on the highway was building and the truck stop was stirring. Jessie walked around the back of the gas station, knowing that morning deliveries were often left for a while. She grabbed a carton of milk, some orange juice, and a pack of rolls for them both. Farther down the road, Jessie pulled over and poured the milk into the metal bowl but Bear lapped only a taste of it and refused the bread. Jessie's dread returned like an unwelcome houseguest.

She fired up the truck and headed out on the southbound highway. It wasn't as fast as the interstate, but there were fewer patrols. By keeping within speed limits she'd save on gas too, which was a big deal. By tomorrow, she'd need to find a way of paying for that—no minor problem.

The pickup averaged 40 miles per hour, which made Jessie an obstruction to be passed. The huge eighteen wheelers were the worst, sixty feet of towering intimidation. She kept the windows shut to stop the clouds of dust from filling the cab. The heat was relentless. Most of the time Bear laid panting on the floor mat; his tongue lolled from his mouth. Occasionally, he'd climb up on to the hot vinyl seat, and pleaded to be let out. Jessie stopped several times and tried to get him to drink water, but she also had a driving need to press on.

Early afternoon she pulled over into a Wendy's, reluctantly leaving Bear in the truck. By now, he just laid on the floor, not awake, but not asleep. Again she wondered about finding a vet. Jessie walked around the busy restaurant and sat down at a recently vacated table. From the leftovers she took most of a quarter-pounder burger, half a club sandwich, and a handful of fries. She tucked a near-full bottle of mineral water under her arm and walked out. The couple at the next table watched her but said nothing.

Back at the truck, Bear ate a little of the turkey from the club sandwich. Normally, he would have devoured it, including the wooden cocktail stick. From a faucet on the wall of the cafeteria, Jessie filled Bear's bowl and watched him try to drink, but he splashed most of the water onto the ground, making the dust turn to small droplets of mud. The low thump of a motorbike engine sounded behind her, but she ignored it.

"Come on, Bear. No rush, buddy. Take your time," she urged.

Bear lay down suddenly, and knocked the bowl over. Jessie's panic returned.

"Please, Bear." She knelt over him and stroked his head. He opened his eyes for a moment. *He's getting worse,* she thought. She needed a vet, *but what could a vet do?*

Grabbing the bowl, she ran back to the faucet for more water and turned back into the bright sunlight, squinting as she searched for Bear laying by the truck. Ahead of her, a figure stood close by, holding a huge map. *Why is he so near the truck?* Then he noticed Bear and walked over to him. Jessie lengthened her stride and tried not to spill the water. Then she recognized the poised stance, the elegant manner. Finch.

"Did you just get here?" she said. "Are you following me?" She tried to guess how he might have done that. *Maybe he fitted a device to the pickup,* she thought. Maybe he'd been tracking her all this time. *Why would he do that?*

"Following? No, I'm on a journey," he said. "It's a road trip." He nodded at the classic Triumph nearby. It was pristine, not a speck of dust on its gleaming paintwork. In an easy motion, he folded the large map and tucked it inside his leather jacket. "But hey, it's great to see you again, Jessie."

He smiled his perfect smile: beautiful teeth and genuine intent.

"You really expect me to believe this is just a strange coincidence again," she said.

"Oh, absolutely not," he said. "I expect you to figure out some logical reason why I've been tracking you." He chuckled. "Because it's easier to invent a sinister plot and turn me into someone who can't be trusted."

"Look, it's just more than strange, that's all." She looked around her. *Maybe I'm in a TV show,* she thought, looking for a camera-crew. Nothing. *Is this synchronicity?*

"Well yes, it is certainly strange," he said. "Anyway, how's it going, Jessie?"

"Oh, just great. I lost my job, plus my place in a band, all my stuff, and oh yeah, my buddy here is *really* sick..." Her voice caught as she looked over at Bear. "Anyway, we'll be okay," she said, putting the water down where he laid. Bear was panting sharply, and she wanted to get him out of the heat.

"An end of something indeed," Finch said. "Still, I don't like to think of a friend being sick." He walked over to Bear. "I prefer to think of them well..."

Finch squatted down next to him. Slowly, gently, he ran his hand over Bear's ribs, only he didn't seem to touch him. His eyes were closed. *Are his eyes closed?* For a lingering moment, Finch was still and silent. Even the traffic noise around her seemed to hush. Jessie found herself holding her breath. She'd heard about healers; maybe that was all part of it, part of whatever he was. He sighed gently and opened his eyes, and she let herself exhale, too.

Finch stood and gazed at Bear. *He's really kind*, she thought. *How can he be so kind just for nothing?* He turned to her. "Please. You must see him well."

They both watched as Bear struggled to stand. Jessie moved forward, but Finch held up his hand.

"In your mind, Jessie, *see him well.*"

He turned to her; his gray eyes were almost silver in the sunlight.

"Okay...right..." she hesitated. "The other day...you said—this everyday magic thing—I still don't get it," she said. "And trust me, I could use some conjuring right now." She crouched down by Bear and stroked him. *He's stopped panting*, she thought.

Finch wrinkled his nose. "Conjuring is based on illusions or party tricks," he said. "You'd need a *trickster* to do those." He used the word with distaste. "And the problem with *tricksters* is that they create illusions; they make the unreal appear... real."

"So okay, but isn't that...? I'm sorry, you've lost me." She didn't want to be rude because he seemed really genuine, but the whole trickster-illusion thing was irrelevant, wasn't it?

"Because only what's truly real is truly powerful," he said, like that explained everything. Then his face relaxed into a smile again. "Spot the illusion, Jessie, that's your quest," he said. "See through the illusion of how things *appear* to be, then you'll know exactly what to do."

That was it, like it was all explained. Jessie shook her head and stood up.

"Look, the only thing I need to do is make things get a bit easier for us," she said.

Finch looked over at the pickup truck. "Well, it sounds as though they couldn't get much tougher, could they?"

She didn't like the way he sounded; it was too open-ended.

"And now, I should go," he said. From his jeans pocket, he pulled out battered leather gloves. He slipped them on, tugging the second one into position with his teeth. Jessie wanted him to stay a while longer. *If he is Native American he could have some old kind of wisdom*, she thought. *Like being able to see the future.* Kicking the engine to life, he shouted over its rumble. "Jessie, you already make things happen, lots of things—think about that."

She watched him pull out and wondered what he meant. *Am I making things happen? So why do I make things so tough?* Seeing Bear well was a good idea, though. Positive thinking, she decided, couldn't hurt. *He's okay*, she told herself. Jessie closed her eyes and imagined him well again. *He's well. Well and healthy, jumping around. I see him well.*

The sound of lapping water made her open her eyes. Bear was up and drinking steadily. *He can stand and he's drinking.* She thought about the last few days, the strange dreams and the feathers. Something tugged at her thoughts, like a child on a mother's sleeve. She searched the road after Finch, but under the beating sun the highway shone glassy like a mirror and all she could see was heat waves.

Ten

Back on the road the sight of Bear sat up on the seat allowed Jessie to relax a little. Her last conversation with Danny played over in her mind. Why had he come to see her with the lyrics? She wondered again if the song was any good. Danny said it was, but then he was probably feeling guilty. As she remembered him walking away from the gas station she realized that could be the last time she saw him, which didn't feel great.

Jessie pulled into an out-of-town shopping mall. With people, purses, distractions, and diversions, she knew that this was a place to find money for gas. She parked the truck close to a side exit in case things got crazy. Once inside, she walked around a few times to make sure she could find her way out in a hurry. In the crowds, Bear automatically tucked in behind her. The sight of his swagger made Jessie smile. He looked so much better now. *See him well*, she thought.

Inside the mall, the air was cool and refreshing. They sat near a fountain, and Jessie checked for security guards. To one side of the fountain's pool, escalators carried people between the floors. Women were distracted by young children; store workers roamed around on a late lunch; there were rowdy teenagers, and only a few cameras. *Nothing too difficult*, she thought.

The trouble was Jessie didn't want to do it. She'd hoped this was all behind her. Taking a bit of surplus food from a diner was one thing, but taking a young mother's wallet felt different. She thought about Finch. He'd said she was making things happen. Jessie wondered if it was possible to make things as tough as they felt right now. *If this is life working from the inside out, it's really messed up.*

She stared at the fountain. Maybe it wouldn't harm to think a more optimistically. She tried to imagine something cool happening. After dreaming about finding her dad in Memphis and then winning the music contest, Jessie decided that "making things happen" was a nice idea, but she needed something a bit more practical in the real world. *I really need some money*, she thought. She watched the fountain flow into the pool. It was surrounded by plastic boulders, bushes, and leafy tropical plants. In front was a white picket fence with a small sign, "Keep Out." From the escalators, shoppers threw coins into the fountain and watched them sink to the bottom.

People were just throwing money away!

She watched one child plead for a coin, and his father lifted him up so that he could throw it. The coin fell short of its target, missed, and fell in the bushes to one side. The father laughed and hugged his son. Jessie checked around her.

"Stay here, Bear. Stay."

She jumped over the low fence and was quickly concealed by vast foliage. In the gloom, she could make out coins shining amongst the earth. She jumped at them, her fingers picking quickly through the soil. In places, small piles had collected. Grinning, she plucked the little stacks. It was money for nothing: nickels, dimes, and even several quarters. *How could someone throw away a quarter?* she wondered. Her pockets soon bulged with a mixture of earth and money.

To her left, she heard the rustle of undergrowth brushing together.

"Gotcha!" A large, weighty hand landed on her shoulder as the burly security guard lunged toward her and grabbed her arm. Still crouched, she kicked him hard on the leg and her boot connected with his knee. The guard went down awkwardly and pitched toward the pool edge. Before he could get up, a low rumbling growl sounded close by. In the shadows, Bear was crouched just three feet from him. The guard's face fixed in terror when he saw Bear: fifty pounds of violence not on a leash.

"Okay...get the dog away—get the dog away!"

The guard covered his face and head. Jessie darted behind him and was out over the picket fence in a flash.

"Bear, come on, move!"

Jessie fled through the shoppers toward the side exit, followed at a distance by the pit bull. She knew they were too fast for the burly guard; plus, he looked like he'd sooner catch scabies than Bear.

They made it back to the truck in about four minutes. Bear got a quick pat and a rub before being shoved struggling into the cab. Back out onto the highway, she tucked into the slow lane between two trucks and watched her mirror for a while. Then she pulled over into the next service station to count the money.

"Thirteen dollars and seventy-six cents, Bear. Good work, huh?" Jessie was so relieved she hadn't had to take a wallet that it took a while for her to register the obvious. *That's not going to buy much gas.*

She'd used all the money left from the fire on a day and a half's driving, and she was still almost a day from Memphis. She put the heels of her hands into her eyes and groaned her frustration.

As they continued east, Jessie figured they had enough gas to reach the nearest town, Sligo, about 60 miles away. At that point, she was going to have to find a way of getting some more money; for now, at least she'd kept them moving. It was no miracle, but it was better than nothing.

To pass the time, Jessie sang loud with the windows rolled down. It felt great to be singing again; she'd missed it. Around her, the flat farmland continued; she knew she was between nowhere and somewhere. And she still hadn't found what she was looking for.

They arrived in Sligo late in the afternoon; it was a dustbowl town, like Dorma, but with a few more trucks and a lot less cars. Again her thoughts drifted toward Danny and so she pulled over at a phone booth; he might still be home. It felt like something to do, a break from being on the road.

Dialing his number, she wasn't sure she was doing the right thing. She felt awkward, exposed.

"Danny?"

"Yeah, who's that?" He sounded tired. "Jess, is that you...? Hey, how are you?"

"Fine. Listen, I don't have much money. I just needed to say, well, about the lyrics thing, it was just...you know." *Dumb, dumb, dumb,* she cursed silently, and waited for inspiration.

"Hey, no big deal, Jess," he said gently. "I'll get over it." Then, "How's your road trip going? Where are you, anyway?"

"Just pulled into a dump called Sligo. Bit of a problem with cash for gas, but I'm working on a plan."

"Jessie, don't go getting yourself in trouble—please."

"Yeah, well, I'm starting to run low on options out here."

Silence fell between them.

"Jessie—what about Bear?" he asked.

"What about him?"

"Well, if anything happens to you, like getting busted, what do you think will happen to him? A dog pound maybe, but destroyed more likely."

"No, no way." Jessie tried to sound brave. She remembered the fire and her stomach lurched with the same despair that she'd felt then.

"Think about it," Danny said.

"Right, yeah."

"And keep in touch, huh?"

"Yeah. Okay. Later."

Jessie put down the phone and crouched down next to Bear. She hugged him and buried her face in his thick neck. Bear squirmed until she let him go, and then licked her face in confusion. *I need to think of something else,* she thought.

Walking down the main street of the town, she sat down on a bench. She called to Bear to sit with her, and he tucked close then looked the other way. She stroked him, still thinking about Danny's warning. Nothing was worth that; no trip to Memphis, no music contest, no finding her father, nothing. She needed a kosher way of getting a bigger amount of cash. The idea came to her as more of a sense of hanging dread. Jessie realized that there was really only one thing to do; she just needed to go and do it.

Eleven

Her father's ring. Jessie knew it was all she had of any value; she'd sell the ring and get the money they needed.

Back at the truck she took the ring from the box, one last time. She lifted the blue bead bracelet up. It was pretty but probably worthless. As she pushed the ring onto her finger it felt cold and had a mist on its surface. The emerald was sizable and if it was good quality might be enough to get them to Memphis and even a place to stay for a while.

In a rough part of town, the pawn broker was predictably well marked: 'Earle's Pawn and Precious Metals.' The storefront was grubby, with an array of strange household objects behind a window with a grille on it. Jessie couldn't remember the last time she'd used a pawn shop to hock something, but she knew she'd remember this day.

Inside, the counter was high with a raised platform area behind. Behind it, a war veteran played solitaire. In army fatigues and a bandana; his T-shirt had helicopters flying over palm trees on it. Down by his wheelchair stood a short-barreled shotgun. He turned cards as he spoke.

"You got something for me?" His voice was reedy, thin. As he looked at Bear, his head tilted to one side.

"Selling this." Jessie held her chin up and put the ring on the counter.

As the veteran picked it up, the ring shone in the dim light. Jessie watched him handle it and felt sick. With an eyeglass he examined the markings and the emerald but his face was unreadable.

Then he put the ring on his finger and as he looked at it he raised his eyebrows.

"I know what it's worth," Jessie challenged. "I know it's special." She didn't know if it was or not, but the thought of losing it weighed heavy.

"Yeah?" he said. "What's it worth?" He stretched his hand out and appraised it from a distance.

"Five hundred," she said, with no idea how close she was. She needed at least half that to get to Memphis and get established.

"Nope," he said. "Tell you what—I'll give you the offer of your life. Two-fifty for the ring and your canine friend here. It's more than they're both worth, but let's just say I'm feeling generous."

"My dog's not for sale." *He's not having Bear.*

"Everything's for sale."

"Yeah, well, the dog's not in this—it's the ring, and it's two-fifty. Do we have a deal, or do I get my ring back?"

Jessie held out her hand. *He can shoot me but he's not having Bear.*

"Fine. But missy... I'm not offering a loan deal here; it's a sale." His leer exposed stained teeth.

"Okay, whatever."

Outside in the dry heat, the cash in her pocket felt dirty and corrupt. She reminded herself that she'd gotten the money that would get them to Memphis, that they had a way out. However, the ring had been her father's, and she'd sold it so soon. Her mother would be disgusted with her. *No change there,* she thought.

From a supermarket she bought dog food for Bear and a soda for herself. As she put the items onto the counter, the checkout lady frowned. Jessie got ready for her to say something but the lady was watching Bear. He was panting from all the walking and his tongue was hanging out. When the lady offered a drink of water for him, Jessie stared for a moment before being able to mutter her thanks. *Why can't I spot nice people?* she thought.

Together, they sat outside on the pavement in the early evening sun. Jessie distracted herself with thoughts of the contest in Memphis. It was just a few weeks away, and arriving in the city with no band, no gear, and nowhere to stay meant finding her father was something to do sooner rather than later. *I wonder what kind of person he is...* she thought.

◎　◎　◎

In Dorma, Ray was serving his first and final customer of the day, but he soon realized that this man wasn't buying or selling. This man was taking. The stranger had approached with a very direct stare, and it was a stare that currently held Ray transfixed. As the man talked to him in low, even tones, Ray's sneakers might as well have been glued to the floor. Running was not an option.

Like a distant recording, Ray could hear his own voice answering the stranger's questions. All he could actually see were the man's black eyes. He felt disassociated, like he was listening as someone else babbled answers.

Ray's voice rose and fell earnestly, as if he was trying to convince someone, as if he was pleading for something. His flabby arms swung as his hands danced to the tune of his own urgent explanations. Ray couldn't actually feel his arms, or indeed any other part of his body, and he reminded himself that this apparent disconnect was a good thing. For when the stranger had first approached, Ray's first instinct had been to get as far away as possible. It wasn't his lean, greasy appearance, or even the stench of the swamp that radiated from him. It was more the thought that struck him like a numbing blow: that if the devil really existed, he was stood right in front of him.

Twelve

J essie parked the truck outside of a bar on the way
out of Sligo. The live music inside had a soothing
rhythm that relaxed her. She wouldn't go in, wouldn't leave
Bear, but it was nice to be near music, even if it wasn't her
kind of thing. They shared the leftover breakfast rolls as a
late supper. Afterward, Bear lay by her side, his body warm
and comforting. Under the harsh wool of the blanket, they
fell asleep to the sorrowful harmonies of country music, a
real-life lullaby.

That night, Jessie dreamed again.

The scarecrow stood humming but the patches on his
jacket weren't holding the straw in and little pieces of it
floated off and turned to candy floss in the soft breeze.
Her work boots had gotten tangled in some curly chicken
wire, and as she fought with the tangles she fell over into
the mud. She pushed down with one hand and that got
snagged in more of the wire, which was weird because
then the scarecrow stopped humming and said in a chirpy
voice, "Hey partner, need some help there?"

"I'll do it," Jessie said, and grunted as she stood up.

"Prefer to go it alone?" The hummingbird that
buzzed around his head was blue and glittered in the light.

There's no hummingbirds in Kansas, she thought. Someone was tutting again.

"I said I can do it," she muttered, as the chicken wire turned into fishing net and wrapped itself around her boots. As her heels jammed together her ankles hit each other hard enough to hurt. Predictably, in the field of troubles, wintry rain fell as liquid tears and loneliness washed over her like an ocean of despair.

Why am I always alone? she wondered.

She still had the exact same feeling when she woke up in the truck. *Why am I always alone?*

After chewing on the question for a while, Jessie drove to the nearest phone booth.

"Hi, it's me."

"Jessie, don't you sleep?" Danny complained.

"No. Listen up, I don't have much change," Jessie said. "Just needed to say I didn't steal anything yesterday. I pawned my dad's ring, the amazing Egyptian one. I told you about it in O'Neill's. In the bar..."

"You did what?" Danny sounded awake now. "Jess, why? Who to?"

"Some greasy 'Nam vet called Earle, a real creep in a wheelchair—runs a pawn shop in a place called Sligo. He wanted to buy Bear, too—I flipped him the finger on that one."

"And are you okay with that? I mean, 'cause it was your dad's?"

"Yes, sort of, look, forget it. It's just some dumb ring." Her words felt hollow. "Gotta go, anyway, it's no big deal."

Jessie hung up. She'd hoped it would feel better, letting Danny know—hoped he'd be pleased that she'd listened to his warning. Instead, it just made the whole thing more real—she'd lost her dad's ring. She wondered about trying to get it back, wondered about finding another way. There was no way that redneck Earle was going to part with it without a healthy profit. *So much for everyday magic,* she thought.

Around them, Sligo groped a start to its day. Against a row of drab buildings, Patsy's Pastries was brightly-lit and inviting. Bear picked up the sugary scent and trotted ahead toward the shop door. Inside, the shelves and baskets were loaded with breads, cookies, and decorated cakes. Jessie bought a coffee and three giant muffins, one for her, two for Bear.

Part Two: Creative Chaos

Thirteen

Danny circled his tiny living room and thought about Jessie. He felt haunted by this girl who refused his lifts, wouldn't let him buy her a drink and even acted wary about him lending her the occasional CD. Danny knew most girls seemed to like him. Jessie seemed to not even notice him, but she called him, didn't she? What did that mean?

He'd wanted to tell her about band practice last night and the realization that they'd done the wrong thing. He knew he should have argued more against Nico's push to fire her, but his feelings for Jessie would have been obvious and that wasn't something he wanted to broadcast. Besides, she'd let him down too; couldn't she see that? Without her the session had been easy-going in atmosphere, followed by easy listening as an ugly result. The contrast of Sophie's vocals with Jessie's was like putting Ma's home cooking next to five star cuisine; it was the everyday next to the exquisite.

With such a short time left until the contest, Danny knew that they needed to make some solid decisions. He reasoned it out; their choice of covers felt strong and the new material they had was fresh, probably good enough to get through the early rounds of the contest. But without

Jessie fronting they were like a horror film without a psychopath, all bark and no bite. Without her fire and determination fueling the performance, they were just a four-piece band.

The night she tried out for the band was still strong in his mind. Her choice of song was unexpected: "Desperado," by the Eagles. It wasn't exactly cool. However, its simplicity showed how flawless her voice really was. Ed knew the old classic too, and his lonely piano accompaniment had created the perfect backdrop to her rich tones. The prickling sensation on the back of Danny's neck sealed it for him. Afterward, they'd all just stared at her. Jessie's confused expression had surprised him even more, because for all her apparent cockiness, it was obvious that Jessie had no idea. Was the band impressed by what they'd just heard, or not?

They were a motley crew: a genius muso geek, a moody drummer, and his rich stroppy girlfriend. Danny knew it was Jessie that was the wild card, the real unknown, and the reason that potential seemed to crackle in the air that night. He remembered how great that moment was, how simple it had all seemed. He'd guessed that Nico would fancy her and Princess Sophie would resent her, but was totally wrong. When it came to musical choices, Sophie tended to agree with Jessie and even asked her advice on how to approach her own backing vocals. By contrast, in any musical discussion, Nico would automatically disagree with Jessie and then everyone else would try to negotiate between them.

In his apartment, Danny stopped pacing and watched as the telephone refused to ring. Finally, he made his decision. He wanted to find Jessie and he couldn't count on her calling back. He'd leave her a message on his answer machine, just in case. Band or no band, he wanted to see her. He knew the route she might take and could travel twice as fast as she could in the truck. Maybe he could get her back in the band. Sophie would approve of his decision; blonde didn't have to mean dumb. Nico would just have to put up with it. Having his girl singing backup in a winning band was better than her leading one that crashed and burned, wasn't it?

◎   ◎   ◎

The morning sun was still cool as Jessie continued her way southeast. She reckoned they could easily make Memphis that day and tried to feel happy about that. However, as the distance between her and Sligo grew, the cigar box on the seat seemed to shout at her and eventually she pulled the rug over it.

The local radio station was playing "Desperado," by the Eagles; a lilting tale of a lonely cowboy. As always, the song made her think of home; her mom had loved it and sang it loudly. It was one of the first songs Jessie had known the words to all the way through.

Her earliest memories of her mom were sunny. She'd played the radio full blast, belting out her favorites. As it became obvious that her father wasn't coming home,

Jessie had watched the light that was her mother fade. The person Jessie left was foul-mouthed and bitter, a woman who got lost in a bottle, silently raging and staring. Back then, Jessie had been angry at her mother. The house was a mess, there was no food in the cupboards, and her appearance was unkempt—didn't she care? What man would want to come home to a woman like this?

As a child, she'd decided her dad left because of something her mom must have done, but the postcards painted a different picture. The stories that had played out in Jessie's head seemed wonky now. Things between her father and her mother seemed to have just ended. He'd gone and not come back.

By now, Jessie couldn't remember things clearly. Maybe what she'd done was the same, Jessie had left his mum like he did, but she'd been kicked out, hadn't she? *Did I make this happen?*

Danny set out on the interstate. It was a faster road than Jessie had taken, plus more direct. The Camaro had twice the pace of the old pickup; he could halve the travel time at least. He'd cut off the main route and head down to Sligo in her footsteps. That much of his plan was solid; the rest he'd have to improvise.

He thought about Jessie; she had some offbeat idea about finding her father, that maybe he was still working in the business. The bonus would be to discover him a success, a player in the industry. She'd also mentioned a younger sister and sounded protective of her. He hadn't gotten much in the way of facts, just a list of random remarks to tie together.

The interstate was fairly clear, and by lunchtime, he'd made good progress. He allowed himself a pit stop at a Taco Bell. He filled up with gas and called home to check his messages. On the machine, his voice was falsely casual.

"Hi, this is Danny Brewer, I'm gone for a few days, so leave a message and if that's you Jessie, don't hang up! I'm coming to Memphis. We need to talk. Meet me at the Pyramid arena. I'll be there by four o'clock tomorrow—that's Saturday... yep, okay, hope to see ya."

Record a message in haste, repent at leisure, thought Danny. Had he given his feelings away? Part of him didn't care. Besides, he told himself, after all the signals she'd ignored over the last year he was probably still safe. He could probably greet her wearing a T-shirt with her photo on it and she wouldn't figure it out.

Behind Danny's Camaro, the driver of a white Dodge kept a cool distance. Kabos had learned patience through years of waiting. He could wait a little longer. While it had been close before, he knew the ring was nearer now.

Kabos thought again of his own country, Egypt, the famous land of the pharaohs, a noble place with a proud history. He'd been in this country America for too many years and was sick of it. The accents, the people—he despised them and their absurd ways. No matter, his long search was almost over, and when he had taken the ring from the girl, he could quit this frustrating place.

He yearned to return home, to his father's mansion in the suburbs of Cairo. He missed the cool marble floors, the sounds of insects at night and the aroma of jasmine floating up from the courtyard. Kabos missed his father too, at silly little moments, like when he'd invented a new illusion, tied his laces extra-tight, or was gutting road-kill. Last night it had been a raven's cry in the dark night that made him stop and wonder. How long his did father's body lie on the terrace in a crimson pool, and how soon would it have been before his eyes were taken by crows?

In the rearview mirror, Kabos clenched his freakishly white teeth into a grin. The row of perfect porcelain veneers was a recent acquisition from a dentist in Reno. The dentist had been reluctant to give a $60,000 dollar treatment for free outside of regular surgery hours. However, Kabos overcame the dentist's resistance by whispering in his ear a while. How the dentist explained the stench of a swamp in his clinic every morning for a week was his problem.

He moved closer to the mirror and pushed up his top lip. Back in Cairo, he would live like a movie star, returned from America to take his father's place as head of the antiques world. He hoped the mansion was being looked after and someone had kept the servants on. He wondered how they'd explained the fall from the balcony, especially as his father didn't drink. No matter, his doting son wouldn't have been blamed, as he'd been sent to America on business when it happened. Of course, there was the minor matter of Kabos sneaking back to Cairo around the same time, but like the rotting stumps of his teeth, it was a small detail, easily glossed over.

Fourteen

essie reached the outskirts of Memphis by four p.m. and, entering the suburbs, pulled over. She wasn't ready for Memphis, not yet. She'd felt a strong urge to stop but now, in the truck, she wasn't sure what to do. She thought again of her father and the Braves. Maybe he was in one of these houses; maybe he had other children now.

From the cigar box, she pulled out a faded photograph. Her mother and father were posed against the hood of a Plymouth. Her mother leaned back on him, his arms hugging tight around her waist, his chin into her neck. Both were grinning. She wondered again what her father looked like now—had he kept his hair long?

Jessie looked at the homes around her. The suburb was clean—no burned-out cars, just pristine lawns and low fences. Bear was eager to get outside, and together they walked down the street, keeping the truck in sight. The sidewalks were broad, swept clean, and Jessie was suddenly aware of how grubby she must look. Nearby, two young girls played on a lawn, as they ran through a sprinkler they shrieked with delight. Jessie wondered if they still believed in magic, or if they'd given up on it too. Their mother walked outside and shouted for them to come in, eyeing Jessie's shabby truck.

Looking around her, she wondered about turning back. Ahead of her, Bear had stopped to wait and sat panting in the heat. Between them on the sidewalk was a feather, white with gray at its tip. She picked it up, and as she tilted it in her fingers, she felt still inside. The softness at its base fluttered, as if blown by a breeze, but there was no breeze. Jessie sat down on the sidewalk and smiled at it. *Feathers are cool,* she thought. *They feel peaceful.*

"Can I help you, honey?"

A middle-aged woman stood at an open garage door, carrying a small plastic table. Her voice was warm and friendly. Jessie stalled, but as she stood up she remembered her dream. *She's offering to help.*

"Can I maybe have a little water for my dog?"

"Why, sure you can, darlin'. Come on 'round back." Her lilting accent was almost a song.

"Hank! We need some water here for this lady's dog. And maybe a long cold soda." She winked at Jessie before sashaying back up the path, the table abandoned. As she walked, she hummed, reminding Jessie of a happy little bird. The sight of the lady's strappy sandals made her own boots feel heavy in the heat. She had the urge to carry the table for her, but was stalled by how that might look. Bear trotted ahead as the woman's song worked like a charm on him and he disappeared around the back of the garage.

"Hey, little fella," came a man's deep voice. Jessie turned the corner of the garage to find the woman's husband squatting down and stroking Bear in a rough, uneven way. Jessie silently urged Bear not to growl or bite the man, but instead Bear just looked up at him.

"This here a fighting dog?" The man looked up at Jessie. She hesitated. *It's a question, not an accusation,* she realized.

"Yeah, well, that's what he was intended for, but I sorta rescued him from that career, didn't I, buddy?" She bent down as well. Bear flopped down and looked up at both of them.

"Hank, will you get the dog some water?" the lady chided him. "I'll go get that soda." She shimmied into the house, humming a chirpy little tune again.

"You're a real powerhouse, ain't ya?" Hank stroked Bear's back and shoulders with both hands now. He stood up, still regarding Bear. "So how did you come by him?" he asked. "He sure is a fine specimen."

"I guess I sorta stole him," she said. "He was just a pup. I spotted him cowering by the side of the breeder's truck." She looked at Bear, remembering the night. "This lowlife was around the other side complaining about the fighting game and how all the money had gone out of it, animal rights protesters, that kind of thing. Anyway, Bear was real thin and weak, shivering; he just didn't look so good…" She stroked Bear's head. "Anyway, sometimes you know something ain't right. So I scooped him up and put him in my jacket. I knew he was better off with me."

"You sure took a risk messing with those guys," Hank said, bending down to stroke Bear again, who promptly collapsed onto the path to allow his stomach to be rubbed. Hank looked at Jessie and nodded. "But then some risks need taking, don't they?"

Bear was soon drinking fresh water out of a plastic container, which moved around with him as it emptied. From the kitchen door, Hank's wife emerged with a glass of lemonade packed with ice. Jessie stared and tried to swallow the lump in her throat, but her face gave her away.

"Honey, are you in trouble or something?" the lady asked. Jessie knew she was scruffy and unkempt. A few quick washes in restrooms hadn't made much of a difference.

"Not really, I mean no. No trouble. I've just been sleeping in the truck. It's only temporary."

"Well, hey now, that sounds like a real adventure."

The lady flashed a look of concern at her husband.

"And it's good to have you here anyhow. My name's Hank." He held out a huge hand, calloused and warm. "And my good lady here is Peggy."

Peggy stepped forward and held out her hand.

"Jessie," said Jessie, feeling embarrassed. "And this is Bear," but Bear had wandered off again.

"Well Jessie, you're welcome to stay for some food. I was just setting up the grill." Hank nodded to a home-built barbeque. "Looks as though old Bear's kinda decided for you, though." He laughed gently as Bear took a position directly underneath a plate of sausage and chicken.

Peggy kept smiling and looking from Hank to Jessie and then back again. Jessie found herself wanting to cry again. She looked at them both and nodded slowly.

"That would be great," she whispered.

"Honey, you keeping that for something?" Peggy looked down at Jessie's hand; she was still holding the feather.

"Well, I was thinking about it..." Jessie said and tucked it in her pocket. She looked behind her. "Would... would you like me to fetch your table for you?"

"That would be real helpful, darlin'." Peggy beamed. "And an extra chair from over by the freezer, one of the newer ones, please."

Later, after some cold beers and food that she'd remember forever, Jessie found herself telling them why she was here, about the contest, even about hoping to find her father. It felt good to talk, to be in conversation again. She felt herself relaxing, and enjoying their easy company. They listened, and she knew they were trying not to interfere. Jessie tried to sound old enough to know what she was doing and tough enough to work things out. However, as they explained that they had had a daughter of their own, grown-up and out on her own, she guessed they were making the comparison.

As the last ember on the barbeque went white, Peggy coughed and sat up a little straighter on her chair.

"Now Jessie, I know you know you've got your own plans, but I can't help thinking that we've got a clean bed upstairs, and what I'd like you to know is that you're welcome to it for the night." Hank nodded his agreement as Peggy hesitated. "And it would be easy for me to run your things through a wash. I could have 'em dry for you by morning."

Jessie clapped her hands together, her mouth wide in mock horror.

"You saying I'm not quite washed and scrubbed here, Peggy?"

Peggy chuckled and began clearing plates.

"Well, that's settled," Hank said, and stood up. "Jessie how about you and me have some more of that ice cream?"

Jessie pulled the feather from her pocket and gazed at it. In the silent space that followed, she felt more at home than she had for years.

Fifteen

anny reached Sligo and pulled off the highway. It was later than he'd hoped, but he'd made it. All around him, the sky was bruised and blackening fast as dark, foreboding clouds gathered. As he killed his speed, he wound down his windows. The engine smelled hot; he'd pushed it to the limit. The warm breeze on his face held a whisper of rain and he wondered how long the storm would take to hit.

The gas station's bright lighting shone against the darkening sky. Danny filled up with gas and ran inside. From the shelves, he grabbed a family pack of chips to keep hunger at bay.

Back in the car, he slowed his pace for the town's speed limits. By now, there was just one thing on his mind: finding Jessie. The journey from Dorma had been a long one, and for much of it, she'd filled his thoughts. At some point along the road, he'd even been thinking of some lyrics for a song about how he felt. That was when he decided to pull himself together and focus on the practicalities of the situation. Around him, Sligo began to close up for the night, and if he was going to look for a hotel, he needed to decide fast.

Overhead, the low, dark clouds stole the last of the light and ended the day early. On the horizon, distant flashes warned of the tempest to come. On impulse, Danny took a sharp turn off the main street and noticed that the white Dodge behind him copied his move. A sign to his right caught his attention: "Earle's Pawn and Precious Metals"—the pawnbroker who bought the ring, he realized. From the look of things, Earle was just closing shop.

Danny parked and jumped out, not bothering to lock the car. He wasn't sure what he was going to say to the guy, but right now he was a definite link to Jessie. He put a hand up to the grille over the door.

"Can I come in?" Danny asked, trying to look friendly. Earle reached up to bolt the door, stretching out of his wheelchair with the shotgun balanced in his lap.

"Closed," Earle said. "Come back tomorrow."

"It's about a girl; she sold you a man's ring. Do you still have it?"

Earle stopped. He watched Danny for a moment and reached for the lock again. As he moved the bolt back across Danny saw an oversized ring glitter on Earle's left hand. *Surely that isn't it?* he thought.

Danny checked the weapon and moved slowly. Inside the shop, the holes in the ceiling indicated how Earle liked to deal with trouble.

"Yeah, thanks buddy," said Danny.

"You interested in the girl or the ring?" Earle wheeled away a distance, then spun around to look at him. "That feisty little filly something to ya?" he said.

"No, it's the ring...I want to buy it back if I can," Danny said.

"Oh, sure. You got three thousand bucks handy, kiddo?"

Earle pulled the huge ring from his finger and held it up. Even in the dim light, its markings gleamed and glittered. Earle's other hand rested on the shotgun stock.

Danny knew it was the ring Jessie had described, but was it worth that much? He had a few hundred; it wasn't even worth trying to negotiate. Earle twisted the ring around in his inky fingers and sneered.

Behind him, the shop door opened with a sigh and suddenly the room was swept cold.

A lean man dressed in filthy clothes crept forward, his movements silent and quick. His crow-like features seemed to soak up the light, and his face stayed in shadow. Earle raised the gun and the black mouths of the barrels swung past Danny.

"You can stop right there, stranger." Earle spat on the floor to his side and wheeled his chair back with one elbow.

Danny turned to see the wraith-like figure step forward in a looping path around Earle. In the half-light, he saw the curved blade of the dagger flash. As the intruder spoke, everything faded a little, and the wall behind him seemed to drop away. The vaguest smell of roses reached him.

"The ring, give it to me. It belongs to me…"

Kabos' hissing echo bounced off the walls. Danny's rising panic numbed his scalp.

Earle twitched his head at Danny and then altered his position in the wheelchair. As he did so the ring fell from his lap and rolled across the floor.

Kabos leapt forward, but Danny was nearer and as he grabbed the ring, Earle let off a warning shot. In the enclosed space, the howling tone reverberated and Danny's ears rang in shock. Kabos glanced at Earle and then walked directly toward Danny.

"Give me the ring. I won't kill you, just the cripple," he said between gritted teeth. "Look at me." As Danny stared at him, the man's eyes seemed to go black. Suddenly, Earle darted forward with a roar and jabbed a fierce blow to the base of Kabos' spine with the stock of the shotgun. Danny knew the strike should have floored the man, but Kabos only shrieked in anger. He spun around to face Earle, and leaning down toward him, he started hissing.

Danny pitched backward to the door, wrenched the door open and ran out onto the street. Behind him, Earle screamed, sharp and shrill. Danny made it into the car. As he twisted the keys in the ignition, his hands shook. He saw the white Dodge across the street and made the connection. Behind him, the shotgun rang out again. His tires screeched out as the car lurched forward, and still Earle screamed.

Danny pulled out over the crossroads, hardly registering the other traffic. Getting back to the highway was his single desperate thought. Terror took hold and he drove the car as fast as he dared. He struggled to think; the white Dodge had been following him. That vagrant wanted the ring, Jessie's ring. In his mirror, he watched for the Dodge. Storm clouds turned the sky black, and the rain was like thunder on the roof of the Camaro. He drove on and was glad for the darkness, for in darkness there might be safety.

◎　◎　◎

On the outskirts of Memphis, Jessie was enjoying the comfort of Peggy's daughter's bedroom. She wore a borrowed bathrobe and slippers. After the longest, hottest shower she'd had in months, she'd used actual toothpaste to clean her teeth. She felt brand new. Not wearing makeup still felt strange but not in a bad way. *I don't have to wear it,* she reminded herself. Bear was curled up on a pink, furry, heart-shaped rug. She rattled him gently with her foot and his soft fur on her clean toes felt delightful. Around the bedroom were a teenager's things. A family of teddy bears jarred with the Chili Peppers poster and heavy junk jewelry. On the dresser was a framed photo of Peggy's daughter smiling, her arms around two girlfriends, all making the peace sign with outstretched fingers. *Lucky girl*, thought Jess. She hoped she was the kind of daughter who called home regularly; the couple deserved that.

Earlier, she'd fetched the cigar box from the truck. Sitting cross-legged on the bed, Jessie gently fingered through the contents. The stones of the blue bracelet felt silky and she pushed them like worry beads through her fingers. It could have been a gift from her father to Mary; Jessie couldn't remember it. Her sister was almost fifteen now; she'd probably be dating boys and listening to music that Jessie didn't know. She picked up the final postcard.

It was the worst one:

November 22nd

Corinne,

This isn't any easier for me babe, but I hope it makes some kind of sense. It's difficult to explain and I tried last night, but this isn't a life for you and the girls, and it never would be. You've always known my heart was in this dream; that's the one thing I never lied about. I'll send money soon.

Billy J

x

For the first time, Jessie wondered about her mother. What it had been like for her? She would have watched the mailman make his delivery, retrieved the postcard from the mailbox. With two young kids back inside the house and all of them waiting for this man to return, or better still, send for them. How had her mother felt as she'd stood reading that card, and why had she kept it?

Sixteen

Kabos drove on through the night. In the darkness of the cab, he measured the situation. The youth had evaded him while he'd been distracted by the cripple. Not for the first time, he'd let his anger rule his head, and as the killing rage took control, the boy had escaped. His temper was something he really needed to control. No matter, Kabos knew where the youth was headed: Memphis. It was a fitting location for his triumph, a city with the same name as the first capital of Egypt. The same city he'd been travelling toward to take the precious artifacts to be appraised all those years ago. His father would approve; he was certain.

In a rich suburb of Cairo, Kabos had grown up in a world of antiques, fine art and sorcery. Both art dealership and the practice of dark magic had been passed down through his family for generations, possibly since the high priests first practiced it in the temples thousands of years ago. As a child, his father's tricks and illusions were everyday events. A spoon apparently floating in mid-air, strange mist taking form as a monster in front of him, even the sight of his orange kitten hanging limp from a tree branch—all were possible in little Kabos' world. His father might amuse Kabos by seeming to float cutlery at breakfast, only to punish him by hanging his only pet by suppertime. Kabos' fear of accidentally disobeying his father was so habitual that he still checked his shoelaces to ensure they were properly tied.

Young Kabos had been carefully molded to see the world another way. His father's mantra still echoed in his ears: "To see the world differently you must live differently." Kabos had slept on the earth floor of the cellar underneath the mansion and his father had fed him raw meat through the bars of his cage. At the age of eight he was made to sleep outside and kill his own food while the servants were told to ignore the master's son or lose their jobs. His physical training began soon after, and in a concealed courtyard he would stand for slow hours under a hot sun holding sacks of grain or metal weights. While most teenagers chased girls, Kabos developed a physical strength that enabled him to curve metal and crush skulls. By showing his beloved father he could do both, he earned the right to sit with his father just before his fourteenth birthday. From then on, killing street urchins and homeless beggars became a regular sport for them both. "Quality time", as Kabos thought of it.

If Kabos had ever had a mother (which he mostly doubted) she was never mentioned. Nothing in the mansion suggested her presence or her existence. Eventually, Kabos had stopped wondering who brought him into this life and decided that he was better off not knowing; after all, if the world belonged to men, what use was a woman?

The emerald ring and the temple dagger were priceless relics entrusted to Kabos' care. Stolen from a looted tomb many years earlier, they had fallen into his father's hands by chance. Careful arrangements had been made to sell them to a Chinese collector for many millions of dollars, based on their being proven to be authentic. So first, the artifacts and other supporting evidence must be appraised by a trusted expert in antiquities. Following detailed instructions, Kabos had traveled to America to meet the contact in the city of Memphis. He was to travel overland, undercover, and pass through no border controls that might trace the illegal export of rare Egyptian artifacts. For someone schooled in fakery and illusion, it became an entertaining game. So gifted was Kabos at hypnosis and mind-control, he could walk past customs officers waving his arms and they wouldn't stop him.

Kabos' arrival in America had been more enjoyable than he'd expected and his father's hatred for the country and its people had seemed misplaced. Feeling a lightness and sense of liberation quite alien to him, Kabos had been initially charmed by its occupants. He liked the friendly way they talked to him and how they appeared genuinely interested in where he was from. After living under his father's rules for almost twenty years, America truly seemed like the land of the free. Now that he'd been living in the country all this time, he'd developed a deep loathing for everything about it.

After the theft, Kabos had struggled to imagine the biblical force of his father's wrath. Whichever way he looked at it, priceless treasures entrusted to him had been stolen by a bunch of rednecks from Kansas, which was why as soon as it happened, Kabos had returned to Egypt and killed his father before his father had time to find out.

These days Kabos traveled light, slept rough and used basic sorcery of scented vapors and mind control to secure food or transport. Cash money was always easy to obtain, but Kabos preferred to practice his tricks. The white Dodge he was currently driving had been taken by convincing its owner that he'd mistakenly been driving the wrong colored vehicle. The burly cowboy was probably still looking for his pink pickup even now.

Tonight, as he drove, he tried to cheer himself up by humming a happy tune from the Disney Channel. On the TV show he'd watched in the Wal-Mart store, the presenter had said that singing happy tunes released feel-good hormones to create a sense of inner harmony and well-being. It wasn't actually working yet but then, Kabos reminded himself, he did need to be more patient.

Seventeen

On a Memphis suburb, Jessie fell to sleep to the sound of Hank and Peggy laughing at a comedy show downstairs and Bear's gentle snoring. Returning to a field of dreams, she frowned as she slept.

The hummingbird had unpicked the fishing net and was currently tying the laces on her work boots. Jessie chuckled at the little bird and it came out as a wobbly burp. *I got help,* she thought, feeling pleased. Around her, the hill flattened to a gentle slope and it had stopped raining. *That's weird.*

"Hey thanks," she whispered and stroked the hummingbird's head with a sparkly feather.

"Not on your own, then?" said the scarecrow and waved at the bird, which waved back. Then everything got brighter so he took the round, blue sunglasses from his top pocket and placed them on the back of his head.

"I don't know anymore." Jessie wanted to tell him something, but couldn't recall just what. *Maybe if I could just explain how I really feel,* she wondered, *maybe someone will actually like me.* But the scarecrow was busy rubbing his chin and so she left it for another time when the whole thing didn't seem so Sergeant Peppers.

Jessie woke in the strange bedroom and sat up in bed. As she looked around, she saw the dressing table and in the mirror, her dazed expression stared back at her. The dream faded away. Bear padded around the room, asking to be let out. She slipped the bathrobe on and made her way downstairs as the smell of potatoes frying rose up to meet her. Jessie smiled as she realized that Peggy wouldn't let her leave without a decent breakfast.

At Hank and Peggy's front door, Jessie said goodbye to the couple, and accepted the bag they offered her with a shy grin.

"It's just a little packed lunch—some of the leftovers from last night. No sense in good food going to waste," Peggy said.

Its heaviness suggested more, but they both knew that. Peggy hesitated, then stepped forward and hugged her, rocking slightly.

Hank held out his hand. "Look after that dog. I know he'll look after you."

Jessie's hand felt small in his, but she shook firmly. Stuck for adequate thanks, she nodded, and wished she could do something in return.

"You've been great, both of you, real lifesavers…you know…really helped…thanks." Jessie hesitated, but the couple's smiles were unconditional. Hank opened the door and put a hand on Jessie's shoulder in mock warning.

"Don't forget, look after that dog," he said.

Jessie grinned. "Okay Hank, I got it. I'll look after him!"

Outside, Bear trotted off down the path towards the truck.

"And good luck in your contest!" shouted Peggy. "Sing 'em one of them old ones for me; the old ones are the best ones, remember!"

"Maybe I'll do just that," Jessie laughed and looked back to see Hank with his arm around his wife's shoulders. *OK Memphis, here we come,* she thought.

Jessie traveled the last few miles toward Memphis in the morning traffic. In the distance, a scattering of skyscrapers marked the city skyline. It was hardly a metropolis, more a smaller cousin, but Jessie scarcely noticed. Her thoughts were on her dream last night. *What did I want to explain to the scarecrow?* she wondered. She reached the Frisco Bridge, with its walls of gray crisscross ironwork. Underneath, she watched the mighty Mississippi as it guarded the west of the city before sweeping down south. Driving over the famous bridge made her smile, as if it was a grand gateway announcing their arrival. The river below seemed vast and unstoppable. Jessie found herself grinning and began to laugh.

"Hey Bear, we made it to Memphis!" she sang out. "Watch out for Elvis!"

She turned on the radio. They were playing Rihanna and Jessie sang along loud and banged the dashboard to the rhythm. From the passenger seat, Bear watched her and so Jessie turned to sing at him. She had no plan for when she got over the bridge; she decided it would be great just to get lost for a while.

They made it through the morning traffic and over the bridge into the city. The river marked her crossing from Arkansas into Tennessee. She wanted to remember everything and wondered where to begin, but she also needed to check the venue for the finals of the music contest, the Pyramid Arena.

Turning right onto the expressway, she circled the city for a while then headed once again toward the Mississippi. A flash of light drew her attention. Ahead of her, a vast pyramid shone like silver, its surface completely mirrored. The sight of it made her gasp.

"Oh wow..."

The Pyramid Arena was colossal, the third largest pyramid in the world. The landmark was the venue for the finals of the music contest. More than thirty stories high, it was a rival to Khafre's pyramid in Giza. *How did I miss this from the bridge?* Drawing closer, she pulled over and killed the engine. She'd heard it was a real pyramid, but had imagined something much smaller. As the morning sun flashed across its steel faces, the contest felt more daunting than ever. *That's where it all gets decided,* she thought.

"Come on, Bear." She started the engine up again. "Let's get going."

Jessie turned back and drove a little way then turned onto Madison. She found a space near an old theater and parked. Compared to Dorma, Memphis seemed huge and Jessie twirled as she walked, grinning up at the buildings around her. Some were renovated, some were left empty, but she decided they were all cool. Her smile was constant. *Right here, right now, everything is okay,* she thought.

Eighteen

essie walked around Downtown for a while. Its various stages of repair included boarded over to lavishly restored: the new and the old, the good and the bad, loved or unloved. After Dorma, it was great being somewhere different. Jessie felt like she'd cast off a heavy old coat.

By lunchtime they reached Beale Street and Jessie knew that if Memphis had a musical soul, then here was its historical heart. Her dad had been there too, and the thought of that felt strange. The street was just as Jessie had imagined it; groups of locals and tourists milled around and the atmosphere felt bubbly and light. Music bars were a regular feature; Slinky's competed with Mitch's Bar, alongside the Rum Boogie Café and Bar Cuba.

Elvis was everywhere, if nowhere. The tourist shops sold the King in every shape and size. In one shop's doorway, Jessie stood face to face with a full-size model of Elvis dressed as an Indian chief. In a leather and suede outfit, his headdress was a mass of white and dark turkey feathers. One feather sat on the King's moccasin, and Jessie bent down and picked it up.

"Hey Bear, maybe this one's special," she said. The appearance of feathers felt like a good thing now, and made Jessie smile.

From a kiosk, the smell of fresh coffee and warm bagels had slowed Bear's walk. Jessie turned to see him slumped on the sidewalk. He looked back at the kiosk and then at her.

"All right Bear, you need some food, don't you, buddy?"

She bought coffee and raisin bagels and looked round for somewhere to sit. She was spending precious money, but for now that was okay.

Farther down the street, a bronze statue of W.C. Handy marked the entrance to a small park. More concrete than park, it was still inviting, a few trees giving shade to the benches beneath. A small group of musicians was setting up to play, not for money, just for tips. It was the perfect place to sit for a while, maybe even a place to figure out a plan. Jessie steered Bear across the road by holding the bag of bagels in front of him. As he trotted along his tail stub wagged constantly. *If only it were that simple*, thought Jessie, *just a few bagels to solve your problems.*

She searched for an empty bench. In the lunchtime heat, most were taken. She spotted one with a lone occupant. A hippie-looking guy in a tie-dye T-shirt and cobalt blue Beatles sunglasses perched at one end. He stared at a copy of *Time* magazine. She sat down, keeping distance between them. Jessie took a drink of the coffee and balanced the cup on the edge of the seat. She reached into the bag for a bagel.

"Come here, Bear…sit."

Bear had wandered off toward the hippie. He wore

sandals, and Bear seemed interested in his feet. She began to smile an apology, but then noticed his posture; he sat entirely upright and looked down his nose as he read. Jessie sprang up, and knocked the coffee flying.

"Jesus Christ!" she blurted and grabbed at the overturned coffee cup. "What...what are you doing here?"

Finch swept off the little round sunglasses with an elegant stroke.

"Aaah, buenos dias," he placed the magazine to one side. On the front cover of the magazine was an ancient Egyptian scene by a river. His hippie outfit included a bead necklace and leather bracelets. His dark mane was tied back, and his goatee beard was long enough to be braided. It was held in place with a vivid blue bead. *How is he doing this?* thought Jessie. *Or did I just find him?*

Her mouth hung open. "I can't believe you're in Memphis..." she said.

"I know, you might say we're virtual travelling companions. It's almost like you're following me," he smiled, and gestured with his sunglasses for her to sit beside him. "So partner, how's your trip going?"

Jessie sat down gradually, still clutching the bag of bagels. Bear squatted to attention, his nose inches away from the bag.

"Yeah, okay. Few ups and downs. Finch—how are you here? I mean, did you know I was coming...?" she watched him carefully. His gray eyes glittered; with mischief or danger, she couldn't tell.

"Yes...it certainly seems like an unexpected coincidence, doesn't it?" he said. "It's almost as if our paths are destined to cross..." He played with the bead on his goatee, and then shrugged. "So Jessie, do you still make things tough for yourself?" he asked.

"Dunno, guess so—not all the time, though." *Last night had been different*, she thought. *Maybe that changes things.*

"And what brings you to town?" he asked.

"A music festival, a potential break...my father, maybe." Jessie watched him. *Does he know that already?* But his face was unreadable.

"Ah, well, I wish you good fortune. It seems our friend here has more simple goals," he chuckled. "He just wants his lunch."

Bear's nose rested against the bag. His great brown eyes were fixed on Jessie's face, but Jessie ignored him. The soft tutting sound from Finch interrupted her thoughts.

"Yeah, right. Hey Finch, can you make things happen? I mean – could you make something happen for me and Bear, maybe..." she ventured. She didn't want to sound desperate, but right now, she needed a break.

"Or maybe you can just make something good happen yourself, Jessie. Maybe you're the one who knows what to do."

He stared at her for a moment and then stood up. *I thought I was supposed to ask for help*, she thought.

"Oh, and please be careful." Finch opened his sunglasses and blew on them gently. "Watch out for tricksters, Jess; they create illusions, remember," then he paused. "They want you think their magic is real but actually...it's not." Then he looked at her and winked. "Remember now, only what's truly real is truly powerful."

She stared at him. "So is that a warning?" she asked. *He's not making sense.*

Jessie began to stand just as Bear jumped and tugged at the bag. It ripped, and the bagels tumbled onto the sidewalk.

"Bear, for Chrissakes..."

The bagels rolled into the path of some kids on skateboards, but she retrieved them just in time. She looked behind her to see Finch at the entrance to the park, about to disappear among the crowds. Bear trotted behind her as his tail danced a heady jig. Jessie tossed the bagels over onto the grass.

"Here, you hog."

She was confused by Finch's warning. *Why did he mention tricksters again?* She sat back on the bench.

Finch's magazine sat on the bench, and a small card poked out of its pages. Jessie pulled it out, and a bright yellow smiley face stared up at her. On the other side was his latest wisdom:

Have a nice day.

Bear laid flat on the grass, he'd trapped a bagel between his paws and was gnawing at it. From the back of the park, the band of musicians struck up and launched into loud, happy jazz with easy relish. Jessie put the magazine to one side and concentrated on the card.

"Yeah, great. Cryptic," she said out loud, and tried to guess what a yellow smiley face might mean. The cheery trumpets in the background taunted her. She sighed and picked up the magazine; ancient Egyptian history wasn't really her thing. Under the river scene the headline read "Egyptian Temple Sorcery: A dark art or illusions and trickery?" *He probably studies this stuff,* she thought. While the band played on, Jessie finished the remains of the coffee and thought about Finch. *What if I could make something happen?* She tried to imagine something lucky, like a big break or something, but she couldn't figure out whether she was supposed to *think* about being lucky, or try to *feel* lucky. Meeting Hank and Peggy had been lucky, she reasoned, and tried to remember what she'd been doing just before that. *Did I make that happen?* Hanging around in a park didn't feel like progress. *Plus he said I know what to do.* She put the smiley card in her pocket and watched as Bear finished the last bagel, and then looked around himself for crumbs.

Jessie remembered that she'd first met Danny because of Bear. In the music shop, Bear had followed Danny around the aisles. Chuckling, he'd had tried changing direction a few times but Bear had trotted after him, then sat at his feet when he stopped.

In the end, Jessie had gone over to try and halt the weird behavior of her scary-looking dog. Bear was an instant Danny fan and Danny turned out to be a dog lover too. They'd talked about music, about bands, and eventually about his own band, which was looking for a lead singer and guitarist.

She spotted a phone booth over from the park, and realized that she should call Danny. *Call him.* The thought was clear, like there was nothing else she would do. She picked up the magazine and deposited it in the trash as she left the park.

She walked to the booth with just that simple idea—call Danny. After a few rings, the answering machine clicked on with its hollow echo. *Just when I acted on impulse,* she thought. Jessie had expected his cheery greeting, and now it was simply his cheery message machine.

"Hi, this is Danny Brewer, I'm gone for a few days, so leave a message and if that's you Jessie, don't hang up! I'm coming to Memphis. We need to talk. Meet me at the Pyramid arena. I'll be there by four o'clock tomorrow—that's Saturday... yep, okay, hope to see ya."

Jessie replaced the handset and stared at the phone. *It must be something to do with the band,* she thought. Her heart jumped at the possibility of that, *maybe they've had second thoughts.* As she walked away from the phone booth, she couldn't help but dance a little jig. She'd made something happen! Jessie strode ahead, then turned to watch Bear trotting behind her. His tongue was out to one side and bounced as he walked.

"Pick it up, will you?" Jessie laughed. All she had to do was to be back at the arena by four p.m. She was going to see Danny again, and that felt fine.

Nineteen

utside the Pyramid Arena, Danny had kept watch for two hours. He'd circled it, located all the entrances, and then decided to ditch the car; it might get spotted. He hid the Camaro beneath an overpass and then walked back. Across the street from the pyramid, he sat with his back against a mesh fence. He couldn't figure out what direction Jessie might come from, or if she'd be in the truck or on foot. Every white truck he saw made his heart thump in his chest until he realized it wasn't the Dodge. By one p.m. his stomach rumbled with hunger and he decided there was no point hanging around for another three hours. His whole plan assumed that Jessie had heard the telephone message.

He walked toward town behind a gang of teenagers. One youth danced around the group like a court jester, joking and clowning with endless energy. Danny watched them for a while, and then he glanced across the traffic and froze. Three lanes over, a white Dodge truck sat in a line waiting for the lights to change. The driver was unmistakable: lank hair, mirrored sunglasses, wearing a military cap and a scowl. From the angle of his face, he hadn't seen Danny walking behind the gang. Danny walked faster toward the group and tucked in alongside them. Maybe they would help him disappear for a few valuable seconds. He tried to ignore the fact that they were black, and he wasn't. He hoped the Memphis tradition of "no race line in music" still held.

"Hey fellas!" He cringed at how ridiculously cheerful his tone was. "So hey, I'm looking for a decent bar to go to, or maybe a good restaurant—do you guys know anywhere like that someplace?"

The tallest of them scowled and pouted.

"You askin' whuud?" he said.

The court jester followed suit. "Yeah, dip out, cheese boy..."

The tallest held his hand up. "Hush up, Slix."

He had his jaw up, waiting for his answer. He wore a white oversized vest hung out over mammoth jeans. His lean arms were tight with muscle, and dark tribal tattoos shadowed his skin. The black scarf on his head was worn taut and smooth, a perfect petite knot tied at the back. The others wore a similar uniform of hoodies, Converse sneakers, and hats. Their junk jewelry included flashy crosses and heavy bracelets with thick gold chains. They looked at each other and then two of them started to watch the traffic. *Just keep moving*, Danny thought.

"Um...you know, a bar or something. A good one?"

Their pace slowed as they paused to examine him, then they began to circle him a little. The scouts searched behind them, and drew attention he badly didn't want. He stole a glance at the white Dodge. The light turned green, but it didn't move.

"White boy, you're in Memphis and you're looking for

a bar—are you fo' real?" The tall guy's tone was playful, as his open palms marked the pace of his words. The others sensed sport and grinned.

"Oh, yeah, yeah I know." Danny tried to sound cool. "I'm a musician, here for the contest in a couple of weeks." He pulled a hopeful expression. "My band still hasn't gotten here. I'm checking out the venues for the qualifying heats."

Across the traffic, the white truck pulled away. He glanced over to make sure it kept moving.

"Okay, that's cool, man." The tall guy spoke again. "Yeah, you need to be heading down this way, bro."

The others nodded, one of them adding, "Yeah man, you need to be breaking down onto Peabody."

The teenagers changed both their attitude and their walk, as each vied for eye contact with the guy from the band. The smallest gang member was dressed all in black. He bounced as he walked.

"So what's your style, homey? What kinda tunes you puttin' out?"

"Well, it's rock, with a bit of bite. We've got kind of an edge, plus a cool girl vocalist with attitude. You know, Green Day meets Pink."

Danny knew it wouldn't be their thing, but at least they wouldn't kill him for it. They all nodded in semi-approval.

"You guys more into hip-hop, though, I guess?" He looked over at the traffic again. The truck was long gone.

"It's God's own message, brother."

The tallest guy was obviously the preacher, too. He pointed at the small guy in the black hoodie.

"Hey, Yo-yo, show this white boy some moves."

Yo-yo stopped walking. "Sure thing, Milk."

He spread his legs wide and struck a pose. The others fanned out around him, as the one called Slix struck up the pulse, making a staccato, blasting noise. The others joined in, adding whumps, clicks, and smacks to the thud of Slix's beat.

"Aw, yeah…"

Then, "Lock it down…"

Yo-yo nodded sideways at his backing track like a skipper in front of a twirling rope. On a half beat, he made a lazy jump in:

This town is home but it ain't for homeys,
You think you know me but you'll neva own me,
You come out running just like a little cat,
You're looking round searching this an' that,
Some record deal that ain't worth the taking,
That girl o' yours the only thing not fakin',
She got the keys to a mansion and a pool,
But wise up quick, boy—you're looking like a *fool*!

Yo-yo pointed directly at Danny and exploded into laugher, his teeth bright and smile genuine. The others clapped, while Milk cuffed Yo-yo playfully around the head.

"Right in the pocket, man," he said.

Danny clapped too, not sure what he'd just heard, but enjoying it just the same. "Will you guys enter the contest too?" he asked, and was met by laughter that faded quickly.

"We don't have no money for the entrance fee." Milk hunched his shoulders. "Maybe next year, you know?" He nodded at the others. "But we got our own scene going; there's open mike venues out on McLemore. We go freestyle down there."

They walked and talked further into downtown. Milk introduced Vinnie, Yo-yo, Phat Boy, and Slix. Milk's father really was a preacher, which to Danny explained his easy ride with these boys. He listened to how they had become disheartened by a church scene that didn't relate to what growing up was like for them.

"There ain't nuthin' they got that we want," Milk explained. "Just some ancient ideas and a bunch of crazy rules, that's all."

They parted at the corner of Union. Milk touched fists with Danny and the rest gestured casual farewells.

"Hey, yo contest boy—be lucky, bro!" Milk smiled.

"Yeah, that girl of yours sounds like a bad ass," Yo-yo added and grinned. Milk pulled him close in a neck hold and laughed as Yo-yo struggled to get away.

"You wantin' a bit of white booty, brotha?"

They all laughed and gestured casual farewells as Danny looked around before crossing the street. The white Dodge was nowhere to be seen.

Kabos circled the arena. He drove with the calmness of a cold heart. According to the imbecile in the Dorma music shop, this was the place of the contest. Not that he'd wanted to delve too deeply into that freak's mind. The crazy had babbled out all he knew about the girl musician and the contest. He'd even shown Kabos her friend Danny's telephone number on a music poster in the shop. After that, he'd left the idiot to his ramblings. A call to the youth's answering machine had told Kabos where to be and at what time; it was almost too easy.

With no immediate family left, Kabos conversed with the dead instead. As one of a long line of practitioners of the dark arts, he imagined his ancestors to be proud and worthy noblemen. Kabos spoke to them often, muttering salutations or just trying to stop them being angry for the loss of the relics. It seemed to work and they often responded to him in encouraging tones. He was frequently upset that his dead father didn't talk to him, but Kabos hoped he was halfway toward fixing that.

It was actually working out pretty well, he reasoned. Once back in Cairo, he'd be the head of his family and man in his own house, which meant he could live like his father, wear expensive suits and smell of exotic oils. He could have an enormous bedroom and sleep on a vast bed, swathed in silk underneath a mirrored ceiling. He'd have a swimming pool, shaped like the Eye of Horus, and lie on Beverly Hills-style padded loungers. Why not? The voices in his head said that he could stop living undercover once he had both items back.

Kabos parked the vehicle and walked up to the arena entrance. He felt calmer all the time and the breathing techniques he'd seen on the yoga channel really seemed to help. The Pyramid arena was impressive and yet incongruous with its surroundings, something fine amongst such trivia. Kabos wouldn't go inside such a building; pyramids were for dead people. Plus there might be dark energies in there; it wasn't worth the risk. He would find another way to stalk and catch his prey. By now, he almost relished the complexities of this hunt. No sense in rushing to a hasty conclusion. Move too fast and there would be little time to savor the delight of the chase, or the thrill of the kill. Kabos checked all the exits to the arena before getting back in the Dodge. He hoped the youth called Danny might be naive enough to walk around on foot.

Twenty

Jessie decided to go early to the arena, but she needed to find her pickup first. She remembered parking near a theater, but she'd seen a few since then. As she walked, she watched for any man who looked like the right age for her father. She continued down Beale Street until she ran out of music venues. Churches were now more frequent than bars and they were neatly kept, with manicured grass and spotless paths. Her attention was drawn to an imposing wooden chapel painted sky blue. On the roof, a white cross stood tall like a mast. Its main window was a multicolored patchwork of leaded glass. In its center was a huge yellow smiley face. Jessie stared at it, motionless.

"No way," she whispered. Underneath in crooked white lettering were the words "Jesus smiles on the brave"—or was that "braves?" Apart from the window, the church looked like most of the others that she'd walked past. It was just a church, wasn't it? She strode up the path, a little self-conscious, and wondered what she'd say to anyone inside.

The door swung inward with a gentle push. Inside, rows of white painted pews stood on a varnished board floor. The air was cool and smelled damp. At the front, the altar sat on a raised stage with a carved wooden pulpit to one side. Jessie walked the length of the aisle, looking around and above her. In the shafts of sunlight through the windows, dust particles swirled but didn't settle. *There's nothing here.* No information, messages, or signs and no traveler called Finch. In the welcome cool, Bear lay down onto the wood and dog-sighed.

Danny's walk had become almost a jog. He wanted to check farther downtown before returning to the pyramid. As he scanned the streets and traffic, the anxious feeling in his chest returned. If Jessie was in the old pickup, she'd be conspicuous and completely unaware of being hunted. Suddenly, the street up ahead erupted as horns sounded and drivers screamed, "Moron!" and "Retard!" and "Get out of the way!" Danny turned to see a flash of white between the cars. In the Dodge, Kabos was driving across two lanes of traffic, and aimed directly at him.

Danny jolted into a run, as cars screeched to a halt, and behind him glass shattered and people yelled.

"Watch out, asshole!"

"What is he doing...?"

An SUV tail-ended the sedan in front. The white Dodge switched direction to head parallel with the line of parked cars between him and Danny. As Kabos drove into oncoming traffic, cars swerved wildly to avoid him. Danny ran faster; he snapped his head right to see the driver draw level with him. Through the open window he could see the driver laughing. Screeching brakes, car horns and angry shouts distorted everything, but the driver of the Dodge only had eyes for Danny. Ahead of him, a gap in the line of parked cars opened up. Kabos swerved left towards Danny into the space, and mounted the sidewalk just as a garbage truck plowed into the rear corner of the pickup. In an explosion of colliding metal and glass, the Dodge catapulted around on an imaginary axis into the side of the garbage truck. Up in the cab, the driver shouted, even though he couldn't see who he was shouting at. The Dodge was embedded in the side of the truck.

Danny sprinted across the stalled traffic and in front of the screaming man in the garbage truck. As his arms and legs pumped, fear flooded his body. Back in the Dodge, Kabos screamed in frustration. Jammed between a four-by-four and the garbage truck, he struggled with his door as his quarry disappeared behind him, but his legs were caught in a tangle of crushed metal.

"Where did he go?" He banged the glass until it smashed. "Where did he go?"

He grasped the steering wheel and pumped himself back and forth, wrenching the wheel loose.

"Somebody release me NOW!" he shouted at the gathering crowd of people.

Danny sprinted down a street to his right and then turned sharp right again alongside a warehouse. Alongside a truck, two packers stopped loading boxes to watch him race past. Fear urged him on, but his breath faded as his lungs heaved to keep pace. The ache under his ribs turned to a stabbing pain and he looked for a place to hide. Glancing behind him, he allowed himself to slow a little; the driver of the truck wasn't following. Across the street, he saw what he needed. Checking behind him again, he crossed over and jogged up the path toward the church's entrance. Its hinged door swung open to frame a couple who were just leaving, a young girl and a dog.

"Jesus! Danny, what are you doing?"

Danny stumbled forward, bent over, and looked back to watch the door close. With one hand on his chest and the other stretched out in front, he motioned for them to walk back inside.

"Just a minute, give me a minute," he gasped.

"Danny, are you okay?" Jessie said. "What's going on? Why have you been running?"

Danny nodded and began to stand up.

"Yeah, s'bad. Sit down. Sit down, Jess."

He clutched the end of a pew, as his breath came in gasps. His face was blotchy, and his eyes wide with shock. He looked behind him again.

"Christ Danny, you look scared shitless. What happened?"

Jessie flinched at her second blasphemy and looked at the altar. She sat down on the pew that Danny was holding. His hair hung over his face, there was a line of sweat on his cheek and more running down from his hairline. It took a few minutes before he would sit down, and even then he kept checking the door behind them.

"Hey look, chillax. You're scaring me," she said.

"Why are you looking at me like that? And how did you find me?" She tried grinning at him.

"Jessie, where did your father get that ring?" Danny's tone was urgent.

"The ring, what's the big deal with the ring?" Jessie still felt bad about selling it. "Look, I don't have any idea about the ring, or any of the stuff Mom sent—it's just stuff, isn't it?"

He shook his head.

"For Chrissakes, just sit down, will ya?"

"I will, if you'll stop swearing in here," he said.

Danny sank down onto the pew and began to talk about a man in the white Dodge, a fight with Earle in Sligo, racing to Memphis, and a lot of craziness in the street with the cars. He kept interrupting himself to start explaining something else and then didn't actually finish any of it. Some of it Jessie understood, but much seemed fantastic—had a man in a white Dodge killed someone because of her father's ring?

When he'd finished, Jessie tried another question. "But how did you know I was here?"

Danny shook his head. "Know what? I have absolutely no idea, but it seems like the biggest piece of freaking luck I ever had in my life."

Jessie felt that familiar weirdness creep over her. She looked up at the window with the smiley face. Just like Finch's card said: *"Have a nice day."*

They sat for a while longer. Jessie tried to check details. She still couldn't figure out how the man in the white Dodge had found where Danny was. He must have known about the telephone message, but tracking those facts back made no sense either, unless someone had told him about the band? The disjointed information just didn't flow: a man in a white truck, Earle with the shotgun, the fight for the ring, a chase down the sidewalk a few streets from where they were, and the unbelievable link back to her.

"Danny, you're staring." Jessie wished she was wearing makeup.

"Well, yeah, so I had this whole speech planned, but now it's all kinda..."

"What?"

"Jessie, who knows that you're in the band?"

Used to be in the band, she thought.

"Well, my little sister back home does, so that means my mom too, and Ray at the shop, of course." Her eyes went wide. "You don't think that nut job could have hurt Mary or Mom, do you?"

Danny just stared back at her.

"Shit! Danny, we need to call my mom." She sprang up and strode toward the door.

"Hey, stop! We need to find a back exit or something!" said Danny, following her. "That guy could be right outside…"

Jessie was on a mission and marched straight into bright sunlight. *Some risks you need to take*, she reminded herself.

Twenty-One

"Hello? Yeah, Mom. It's me again." Jessie's manner was brusque and businesslike. They'd found a phone booth in the lobby of a hotel. Danny stood a discreet distance away with Bear. He'd said that a hotel would be safe, but still he watched every face around them.

"So soon? Is it my birthday?" Her mother sounded sober.

"No. Listen, Mom, has anyone been around asking questions about me?" Jessie asked.

"You in trouble with the law again, Jessica?"

"No, no way. Just answer the question—did anyone come around?"

"Don't think so." She sounded confused. "But maybe some guy did. Hell, I don't know…"

The line went quiet for a while.

"Well anyway, I don't remember," she snapped. "But seeing as you're on the phone, you may as well know we're movin'. We're packing up, going back to Colonna."

"You're going back?"

This was major. A return to where they'd lived with her father was not something her mother would do on impulse.

"Why? When did this happen?"

Danny walked a little farther away into the lobby.

126

"Well, we are still having a life back here, Jessie. Things do move on, with or without you being around."

"Okay, right. So where will you be? I mean, how will I call Mary?"

"You'll have to use my cell phone."

"You got a cell phone?" Jessie almost laughed. Her mother certainly was moving on.

"Yeah, Mary mailed you the new address and number." Her tone was dismissive; she was done with this conversation.

"No, wait. Give it to me again. Hold on, there's a pencil here."

She wrote the details on the hotel notepaper. The place was called Pastureland. It sounded like her mother had gotten a live-in job in a nursing home or something— nice.

"And Mary—she's okay still?"

"Why shouldn't she be, Jessica? She's got me, ain't she?"

Jessie wasn't ready for that.

"Yeah, right, whatever." *Don't let her get to you*, Jessie thought. *It's what she wants*. "Look, did someone come around asking about me or not? Can you think again?"

Her mother paused. "Like I said, maybe. Some odd guy—what with all the movin' an' all. Look, can we do this some other time? I'm surrounded by boxes and there's a cattle truck trying to park itself outside that looks like it's going to hit the front fence. Things are a little stressful right now."

Jessie's mother didn't sound stressed. In fact, she sounded breezy, almost happy even, which was double-weird.

"OK, well..."

"Yeah, I know—tell Mary you said hi," her mother intoned, "and you'll send a letter soon."

The remark stung. Jessie didn't write as much as she'd promised. She couldn't bring herself to. Jessie put the phone down and sighed.

Danny, Jessie, and Bear walked in silence and turned back onto Main Street then headed back toward the river. Jessie brooded over the conversation and wondered what had made her mother want to move back to Colonna.

Danny's patience eventually evaporated. "So has the guy been around? Did he talk to them?"

Jessie frowned. "Dunno, but if he did, my mom was wasted at the time."

"Listen, I really think we need to get out of this area. How far is your truck?"

Jessie realized they were walking in bright sunshine, exposed. With Bear, they were even more conspicuous. "Over that way I think, not far." Jessie spotted some scaffolding she recognized. The theater was farther down.

"I'm hungry — you hungry?" Danny asked.

"Yeah, maybe, I guess. I think we've got some food in the truck."

Danny looked behind them and scanned the street. In the distance, they heard the sound of sirens and a helicopter hovering into position. The sounds came from the site of the wreck.

They drove as far as the outskirts of the city and chose a motel set back from the road that was almost obscured by a newer, taller building. Danny said that if they nearly drove past it, then so would most people. Jessie was too preoccupied to argue. They parked the truck behind the main building. The whole area was fenced off, so if anyone drove around the back, they'd see them from the room.

They booked a twin-bedded room and didn't mention Bear. As Jessie opened the door, she was greeted by hot, stale air. Inside, fuchsia walls clashed with a stained tan carpet. Rose nylon sheets were covered with a tufted yellow bedspread. The shade over the center light had once been white and the light it cast was as meager as the surroundings. Jessie wandered over to the lamp by the nearest bed.

"Just like home," she muttered, blowing a layer of dust off the bedside table.

"Yeah, well it's only for one night," Danny said, and collapsed on the farthest bed. He lay down and kicked off his sneakers.

"Man, what a day," he groaned and closed his eyes. Jessie and Bear stood and watched him.

"You're just gonna sleep?" she asked. Gradually, Danny opened his eyes, then held out his arms.

"Got anything else you want to do?"

Jessie snorted and sat on the end of her bed, grabbed the remote and kicked off her boots. By the time she'd found the news channel describing a crazy car chase, Danny was snoring gently. The overwrought female reporter was all highlights and vast mascara. The piece to camera was live and the woman posed in front of a tow truck and a fire engine with lifting gear. Jessie watched as an SUV was hoisted onto the flatbed of the vehicle carrier. Its mangled front end swung around and one wheel hung down.

The reporter's eager delivery managed to convey horror, shock, and amazement, as she emphasized the sensational details. Her conversation was with the male anchor back in the studio.

"Bob, the driver of the vehicle was thought to be part of a *drug* gang. Potentially a *hit man* chasing a *mark*," she said, her eyes wide.

She explained eight vehicles had been damaged in the incident and three people treated for minor injuries.

"And Bob, *remarkably* no one was killed in what must have been a *terrifying ordeal* for anyone in the immediate area."

Jessie wondered if the journalist actually would have preferred a generous blood splatter across the windshield of the SUV. Aside from a few bent cars, there was really nothing to justify her traumatized tones.

"Alarmingly, the *crack-crazed driver* of the pickup ran from the scene, and I have to tell you, Bob, at this time a potential *killer* is on *the loose!*"

As the reporter nodded her warning, the camera panned to the white Dodge, and Jessie realized what she was watching. This was downtown Memphis. She looked at Danny, then back at the screen. In the church, she'd thought he was exaggerating, or just too freaked out to make sense. Danny's edginess was the result of that street scene; he was the unnamed "mark" that had fled for his life.

Jessie locked the door and drew the curtains. After checking that the bathroom had no window, she walked back to the TV and turned the volume down; Danny probably needed to rest. Even asleep his frown still creased his forehead, she watched him for a while, but then realized if he woke up to see her staring at him, that would be really weird.

She channel surfed for a few hours, and watched as the news coverage of the car chase subsided. Pulling her belt from its loops, she slipped under the top cover, and turned out the light. A moment later, Bear jumped up on the nearby sofa and grumbled as he settled.

In the darkness, the situation felt emphasized. She was in a seedy motel room with Danny in the next bed. The feeling that someone was following them just to get the ring was really odd and Jessie tried to work through the events in sequence. Eventually her head hurt with it, and the heat in the room didn't help.

She ducked under the covers, pulled off her combat pants and then left them in the bed. Checking that Danny was still asleep, she pulled the sleeves of her T-shirt outward and slipped her arms inside then shoved it over her head. Then she was aware that her bare arms were in full view, which felt strange, so she slunk down and tried to get comfortable.

In the gloom, she watched Danny for a while and wondered again why he'd made the trip. Was it just about the contest? The first prize was cash and studio time, plus air play—maybe it was worth another row with Nico to put them all back in the running. Strange guy, though, she couldn't figure Danny out. He worked hard projecting the uber-cool musician thing, but it didn't really fit. Now, in sleep, he looked almost childlike. His shaggy hair made him look less like a trendy guitar player and more like an awkward adolescent, though how he could sleep when there was so much to think about was incredible. She watched him for a while longer then closed her eyes.

The scarecrow was trying to shout a warning at her but the wind howled so loud she couldn't hear him. It didn't matter because he was spinning around on his pole, which made everything go hazy and crazy and the dizzier she felt, the more she could smell tires burning. Fear and fright shook with all its might as terror took an icy cold hold on her hair. Then someplace a girl screamed and screamed because someone really bad was coming and Jessie looked at her feet again, which was lousy because then she realized that the screamer was her.

Twenty-Two

Jessie woke bolt upright, trembling and fixed by terror. Danny stood over her, still in his denim jacket, one hand on her bare shoulder. Automatically she knocked his hand away.

"All right. S'all right. Go away." She looked wildly around her. "That smell, can you...?"

Jessie's heart thumped loudly in her ears—could he hear that? She tried to grasp the situation: it was a dream. She was in the motel room, and this was real. Instinctively, she shoved her arms back under the covers and pulled the sheets up around her neck.

"What smell?" Danny said, still bent toward her.

She stared at his face. It was Danny. Her fear faded to a slight tension in her chest. Bear jumped down from the chair and padded toward Jessie.

"Jessie, what the heck was all that?" Danny asked and rubbed his eyes. "I mean, you look totally freaked." He half-smiled. "What were you dreaming about?"

"You know, I don't know. I mean, I'm not sure." Jessie's tone had lost its hostility. "Go back to sleep, yeah?"

Jessie stroked Bear for a while, until the nightmare faded enough for her to risk lying back down.

When Danny finally woke, Jessie and Bear were sitting together on the other bed, watching him.

"Do you two do everything together?" he said, and propped himself up on his elbows.

"Yup," Jessie smiled. "'Cept Bear's not a fan of showering." She patted Bear the head.

"You showered already?" Danny looked at his watch. "Man, did I sleep right though?"

He jumped out of bed and headed toward the bathroom.

"Well, apart from creeping around the room and giving me frightmares, yes, I guess so."

Danny turned back. "Now hey, you were already..."

"Yeah, I know. I've been having funny dreams for a while. It's just that last night's was bad... really dark," she admitted.

Danny paused by the door.

"No. Go ahead and get your shower, I'll tell you later," she nodded.

Lying on the bed with Bear, Jessie passed the time by watching morning TV. The car chase in Memphis was still a regular item, but it was now usurped by the vice president's alleged facelift. In the background, she tried not to listen to Danny's showering. His tuneless whistle changed notes as he went through the motions of washing. *He's making a good job of it*, she thought.

When Danny walked back in to the bedroom, Jessie concentrated on appearing fascinated by the Katy Perry video on MTV. He paused and seemed to wait for her to look over, but she didn't.

They ate breakfast at Denny's about ten miles east of Memphis. Danny made Jessie check inside before he'd venture in, which felt a little freaky. They smuggled Bear in to nestle silently under the table, and Jessie fed him sneaky pieces of toast and bacon and complained about the prices. Gradually, she told Danny about the dreams, about Hank and Peggy, but not about Finch, or the weird coincidences like the feathers. That felt like a fragile spell that she didn't quite want to break just yet. She played most of it down but Danny appeared fascinated by the dreams.

"Who do you think the scarecrow is?" he asked. "I mean, what does he represent?"

Jessie was still trying to figure the dream out herself. "Dunno; he does sort of remind me of someone I met, but I'm not sure."

At the rear of the restaurant, Jessie spotted the waitress disappear into the kitchen and she leaned forward.

"Hey, are we paying or going?" she grinned.

"We're paying. Sit back down," said Danny, glaring at her.

An older couple at the opposite table watched the exchange. The woman muttered something to her husband and nodded. The man turned to look at Bear under the table and frowned.

"What are they staring at?" Jessie said loudly, her chin up.

"Jessie, quit it, will you?" Danny's voice was hushed. "Why are you always so ready to fight? Whatever happened to 'have a nice day'?"

Jessie looked back to him. *That's what the card said.*

"What did you say?"

"You know, a kindly thought for others, gestures of harmony and peace—'have a nice day'." It's a pretty common expression," he whispered.

His face was fixed in a scowl and Jessie leaned forward and opened her mouth but then she stopped herself. *Why am I angry?* she thought.

"You know, I think I get it," she said.

Jessie half-stood and turned toward the couple.

"Sir, ma'am, I'm sorry I was rude. It's an automatic thing. Please excuse me." She nodded at the surprised looking pair. Danny looked at her, then at the couple, then at her again.

"Let's get the check then," said Jessie, miming a scribbling gesture to the waitress. "We should probably get going."

Her tone was light, friendly even. Danny frowned and seemed to be checking the silverware. Jessie stood up.

"Get going where?" he asked.

"Well, to find my dad of course," she said. "Seems like he's the person we need to speak to, and if he's still a musician, there's a fairly logical way to find him."

While the server went to get the check for their order, she hustled Bear out to the truck, smiling at the couple as she passed.

Kabos had spent the night in woodland north of Memphis. He mulled over the outrage of the previous day and wondered again where the youth was now. The youth had had the ring with him. Kabos felt like it had been stolen from him all over again, and the idea of that brought back fiery frustration. He reminded himself to stay calm, and also that a clear mind demanded cool thoughts. The flashing lights in his head didn't help with that, though, and his constant muttering didn't even make sense to him.

He wondered what he'd do once he had the items back. He'd be rich certainly, rich enough to live in the Cairo suburbs. It would be nice to return to his father's house, he mused, or maybe he should branch out and get a place of his own. It was at times like this he really needed someone to talk to. He chanted salutations and tried again speaking to his father, but as usual his father didn't answer. Kabos reminded himself that his father was a man of few words and liked actions rather than conversation. He was making progress though; he'd got the temple dagger back and killed the thief called Scuz, which felt good. However, the job wasn't complete until he had the ring. When he had the ring, he was sure that his father would speak to him.

As he used the jeweled dagger to gut a rodent, his mind wandered to his dream-vision; the images always soothed him at times of screaming frustration. He imagined building a simple altar to his father under a full moon and placing both the ring and the dagger at its base. Then he'd sink to his knees and bow prostrate, to hear his father's deep tones, telling him that he'd done a good job and it was time to return to Cairo. He played the sequence over a few times, making everything as real as possible in his mind. Positive visualization, the Americans called it; he'd seen it on TV. Feeling a little better, he skewered the rat onto an alloy tent peg and placed it over the fire to cook.

Twenty-Three

Jessie and Danny wandered down Beale, mostly in silence. Without neon lights and with most shutters closed, the place had the feeling of a hangover, a bit self-pitying maybe. A few early-bird tourists had made it out and were meandering around looking for places that were open. Vehicles weren't allowed on Beale, but that didn't stop Danny from checking behind them constantly.

As they walked some places began to awake; Venetian blinds were twisted open and fluorescent lights blinked on. Doors were unbolted, entrances were swept, and the smell of espresso filtered into the air. Somewhere, someone was playing a piano; lazy jazz was a gentle wake-up call.

The three of them meandered in a semi-comfortable silence. Jessie thought about her father. She didn't have much of a plan for finding him, just the vague hope that she could make something happen. *Come on someone... give me a break here*, she thought. She glanced sideways at Danny. He still had that tense look and permanent frown. The threat of the man from yesterday loomed over them like a storm cloud that Jessie didn't feel she should mention.

The reflection of their little group in a bar window didn't look especially strange, but it sure felt it. A guy, a girl and a dog. Jessie checked the image a second time and then noticed something else; she stopped walking and stared at the name across the bar window: "Mitch's Bar." Yesterday she'd walked past this, but today the name struck a chord. On her father's postcards he'd written that one of the Braves was called Mitch. A guitar emblem accompanied the lettering on the window and a standing sign offered breakfast.

Jessie took a few steps back to consider the frontage; it was wide, with a black awning repeating the bar's name. To one side, painted metal tables were chained and stowed against the wall. As they watched, a bar boy emerged, un-padlocked the furniture, and began arranging it in front of the window.

Jessie stepped forward.

"Come on," said Jessie, "we might just have gotten lucky." The boy smiled and stood to one side. Danny followed Jessie and Bear into the bar.

Inside, Jessie's eyes strained into the gloom. There was a stage, two separate bar areas, and a dance floor. It smelled of beer, sweat, and cleaning fluid. They looked around, taking in the sights of the hanging flags, pennants, and bright signage.

"Hey, great place huh?" said Danny. The main bar area was a frenzy of music memorabilia, a huge collection gathering dust. The polished surface of the bar was covered in bottles, while tables were littered with empty cigarette cartons, plastic cups and spilled beer. A posse of staff was already busy tidying tables and sweeping the floor. "Looks like we missed a good night," Danny said.

Jessie approached a man polishing a toughened glass

case that hung behind the bar. Even in the dim light, the powder blue jacket inside sparkled. It was covered in rhinestones and had a narrow silk scarf at its neck.

"Is Mitch in?" Jessie asked, *be friendly*, she thought. "Sorry, I mean please?"

Danny looked at her sideways and raised his eyebrows.

"Little early for Mitch," said the man. His Irish accent was soft and lilting. "Now, is he expecting you?" His blue eyes twinkled.

"Mitch? No, not really. I mean, no," said Jessie.

"Someone looking for me?" The deep voice behind them was a mild warning.

"Yes sir," said Jessie.

Mitch stood around six feet four and was built like a farm house. His leather vest and white Stetson would have looked just as good on a cattle ranch as in a music bar. The buckle on his belt was bull's horns, almost obscured by a generous waistline.

Jessie took a breath. "I'm Jessie, this is Bear and, aaah, Danny."

Mitch's expression softened as he saw Bear.

"You know we don't allow dogs in here," he said, and began to smile. "Even if they do kinda suit the place."

Bear padded a few steps toward him and Mitch crouched down to meet him. Jessie watched as Bear sat down and allowed his shoulders to be rubbed. Mitch carried on stroking Bear, his heavy gold jewelry flashing in the dim light. He looked up at them.

"So, Jessie? Was it about the bar job?"

Danny looked at Jessie for an answer. She remembered that he still didn't know why they were here.

"It's about my father. I think you know him…" her voice drifted off. "Well, if you're the right Mitch, that is…"

She'd considered some maneuvering but she just wanted to know. Since she was seven years old she'd waited for an opportunity to ask someone where her father was, and this seemed like it.

Mitch stood up and became towering once more.

"Honey, I know lots of people." He squinted in the half-light for a while and then pointed to a nearby booth.

"Listen kids, sit down for a minute." He nodded to the man who had been pretending to clean a nearby table. "Casey, seein' as we have your attention, some coffee here, please."

"Sure, boss." The man looked embarrassed.

The three of them sat down on the padded benches. With a nod from Mitch, more lights were switched on, and Jessie was glad for a better look at him. *He looks kind,* she thought.

"So you're looking for your dad?" said Mitch. "And for some reason you think I can help?"

Danny glanced sideways at Jessie, but she'd already decided Mitch was stalling.

"My father was in a band called the Braves, and I think maybe you were in it, too."

Twenty-Four

The coffee arrived and was poured before Mitch spoke again.

"The Braves...now that's a piece of the past I wasn't figuring on hearing today," Mitch sighed. "Feels like a lifetime ago. And here you are, Billy's older girl, if I'm not mistaken."

"You can tell?"

"I'd decided by the time we sat down." He shook his head. "How's Corinne? She still write songs that would tear your heart out?"

"No...I mean I don't think so..." *Did my mom used to write songs?*

"So you were in the band?" said Danny.

"Yes son, I was. Played a pretty good guitar and wrote a little myself in those days. That was before all this, of course."

He's about to tell me what happened to my dad, Jessie realized. She tried to appear relaxed but her hands started to shake, so she held onto her coffee mug. Mitch began the story, saying that the whole trip was doomed from the start. He explained that in a bar in Colonna, Billy and Scuz had cooked up a crazy notion about making it big in Memphis. He said that in the end, they talked about little else, creating dreams that grew like weeds in a wet spell. They'd fantasized about easy money, having a wild time and a lucky escape from a predictable future in Kansas. For weeks, Billy had used his charm, and Mitch ultimately had been persuaded to go along. Fiery dreams had overturned cold logic. Mitch said that Billy was an unyielding optimist and charm was his greatest asset. With a wholesome smile, easy manner, and blue eyes that gleamed with mischief, his argument had actually made sense. Kansas sounded better as a place you were from, not headed to, and a life without risk was a victim's choice.

Originally they'd been four, but Gabe the keyboard player had been reluctant to go and chose to stay behind to work on the family farm. Mitch mused that he'd probably have inherited the place by now. Billy had tried to get Gabe to go, but eventually gave up on him, bidding him farewell with a warning to stay away from Corinne.

"Gabe had this real sweetness for your mother. He used to try and hide it. He didn't mean no harm," Mitch said. "Gabe was just a man smitten by a beautiful woman."

He explained that from Colonna, the trip had felt like such a big adventure. They had big plans to tour around a little first and earn money by playing in bars, but things had gotten tough and quitting had become an option. When they'd finally arrived, they'd discovered a big difference in playing the local bars in Colonna and competing in a musical mecca like Memphis. The sound of the Braves had been something special back home, but it was amazing what a change of location could do to the resonance of two guitars, three voices, and a set of drums. Ten years later, and Colonna was now a world away. Mitch said he was glad he left, although for different reasons now.

"But we were done as a team before we even got here." Mitch suddenly grew more serious. "The guys did something I didn't like, and that was the end of it for me."

"What happened?" asked Danny.

Mitch frowned. "Scuz showed his true colors, I guess. And Billy J. made a choice between one way and another."

Mitch explained that the trip to Memphis had been hot, frustrating, and pressured. Scuz's fiery temper was unpredictable, and the constant fights between him and Billy J. made for a tense atmosphere on the road. By Tennessee, they'd run out of money and were sleeping in the station wagon. The worst of it was that they began stealing to get by. At first it was just a few food items from a 7-Eleven, but then Scuz grew more ambitious. In a town called Cairo, Scuz stole a backpack from a traveler and Billy helped him hide it. Then the arguments really started.

"I wanted no part of that," Mitch said. "A few chocolate bars and a can of soda is one thing, but to take stuff as valuable as that off a person is a whole different ballgame."

"Valuable stuff?" Danny said.

"Some of it, sure – I'd say worth a lot more than Scuz realized."

He remembered how pleased the boys had been when they got back, whooping as they showed off the loot:

jewelry, old artifacts, and weird objects. Scuz had gloated over his haul and explained the easy theft.

"You should have seen this guy," Scuz had laughed. "Some kind of badass, that's for sure. That's what made me watch him. But he sure clung to his knapsack tight. That's when I knew he'd be going home a tad lighter."

Scuz was animated, as his adrenaline still flowed. Then the atmosphere had quickly changed as Mitch made his feelings known.

Mitch had wanted no involvement in what Scuz had done, and no share of the stuff, but the value of the stash was clear, and Billy J. saw a chance to get ahead. He argued that his efforts deserved a fifty-fifty split; after all, Scuz wouldn't have gotten the bag away if it hadn't been for him. However, Scuz knew that he could go a long way on the contents of the backpack and chose fortune over friendship. He'd held onto the bag and most of its contents, aside from a few items given to Billy as appeasement. The ring was probably valuable, but the child's bracelet looked worthless. Billy complained bitterly and grew morose and brooding.

As Jessie listened, she felt that familiar feeling, the one where the bottom seemed to be dropping out of her life and she tried to hold on to what was left. Her stomach lurched with nausea. Where was the father she'd built in her mind, her father—the really great guy?

Mitch described the awkward last leg of the journey. They made it to Memphis without argument simply though a lack of conversation.

"We pretended that it just hadn't happened," Mitch said. "Scuz provided money for provisions and fuel, and we acted like we didn't know where he was getting it from. In the end, I sold the better of my two guitars so I could stand on my own feet for a while. Food bought with stolen money tasted foul to me. So after weeks on the road, we arrived in Memphis. That was supposed to be a beginning, but really it was the end." Mitch described the hollowed-out sense of it, and how when the Braves reached Memphis, their dreams had evaporated in the heat. Tryouts in several bars and clubs had ended in embarrassment as often as disappointment. They'd also discovered how little they had in common. Music and the band were the last thread holding them together and after a few more weeks, each had gone their separate ways.

"It was as if the pressure of the road had tested our characters and we'd all found ourselves wanting," he said.

Mitch had gotten a job in a house band at a music club. Billy J. worked bars and got occasional singing work, before eventually deciding to move on. Mitch said that he'd seen the distance between Billy and his family grow wider. After a long pause, Mitch opened his mouth to say something and then put his hand up. Danny and Jessie waited for him to continue, but he just stared down at the table. Eventually, Mitch sighed and then attempted a smile.

"And that's kinda it, I guess. Your pa just left town." He paused. "It just seemed to suit him to keep on moving."

Jessie tried to hold her voice steady but the tremble was still there. "Didn't you tell him to come back home... to us, I mean?" she said.

147

Mitch stared into his empty coffee cup. "The thing is, Billy J. never did really heed advice. He was kind of a loner in that way."

So far, her father sounded egotistical, shallow even. It was like Mitch had taken the facts of her life and rearranged them.

Danny broke the silence.

"Can I ask a little more about the robbery?" He sounded casual. "What did they do with the stuff?"

"Well, sold most of it I guess. It was old stuff, artifacts; the guy they stole it from was probably a dealer in that," said Mitch. "I think maybe Scuz kept the knife for a while, grew attached to it. He liked to show it off on his belt."

"What kind of knife?" Danny said.

"Again, same kind of thing. Old. Very old, probably. Jewels in the handle. Could have been fake, I guess," he said. "Scuz liked to spin stories about where it was from, used to let the ladies hold it a while." Mitch shook his head.

"So where is Scuz now?" Jessie asked.

Mitch shook his head. "He took off for Nashville and said that he'd stay in touch, but he never did. Don't think he's in Nashville, though; I would have heard about it if he was."

Then Mitch leaned forward and coughed.

"I did hear once from a brother of his. Seems their mother took sick, but I couldn't help him, either." Mitch gestured for another coffee. "Some folks just like to disappear, I guess."

Under the table, Danny nudged Jessie but she ignored him.

"Mitch, what is my father's last name?" Jessie asked quietly. For a long moment no one moved.

"Damn, Jessie, your mom never told you that? She musta been mad. Musta stayed mad, I guess. Heck, your old man's name is Billy Jessop, but he shortened it to Billy J. Liked the sound of it, I guess."

Mitch had told the story as gently as he could, but the tragedy of it was haunting. Jessie held Mitch's gaze. *I got this so wrong,* she thought. The name Billy Jessop seemed to seal it. *My dad sounds like a flake.* She looked down at the table and got ready to bolt. *I just need to get past Danny.* Suddenly high heels clacked across the board floor and a woman's voice called to the bar staff.

"Morning Case, morning Stevie. Hey, your ears still ringin' after last night? Mine sure are!"

Mitch spun around at the sound of the smiling brunette, all curls, bright lipstick, and sweet perfume. Jessie put a palm up to her cheek and wiped a rogue tear away. Instinct told her to hide her feelings, but she knew Danny had already seen her. Taking a breath, she steadied herself to greet this bouncy newcomer. Danny nodded at Jessie, leaned forward across her, and smiled at the approaching woman.

"Hey, darling." The woman bent over and kissed Mitch with a relaxed fondness that made her think of Peggy and Hank. "Hope I'm not interrupting here..." The lady only had eyes for Mitch, and made the harmless question seem like a tease.

"'Course not baby doll, come and join us. I'd like you to meet these two youngsters. Jessie, Danny, this is the reason I stayed on in Memphis." Suddenly Mitch looked boyish. "This is my Bella."

Twenty-Five

Mitch patted the booth beside him and Bella wriggled in close. Jessie realized that Bella was actually older than her first impression. She was probably older than her mother, but a lot better kept, or maybe the years had been kinder.

Soon, they were all introduced and Bella made a fuss over Jessie, as she remembered her father well.

"Well, he sure was a live one, that Billy J.! Always quick with a joke. Made us all laugh, that's for sure. He was attractive, too; you look a lot like him." Then, as if in answer to Mitch's playful frown, she continued, "But I wanted me a man I could depend on, and I reckon I got me the pick of the bunch."

Mitch beamed and winked at Jessie.

The conversation that followed was a mixture of the old and new. Jessie tried to appear friendly, but she was glad Danny kept the discussion going. His easy manner and genuine interest soon had Mitch and Bella reminiscing about the old days. They heard about how they'd met in Slinky's, where Bella had been waiting tables. She squealed as she remembered spilling a full pitcher of beer over Mitch and then refusing to apologize. Mitch said that in the tussle that followed he'd been well and truly smitten.

They'd bought this bar three years ago from Mitch's uncle and now Mitch's Place was doing well thanks to a regular music crowd and the trade from tourists.

After a while, Danny turned the conversation to their other reason for being in Memphis.

"Mitch, do you know anything about the newcomer contest held at the music awards festival?"

"Sure I do. Helped organize last year's. That was some party," Mitch said. "You interested in entering?" He looked at them and raised his eyebrows. "You guys have a band?"

"Kinda," Jessie admitted. "We had a bit of a fight," she added.

"Well, you wouldn't be a band if you hadn't," laughed Bella. "But the awards are only a couple of weeks away, so you'd better settle your differences quick."

"Yeah, we need to work a bit on that one," Danny said. Jessie looked over to him, glad again for his company and the relaxed way he'd dealt with the situation. They talked a bit more about the contest and the other bands, and Mitch described the excitement of the final "playoff." After two days of judging, the entrants were reduced to three bands. Those bands got to play one song each before the start of the Memphis music awards. Mitch said it was always close but that was half the fun. The winning band got a cash prize and a week in a studio, plus air time on local radio. Mitch explained that the real opportunity was in the A&R guys in the audience, sent by the record companies to scout fresh talent.

"People's lives get changed that night," he said. "I've seen it happen."

Jessie tried to forget about her father for a while and concentrate on the music awards. Mitch was an authority, not only on the contest, but also on the local music scene, and he described the local bands and talent with familiarity.

"Onyx seems to be a band to watch. They did really well last year and they've got a good sound, but they needed a bit more experience. Other bands that are bound to play are the Mandevilles, Sacha and Teen, and Holly and the Italians—that's Casey's band." He nodded over to his bar manager. "Or maybe wild cards like Peeko—those guys are South American—or Mission Trivia—they're more heavy metal and thrash. It's not really my thing."

Jessie concentrated on the group's names and wondered how good they were.

"Mitch, do you know any of these bands? Well, I mean, do any of them play here, maybe?" Danny said.

"Sure," he laughed. "Why, most of 'em. In case you didn't notice, son, I got me one of the best music clubs on Beale." Then he chuckled at Danny's discomfort. "And if I read your thoughts right, the next answer is that at least three of them are booked to play here before the event—that's if you're interested…"

Danny grinned at Jessie, who gave up trying to look cool and smiled back.

"Hey, you didn't say what your band was called," said Bella. "You folks got yourself a good handle?" Seeing them look at each other, she squealed with laughter. "Or is that something else that you couldn't agree on?"

Jessie cringed. Political Love was a dumb name they all hated, but the democratic process hadn't produced a better option. Neither she nor Danny would reveal it, but Bella's teasing felt friendly and Jessie decided she really liked her.

"Say, you guys want to try some Mississippi mud pie—the real stuff?" said Bella.

Mitch kissed his wife on the cheek. "Ain't she something, fellas?"

He raised his hand and began the process of ordering pie for five, Bear included.

By the time they'd finished eating, Jessie not only had a job in the bar, she also had an apartment above if she was willing to clear it out. Jessie guessed that Mitch's offer had more to do with loyalty to Corinne than any fondness for her father, but she said nothing. Weirdly, she found herself smiling more brightly than she remembered being capable of. If life was dealing her a mixed hand today, maybe she'd ended up ahead. What didn't match was that Danny couldn't seem to look her in the eye for long, and Danny could normally win staring contests, so that was odd.

Twenty-Six

Outside the bar, Danny explained his latest logic, while Jessie scowled at the sidewalk. He was going back to Dorma and needed to leave now.

"I need to sort things out, Jess, especially with the band. If we're going to enter this contest we should all do it together." He watched her face. "I want the band back as it was."

Jessie faked a shrug. "And what does the band want?" she said.

"Look, we all want to win, and we stand a much better chance with the lineup as it was," he said. "You know, with you as lead."

"Well yeah, I guess... that does make sense," she said. "I mean, I'd like that too." She bent down and took Bear's neckerchief off, folded it again, and then retied it.

"Or can't you just call everyone?" She looked up. "Things are going so well; can't you just get the band to drive here?" *Everything was coming together*, she thought, and *now it was fragmenting again*.

"Jess, I don't think it's going to be that easy. And if I mess this up, then it's over before we got started."

Jessie pouted.

"Look, I'll get back as soon as I can. I might be just a few days."

Jessie stroked Bear's back hard, while Bear stared at her.

"Yeah, fine. It's no big deal. Don't worry about us." Then she stood up and smiled brightly. "We're going to be busy anyway."

Jessie walked with Danny to his car. They walked in silence, with Bear ambling between them. A little way out of town, the Camaro was hidden behind an abandoned auto wrecking yard. Danny unlocked the driver's door, and then bent to stroke Bear. Then he thumped Jessie softly on the shoulder.

"Okay, well, see ya in a few days, Jess?" he said.

Jessie forced herself to sound upbeat. "Right. And hey, watch out for hit men in your rearview mirror," she said, and thumped him hard back.

"Look Jess, don't joke about this guy..." Danny frowned and rubbed his arm. "He's bad news, really. I think he could be the guy that Scuz stole from. Didn't you guess that?"

"So he's a serial killer?" Jessie stopped. "Okay, I get it, I'll be careful. I did see the news report, you know."

Danny hesitated. "Look, I guess you'll want this back." He reached into his jeans pocket. "Maybe keep it hidden."

Earle had cleaned the ring, and the hieroglyph markings were clear and bright. Jessie held it up to the light and whistled softly.

"I don't know if I'm glad to have this back or not."

Jessie watched Danny go, having promised to call

him in two days. She'd also agreed to get a cab back to the bar, which felt extravagant, but Danny had insisted.

Back on Beale, Mitch's wife showed Jessie the apartment.

"It ain't much, honey, but I guess it's better than life in a truck," she said. Bella looked around at the clutter and frowned. Broken bar fittings were piled onto boxes that stood on furniture. Every surface had a carpet of dust. Bella picked up a dirty ash tray, recoiled, and quickly replaced it. Strolling around the room, Jessie really liked it. It was filthy and needed some maintenance, but after Vera's trailer, it felt like freedom.

"I'll bring you over some bedding. You might want to give the mattress a beating," Bella said, and shuddered. She retreated back out of the door, brushing imaginary dirt off her blouse. "Speak to Casey downstairs. He could clean the whole of Beale with what he's got in that store cupboard. I guess you'll work things out. Stow the stuff you don't want in the spare bedroom. By the way, Mitch says you can start work tomorrow night. Just take your time and settle in."

Jessie walked over to the window and looked out onto Beale. "It's fantastic, Bella, just perfect. I love it."

Bella waved away the comment and chuckled. She took the narrow stairs back down slowly and held onto the rail tight.

Jessie cleaned for the next eight hours straight. By the time she'd finished, even her fingertips hurt, but she liked the result and wished Danny was here to see it. She checked it over: bedroom, bathroom, open kitchen, and living room. The view from the living room was her favorite. Outside, Beale Street was in full swing, with a party happening in every bar. Jessie stood at the window a while, her hand on the freshly cleaned glass. Under her palm she could feel the thump of the music from downstairs. Now that she'd stopped working, fatigue ached through her, but she couldn't go to bed without moving the truck. Besides, she'd left her stuff in it. She looked in on the bar and wondered if she should tell someone where she was going, but everyone was busy serving customers.

The walk back to where they'd left the truck was longer than she'd remembered and for a while, Jessie thought she might have gone wrong. Was this the direction they'd walked in? The stroll with Danny seemed like days before, not hours. They'd parked near a tire repair shop. This morning there had been enough traffic to take attention away from the old pickup but now, late at night, the place seemed deserted. *Why didn't I do this earlier?* She was glad for Bear; not much was going to take him on, she reasoned. As she approached the truck, she tried to focus. *Just get in and get back to the bar,* but her tiredness made her heavy. *I need to sleep,* she thought.

In the shadows, a hooded figure watched and waited. The knife he held was pointing toward the floor. Bear shambled ahead of Jessie; the long walk had brought his limp back. Just ahead of them, the man leaned a little farther back into the shadow of the streetlight. The cab of the pickup truck was almost in darkness, and Jessie fumbled with the key in the gloom.

Bear's low rumbling alerted Jessie but by the time she spun around, both the dog and the watcher had made their moves. Bear launched himself at the figure, snarling and snapping. His bite was quick and sharp, a warning only. The man's shout was more of a scream, youthful and shrill. He dropped the knife to the sidewalk. Jessie jumped at Bear, found his collar, and tried to drag him away from the mugger.

"Off Bear, now. OFF!"

Bear lunged forward again, snarling, and she had to pull him back hard. The knife lay on the ground between them and the youth was shrieking.

"Jesus! Aw, fuck! My leg, my fucking leg!"

On the sidewalk, the stubby blade glinted in the dim street light. The boy backed up against a security fence.

"The fucking dog, the dirty fucking dog..."

He hopped around with his foot outstretched. As he turned toward the streetlight, Jessie could see how young he was. She picked up the knife and put it in her pocket.

"Little knife for a little guy," she sneered. "Fella, you need to pick a fight you can win." She unlocked the pickup door. Bear growled and began to advance toward the mugger once more.

"He's gonna bite me again! He's gonna do it again!" he shrieked and pushed back up against the fence, and the metal wire clashed against itself. Under the streetlight, the youth's face was pale and thin.

"In the truck, Bear," she said. "Bear, get in the truck—now!"

Eventually, the dog turned his head toward her and obeyed the command, checking the mugger again before hopping up into the cab.

"Good boy." She rubbed Bear's neck and head hard to try and calm him down. "Good fella, good dog." *Just get him back to the bar.* She started the engine and looked over at the youth as he examined his leg under a street light. Blood dripped down his shin and the wound had begun to swell. *He should probably have a shot.* She sighed and rolled down her window. From the seat beside her, Bear began a low growl.

"Look, can I give you a ride somewhere? I don't mind taking you to the hospital, but you'd have to tell me the way."

The young man's eyes grew wide.

"What?" he said. "Get in there with that freak of nature?" He stood up straight and placed one foot down carefully. "No way, man. Fuck that." He limped away and didn't look back.

As Jessie drove, she began to tremble and her foot shook as she pushed down the pedals. As she checked her rearview, Jessie realized that she didn't know what vehicle the guy after the ring was driving. Back at the bar, she parked the truck in the rear lockup area, away from the entrance.

She grabbed her things, including the cigar box and the stuff from Peggy and Hank. The carrier bag was lumpy and rattled as she walked. Danny had shared the sandwiches with Bear. *What else is in here?* she wondered.

In the apartment, she emptied it out onto the kitchen table. Wrapped in an old T-shirt of her daughter's, Peggy had put soap, shampoo, a new toothbrush, and a comb. The T-shirt was a tribute to Shakespeare; on the front was a quote from Romeo and Juliet and on the back was a huge feather quill pen. Jessie held it up.

"Peggy, Peggy, Peggy..." she said out loud. "You gave me a feather to wear..."

There was also bag of mini-Snickers and an oversized jar of vitamin pills. On impulse, Jessie popped off the top. The rolled up twenty dollar bill inside reminded her of her money can. Hank's practicality, she guessed. Peggy had written a card wishing her good luck and telling her to call, leaving one land line, two cell numbers, and an e-mail address just in case. She put the card on a windowsill and its golden sunflowers shone in the shabby room. With a can of soda she toasted the street outside, *here's to arriving on Beale,* she thought.

In her freshly-swept bedroom above the bar, Jessie slept soundly, relaxed by the pounding music downstairs. At the foot of the bed, Bear was a snoring curled bundle. Through the curtains, the neon lights of Beale blinked off, as even the street called it a night. As she wandered through her dream, Jessie's eyelids pulsed; she was a lone traveler continuing a journey.

Twenty-Seven

Jessie gazed at the meadow at the bottom of the hill but couldn't figure out in a hundred years how to meander down the slope to reach it. A cobalt blue dragonfly paused then glittered on his way past, and Jessie tried to point the way forward but couldn't seem to lift her hand. *Tedious,* she thought, *but then tedious isn't always obvious.* Down in the meadow huge yellow sunflowers turned their hippie, happy faces toward her and smiled an invitation to join them. Somewhere, the flower-child scarecrow hummed a jolly tune but she couldn't see him any more than she could understand him. *He's a real nowhere man,* she realized. *Sitting in his nowhere land.* The meadow whispered on the wind for her to join the fun and the sunflowers began singing, and that would have been a happy song too if she could just go down and give them a merry melody.

Jessie woke in the apartment, with its seventies' furniture, patterned curtains, and the door covered in yellowed paint. At the foot of the bed, Bear waited for her to wake. *I'm in the apartment,* she thought. Bear shuffled toward her, staying low, as his tail stub wagged gently.

"Hey, Bear." She stroked his head. *That was so real.* Maybe her dreams were so weird because of all that had been happening lately, but hadn't they started before that? She tried to remember if the dreams began before she met Finch or after. *Maybe it was when I started my journey to Memphis*, she thought.

◎ ◎ ◎

On the other side of Memphis, Kabos was getting used to the vehicle he'd recently acquired. He'd been sleeping rough in woodland north of Memphis and grown tired of waking up damp and cold. The former owner of the gleaming black Hummer had generously handed over the keys, plus his wallet. On the passenger seat, his breakfast was still warm. The bewildered man was probably still sitting on the low wall. It would take that imbecile several days to remember his own name.

Kabos finished off the man's omelet sandwich and fries, but couldn't stomach the Coke. He drove for a while and then pulled over as his gaze was drawn to a mother and her young son. The boy held a metallic balloon on a string; it was a huge orange kitten and it bobbed in the air as the boy skipped along. His mother talked on a cell phone and laughed a lot and he wondered if she was talking to the boy's father. The child with the kitten balloon reminded him of himself and on the thick leather wheel, his hands clenched and turned white. He watched the wheel begin to move and then released his fingers. After practicing his relaxation breathing, he restarted the engine, and the rumble of its six liter V8 engine felt comforting. He'd drive around for a while, take a tour of Memphis and see who showed up.

Twenty-Eight

In the apartment, Jessie hunted around for a pencil and paper so that she could start writing music again. Bear padded behind her for a while then slumped down in a doorway with a thud. Suddenly Bear began to growl, but then stopped.

"Anyone home?" Mitch called up the stairway.

"Sure is," Jessie said. "Come on up."

In the doorway, Mitch removed his black Stetson and stooped to fit through. He looked around.

"Well now, that's a nice job," he said. "Looks like I hired someone who can work hard… aah, there you are, little fella." Bear walked forward as Mitch squatted down and began stroking him evenly.

"Hey, I can work, Mitch," she said. "Did you want me to start my shift or something?"

His hand went up. "Heck no, just wanted to make sure you're settled in," he said. "Bella was frettin' in case you'd had a rough night or something. Made me promise to call in."

"Rough night?" she laughed. "Oh, I've had lots rougher."

"Well Jessie, I guess you have." Mitch stood up again and frowned. "You know, I can't help thinking what you heard yesterday was difficult." He paused. "I wouldn't want you imagining your old man was a bad guy or anything; he just wasn't good at keeping ties, that's all."

She glanced at Peggy's sunflower card on the window sill.

"Mitch, I've spent the last ten years trying to find some fancy fairytale of a reason why Dad didn't come back for us. Seems like the truth was simple: he just didn't." She looked directly at him. "And that is tough to hear but it's also fact, and that's a lot better than fantasy. So yes, it hurts, but hell, I'm glad I know."

Mitch dropped his gaze and studied his black Stetson. In his oversized hands, it looked small.

"So… what do you think about hanging out with an old man in Memphis for a while? I'm doing the rounds, running errands. It would be a good way to get to know the place."

"We'd love to." She smiled then hesitated. "I'm mean, is it okay if Bear tags along too?" Bear lifted his head.

"Sure he can," Mitch beamed. "But don't let him sit on the seats of the Mercedes, or Bella will have my hide as a handbasket."

Mitch's "errands" turned out to be breakfast in a friend's diner and a number of social calls based loosely around the business of the bar. Jessie watched the effect he had on people and the atmosphere around him; it was as if Mitch was a candle to moths in the night. Men were quick to shake his hand and women would wave hello or come over to chat. The forthcoming music awards were much of the conversation, as people asked Mitch what he thought about this year's lineup and how he thought the newcomer contest would go. Between stops she found herself sharing her life in the trailer and how she came to be in Dorma. She told him about the trailer fire, losing her job, and her place in the band. As she heard herself speak, it all seemed like it had happened to someone else.

In the afternoon, he took her down Madison to a music mall, saying he had something to pick up. Inside St. Blues Guitars, Jessie was quickly lost among the instruments. As Mitch joked with the owner, she walked up and down the rows of guitars, occasionally touching one, or lifting a price tag.

A black Gibson looked similar to the one she'd lost; she slowly lifted it off its stand and positioned her fingers over the strings. "Give you a good discount," the owner called over. It was secondhand, reasonably priced, and still way out of her reach. She placed the guitar back down as if it were glass.

"Aw, no, sorry. I'm not in the market right now."

Mitch had been leaning on the counter. He stood up and began saying his farewells as the owner shook his hand.

"Looks like we're all done here." Mitch walked the length of the shop and past Jessie, who stood gazing at the guitar. "Come on, there's a great place down the street. Let's have some coffee and pie."

In the coffee shop two waitresses rushed up to serve Mitch and both stayed a while, chatting. No one mentioned the presence of Bear, and Jessie's normal hesitation faded. As they waited for their order, Jessie was the first to break the silence.

"Mitch, there's something I want to show you. Don't get mad, okay?" She leaned back and dug in her pocket.

He took it from her and frowned at it.

"Well, if it ain't that old bad penny…" he said and dropped it back down. "You fixing to do something with that?" His voice was stern.

"Look, by now I don't know what to do with it," she said. "Seems like that thing's bad news, but I want to do the right thing with it, whatever that is."

Jessie told him about the cigar box of stuff and about selling the ring in Sligo. He listened as she described what had happened to Danny and what she'd seen on the news. Mitch drank his coffee, but the pie sat untouched. She finished talking, and the ring sat on the table between them like a warning.

"This all you got of the stuff they took?" he asked.

"Yeah, that's it. There were some other things in the box, but they're cards and photos, a bead bracelet, that kind of stuff."

"Is the bead bracelet blue?"

"Vivid blue stones with gold flecks." Her voice trailed. "But that…"

"Scuz gave it to your dad. Billy wanted it for your baby sister; said he'd always given more to you and she should have it." Mitch stared at the pie. "Guess your mom never passed it on."

"I had no idea."

"Jessie, the guy that's hunting down this ring—he could be the guy that Scuz took the bag from. Did you think of that?"

"I didn't, but Danny did," she said. "He's worried that the man could have dealt with Scuz already and gotten the knife back—but that's impossible, right?" She searched his face for reassurance.

"You know, it's funny, but I always felt that Scuz would find real trouble sooner or later." He picked the ring up again. "He was too mean in the heart. An ugly combination of greedy, corrupt, and stupid. I figure that's bound to catch up with you sometime."

Jessie wondered if she should tell him about Finch, about the dreams and the life that worked from the inside out. As she looked out onto the street, a van went past with the slogan "Sleep tight, have a good night on a feather-lite mattress." A cloud of feathers surrounded the picture of a duck asleep on a bed. Jessie smiled and turned back to him.

"You going to eat that pie, Mitch? I know someone who'll take it off your hands if you give him the okay."

Mitch tutted and then looked down at Bear. "I'll give the little fella half," he said, picking up a fork that seemed tiny in his hand. "And given the quality of the pie, that's a damn fine offer."

As they walked back to the car, the music store owner came out and held up a bunch of keys and grinned. "You left your car keys, Mitch." He threw them in a looping arc toward him.

Mitch caught them and then touched his Stetson. "Yeah, thanks friend. I'll be in touch."

They got back to the bar just as Bella was pulling in. Her red two-seater flashed in the sunlight.

"Aaah, there's my girl," Mitch grinned, and pulled the limo alongside.

"Hey, ya big lump," she shouted across at them. "You guys been having a good time without me?"

Mitch and Bella greeted each other like young sweethearts and walked hand-in-hand toward the back entrance of the bar. Jessie and Bear followed behind, feeling unnecessary.

"Hey Jessie." Mitch stopped and handed her his keys. "I left a package in the trunk; could you get that for me?"

"Sure thing, glad to." She walked back to the car. Mitch tugged on Bella's hand then leaned down to whisper in her ear. The couple turned to watch her as Jessie popped the lid of the trunk.

"It's okay," she called over, "I'll get it," and then she looked down. Time slowed by two beats. The guitar case had Gibson written across it, and the amp looked brand new. She stretched one hand out and then pulled back. It wasn't for her. It was for someone else.

"Thought you might need one of those," Mitch called over. "That's if you're thinking of entering a music contest anytime soon." He was clearly enjoying her expression, waiting for the moment to dawn.

"Mitch, it's too much. I don't have the cash for it." She looked over at him warily. Mitch stood grinning like some cowboy Santa Claus, and Bella's smile was one of pride.

"Look, do you want the damn guitar or don't you?" he said.

Jessie understood the gesture and her eyes filled with tears. She nodded and tried to speak.

"Yeah, but..."

Mitch lifted a hand up and turned, leading Bella into the bar.

"You're an old soft shoe, Mitch Hanrahan," Bella said as she pulled him close. "I should have guessed you'd go and do something like that."

Jessie unloaded the guitar hesitantly. The weight of the case confirmed it. She reached the stairs to her apartment, and began whooping like a lunatic. When Casey from the bar knocked a few minutes later, her heart was still pounding.

"Hey, how you doin'?" Casey asked and held out a little envelope. "A fella left this for you downstairs, real nice chap, he was – friend of yours?" She took the envelope from him and read the words "for a fellow traveler in Memphis." Jessie smiled as she realized who it was from.

"Kind of," she said, still staring at the envelope. *How would he know I was here?* she thought.

"Anyways, he reckoned he was going to be out of town for a while; said you'd be fine for a bit."

"Great. Thanks." Jessie grinned at Casey, who shrugged and left.

Inside was a small card. On one side was a drawing of a cobalt blue dragonfly and on the other a phrase:

'Set a heart free and watch it fly'

That's a nice idea, she thought.

The next few days passed quickly for Jessie: a flurry of shifts at the bar, errands for Mitch and Bella, and music writing sessions that lasted long into the night. Bear charmed everyone, especially Casey, who tried for hours to teach Bear tricks in reward for kitchen leftovers. Jessie joked that Bear had really just trained Casey to give him treats.

During the day, Jessie fixed up the apartment, played her guitar, and worked on her songs. The time flew past like a train. Bella stopped by with ugly household items she didn't want. It was an excuse to buy new ones, she declared, laughing. They howled at one lamp with an alligator at the base, a gift from Mitch's mother. Jessie thought it was fabulous and wanted to give it a place of pride in the living room, but Bella made her hide it in the bedroom. At thrift shops, Jessie picked up a few clothes, and soon things settled to a new kind of normal.

Jessie was avoiding calling Danny. Finding out what happened with the band was really important but surely if he'd got good news he'd have called the bar by now? On the fourth day, she resolved to call. It had been long enough and if it was bad news she needed to hear it. Besides, she'd been cooped up at Mitch's Place for days and was used to walking; there was bound to be a payphone nearby.

"Hey Danny. It's me. How's it going?" she said.

"How's it going? Jessie, you're incredible! Where the hell have you been?" Danny shouted.

"What? What's the matter? What do you mean where have I been?"

"Jessie, it's been almost five days! You said you'd call. What did you think I was going to do, just sit and chill in the meantime?"

"Danny, I had no idea what you were going to do. You could have called me, couldn't you?"

"I called twice; I left messages with the chef."

"The chef walked out two days ago..." She heard him sigh.

"Look, there's some lunatic on the loose and you're still acting like that's a minor issue. You have no idea, Jessie, you really don't."

"Okay, okay, I get it. I didn't call soon enough," she admitted. "I've been busy, things have been busy, lots of stuff..." her voice trailed off. She wanted to apologize, but she couldn't get the right way to say it in her head. In the silence that followed, she wondered if he'd put the phone down.

"So you've been busy."

"Yeah, working, fixing my place up. Hey, I got a

new Gibson. It's cool, totally awesome. Been doing some writing. Everything's great, no trouble or anything."

"Jess, I'm sitting here with the number to the bar. I was just about to call Mitch."

Jessie's voice turned to an Irish lilt. "Aaah, you'll be making someone a lovely mother one day, Danny Brewer, to be sure you will."

"Kiss my ass."

"So hey, are you coming back? Did you talk to the band?"

"Let's just say I'm still in negotiation."

Danny explained that Sophie and Ed seemed up for it, but Nico still had issues. Ultimately, he couldn't hear that his girlfriend's vocals were great as backing but didn't have the edge needed for a lead. He said that tonight was a practice night, so he was going to try again.

"Right. I guess it was never going to be easy," she said. "You're coming back though, aren't you?"

"Of course, if only to make sure you keep out of trouble." His voice had relaxed.

"Hey, I'm no trouble. I turned over a new leaf: 'have a nice day,' remember?" she said.

"Jess, look, forget it. Just don't go far from the bar, and call me more often, okay?"

"Okay, Mom."

"And drop the Mom thing."

"Okay… Daniel. Hey, gotta go, Bear's just cocked his leg against some guy's Hummer and he's looking mean."

"A dog with taste, clearly," Danny laughed. "See

you, Jess. Give me a call, okay?" he said, but his slightly pleading tone was lost on Jessie.

"Sure thing. Okay, gotta go." She was distracted; Bear had wandered farther than she'd realized. Thirty yards away, he stood next to the black car; its low roof and blocky shape was sinister even in bright sunlight.

Twenty-Nine

The man leaned against the side of the Hummer as he watched Bear. His face was dark, his features in shadow and his thin nose hawk-like. Jessie gave a low whistle. Bear looked up and trotted toward her. The man lifted his gaze in her direction and registered her with a half-smile. Then he pushed himself off the side of the vehicle and strode directly toward her.

A wave of dread washed over Jessie, like heaviness mixed with liquid fear. There was something in his eyes, the way he was looking at her. *It's him,* she realized, *we need to get away.*

"Bear, move! Now!"

She turned and began to run, but stalled. *Where's Bear?* The dog set off to follow her, but Kabos caught him. In a low sweeping gesture, he picked Bear up like he was a doll. Jessie turned back to watch as the man held Bear up like a trophy.

Kabos' grin became a leer. He looked at her and hissed. Bear held still for a moment but then as Kabos lowered the dog down, Bear twisted and squirmed violently, his whole body thrashed with effort. His snarling was furious. Bear arched his head back and tried to seize the man's arm. Kabos shifted his grip but Bear lunged and kicked then fell free. He tumbled down against the man's legs, and rolled over onto the floor. Kabos stepped back, but Bear leapt quickly. He bit deeply and shook.

Kabos howled with pain and rage and indignation. From a construction site opposite, three workers threw down tools and ran over.

"Hey whoa, what the...!" one of them shouted.

Two teenagers also stopped to watch the action. Kabos dragged himself and Bear back toward the Hummer. Bear's jaws were clamped around Kabos' lower leg as his whole body twisted and jolted. Jessie saw that the man was trying to reach the car, but Bear's attack didn't stop. As he ripped and snarled Kabos lurched backward and reached for a hydrant; Jessie knew if he could get hold, he could get his balance. The flow of blood onto the sidewalk was thick and dark; Bear had gotten down to bone.

Jessie ran and closed the distance between them.

"Bear, let go. Come on, Bear. Here!"

Her shouts were almost cries, but Bear was focused on the man. Jessie reached them just ahead of the construction workers. One of them had a giant wrench in his hand, and Jessie held up her hands.

"No — he's defending me!" she shouted at the men. "This sleazebag was trying to get me into the car," she pleaded. "Get the cops! Somebody call the cops!"

The three men looked at each other, but Jessie knew she didn't look like the type to attract curb crawlers. Plus, the guy Bear was attacking was sinister. He was unkempt and dressed in soiled combats and a hunting vest, which didn't stack up on a Memphis side street. Even from a distance, he smelled like a sewer.

Jessie saw the two teenagers. One of them had a cell phone on his belt.

"Call the cops, will you? This guy is the one they're looking for!"

One worker stepped forwards, and as he got close he screwed his face and cupped his hand over his mouth and nose. At that moment, Bear let go and staggered back.

"Bear, come on. Here."

Jessie kept her distance, trying to get Bear to come to her. One of the teenagers dialed 911, and his fingers trembled. Kabos ran toward his driver's door, and hissed through clenched teeth. He looked directly at Jessie, his face dark with hatred.

Kabos' hiss turned to a low growl. He tugged at the driver's door and pitched himself into the vehicle, as blood splattered onto the pavement beneath him.

"Hey, where are you going?" The guy with the wrench walked around the side of the Hummer. He reached the window just as Kabos fired up the engine and blasted forward. The construction worker stared at the back of the vehicle as it roared away.

On the sidewalk, Jessie bent down to Bear. He sat panting; stripes of blood ran down his face and chest. Bear looked around wildly at the small circle of people around him. The worker holding the wrench spoke first.

"Honey, is he a fighting dog?" he asked.

"Yeah, well, kinda—that's what he was bred for, but

I sorta retired him early…" She looked up at the men and tried to smile. As she stroked Bear, her hands trembled. He still looked dazed. *I need to get him away from here,* she thought.

"He must be what, forty pounds?" asked the other man's friend.

"Nearly fifty, I think," Jessie said.

"Well, he sure sorted that guy. You say the police are looking for him?"

From across the street the site foreman shouted over.

"Yo fellas—you candy asses still work here, or did I fire you already?" The burly New Yorker stood with his hands on his hips.

"Coming boss," replied one, and walked with his workmate. The third guy hesitated, "You gonna be all right, honey?" he asked, narrowing his eyes.

"Yeah, sure, absolutely. I'll just wait for the cops with these guys." She nodded at the two teenagers.

The last guy left and she turned back to the youngsters. One of them held his phone out like a dead bird.

"Ma'am, I didn't actually speak to the cops. I ain't got no cash for calls…" he shrugged. "They ain't comin'…"

Jessie stood up and looked at them; something made her think of Mitch.

"Well fellas, I guess you still rescued us, and I'd like to thank you for that." She dug in her pocket and pulled out a ten dollar bill. "Here, get yourself some credit for that phone."

They looked at each other with wide eyes. The lanky

one nodded his thanks and gently took the money from her, then grinned at his friend. They walked off huddled around the bill and began a heated debate about ice cream or soda.

Jessie hailed a cab. The quicker they were off the street, the better.

◎   ◎   ◎

In the warehouse outside Dorma, the band's practice night had begun. As they sat around on crates and boxes, Danny tried to ignore the tension.

"So we're going to Memphis Saturday. We stick to the original plan, yes?"

Sophie and Ed sat next to each other on drums of industrial cleaner. Sophie raised her eyebrows and nodded, then looked sideways at Ed. Gradually Ed nodded too, but watched Nico the whole time.

Nico sat on a stack of packing crates against a wall. He kicked at a wooden pallet in front of him until it began to split under his boot.

"Oh yeah, for sure," he said. "But we'll be entering the contest without Little Miss Temperamental."

Danny sighed. "And I think that's a mistake."

He looked at Sophie and Ed for backup. He suspected that Sophie was the most in favor of Jessie's return. Danny turned to her and Ed.

"Guys, can you please open your mouths here?"

Sophie looked at Nico. "I'm fine if she comes back," she said.

"No way!" Nico's voice was pure contempt. "How many times have you badmouthed her for being late?"

Sophie sighed.

"Look, I agree she's hard to handle, but is that really the point?" she said.

"No, it's not," said Danny. "The point is that we've got a better chance of winning the contest with Jessie in the lineup. And besides, she's changed a bit. She's kinda... nicer..." He knew it sounded surreal.

"She does have an amazing range," Ed muttered, "big voice really, for a small person..."

"What?" said Nico. "Are you joining the fan club too?"

"Well, no, uh..." Ed looked around.

"Okay, let's vote on it," said Danny. "That's fair, isn't it? Who wants her back in?"

He raised his own hand and looked directly at Sophie, who smiled weakly at Nico.

"Sorry, babe..."

She raised her hand. That just left Ed.

"Aww, that's not fair..." he said. "Why is it up to me?"

Sophie dug him in the ribs. In the silence that followed, Ed raised his hand, but wouldn't make eye contact with Nico.

"Great," said Nico. "Just fabulous." He stood up. "And I suppose you'll want to use my van to move the gear?" He got up to leave.

"Hey, don't you mean *our* van, mister?" Sophie scowled.

Nico threw his sticks down and walked out. They all watched him go.

"Now what?" Danny turned to Sophie.

Sophie hopped off the oil drum, her stilettos clicking on the concrete floor.

"Just leave him to me," she said, then grinned. "Ed, we'll pick you up on Saturday, early—make sure you're ready."

◎ ◎ ◎

At Mitch's bar, Jessie began her evening shift by telling Mitch what had happened with the driver of the Hummer. They sat in one of the booths, while in the background someone played vintage Isaac Hayes, probably because they knew how much Mitch liked it.

Jessie told him what had happened, starting with Danny's encounter in Sligo. She considered telling him about Finch and the dreams, but somehow it still seemed weird to do that. So she kept the story just to the bad guy and the things in the box. Mitch listened but said nothing. When she'd finished, he folded his arms.

"Jessie, it seems to me the best thing you can do is give this fella his ring back, and the bracelet too—if it's his." Under the table, Bear laid at Mitch's feet, his chin rested on his cowboy boots.

"Yeah, I know. It looks like that, but..." She really didn't know where to go with this.

"Is there something you're not telling me?" Mitch had a way of frowning that made her feel ten years old.

"Kinda…look, what I can tell you is that I think that this guy is intent on doing major harm—with or without the ring."

"Sounds like we're mixed up in something ugly." Mitch sounded resigned.

"We?" *He means him and me*, she thought.

"Well, remember, I was involved before you. So I guess the guy has a quarrel with all of us. You, your pa, Danny, and now this little fella." He pulled backwards to check where Bear was. From his waistcoat pocket, he snuck a dog treat down to him.

"Hey, don't spoil him," chided Jessie.

"Aww, a little dried liver won't hurt none."

"So what are we going to do?" Jessie liked the "we"; it felt different, in a good way.

"Leave it with me a while. I need to do some thinking."

Over at the bar, Casey held up a phone and signaled to Mitch. As he stood up, his full height was still a bit of a surprise to Jessie.

"But this guy's freaky, remember. He does this weird shit with his eyes," Jessie said, remembering the way her strength had flooded from her.

"Never mind the guy's eyes," Mitch said, bending under the lamp over the booth. "Like I said, I'll think about it—and maybe you might think about cleaning up your language around me." His frown was playful, but she knew he didn't like her swearing.

"Okay Mitch," she said, feeling childish again. "I hear ya."

Jessie's evening shift in the bar would have been enjoyable if she weren't so worried. They had a good band and a great crowd, but she could only think about the ferocity of the attack. Telling Danny wasn't really an option. The thought of him freaking out wasn't something she wanted to deal with. In the apartment, she fell asleep wondering what the next few days would hold. The band was due in Memphis soon, which felt awkward, strange and exciting all at the same time.

That night, she dreamed of the scarecrow and a heart that wanted to be set free.

The long-haired scarecrow explained that even though scarecrows always tutted, they did always have a heart, which seemed perfectly sensible at the time but the rest of it she didn't understand. He prodded at the stuffing on his chest like she was supposed to know what to do and she did feel bad because after all, weren't friends supposed to help each other? Fortunately that turned out okay because just at the very moment she felt like getting sad again the blue hummingbird came back and pointed at the sparkly key in his top pocket just about where the stitching was coming loose, which was magically-glitteringly-brilliant because that meant she could unfasten the oversized padlock that had been on her chest all this time and had been weighing her down all over and all along. When the padlock fell loose, she let all the sunshine into her chest, just by thinking about it. Then the sun shone outwards from her and that made the stroll down to the meadow to lie by the stream feel like a bowl of soft ice cream and strawberries.

Jessie woke with an odd feeling in her chest, as if her heart was heating up, like someone had poured warm oil into it. For a moment she wondered if she was ill, except that she didn't feel ill at all. In fact, Jessie felt like she'd just woken up on Christmas morning to a mile-high pile of presents. She decided the best thing she could do was dance around the apartment singing and whooping for a while to see if that helped any.

It absolutely did.

Thirty

West of Memphis, Mitch was at the breakfast table. The empty shoebox stood next to a mug of cold coffee. Old photos covered much of the surrounding surface, showing faces, places, visions of the past, some alive, some dead, many forgotten.

"You taking a walk down Memory Lane there, sugar?" Bella put her arm across his shoulders and bent to look at the photo in his hand.

"Me and the boys," he said. "Didn't we think we were somethin'?"

The photo was black and white. They were the only people at a wedding wearing jeans. The Braves posed with the bride and groom. The stage behind was littered with music gear, discarded jackets, and half-drunk beer. Mitch stood tall under a white Stetson; Billy J. was wearing his trademark braces over a T-shirt. Leaning on Billy was Scuz, his greasy hair pulled back by a bandana, with a self-satisfied smile that was almost a leer.

"So, who's the fourth member again?" asked Bella. The youth standing next to Mitch had his shoulders pushed back and his chin tilted up; his smile was polite.

"That's Gabe." Mitch held up the photo so she could see. "Nice guy," he said. "Smart, too. He's the one who didn't make the trip."

Bella leaned forward to study the photo.

"Probably running half the farms in Kansas now," he said. "He was always going to do well."

Bella pulled out a chair and sat down and looked at Mitch.

"Darlin', are you okay about all this with Jessie?" she asked. "I mean, she's a great kid and all, it's just you've been kinda lost in your own little world since she showed up." She stalled.

"You know, I was never really settled with the way that whole thing went," Mitch said. "We planned that trip for almost a year. How it was going to be, what we were going to do, but things went in such a different direction."

"You mean stealing those things and the bust-up?"

"Yeah that was ugly, but it was more than that," he said. "It was as if Billy J. knew he wasn't going back, like he'd planned that part, too." He tossed the photo back onto the table. "Scuz seemed to know. He certainly didn't try and talk him out of it. Corinne got left with two young girls, a heap of debt and no one to help her get over it."

"And now Jessie's here," Bella said.

"Yeah, like the past is catching up to us."

"But you weren't involved, darlin'; you didn't do anything..."

Mitch sighed and began stacking the photos back into the box.

"That's just it," he said. "I didn't do anything. My pa always said to do the right thing over the easy thing." He picked up his cell phone from the table. "Well, maybe this one time I get another chance to do the right thing."

Outside, Mitch's first call was to an old contact in the Tennessee State Police Department, who gave him the direct line of the team investigating the incident on Union. He also advised him how to avoid the call being traced and said that he'd be in touch with an update soon.

◎　◎　◎

In Millington, a lone camper explored the state park. Up here in the woods Kabos could disappear for a while, plus hide the dagger and keep it safe. He needed time for his leg to heal, and besides, there was no rush. This girl was in Memphis for a contest and he knew exactly where she'd be in just a few days. Thoughts of the dog bothered him. He'd always imagined he'd like a dog; maybe he was a cat person after all. The girl's dog had carved and ripped his lower leg into a bloody pulp; which made it dangerous and something to deal with quickly next time. Annoyingly, he hadn't been able to get back to the vapors he needed to create an effective illusion in such a large group of people. Not that any illusion would have worked on the dog. Hypnosis only worked on chickens, and it wasn't like he was in immediate danger from one of those anytime soon.

Around him, hikers, cyclists, and day trippers annoyed him and he began muttering curses on them and their children. He considered changing his vehicle for one of the four-by-fours that seemed to litter the parking lot, but he'd grown attached to the Hummer. Certainly, there were lots of things inside the car to amuse him. The TV, Internet connection and deafening sound system were a great start. The rolls of cash tied with rubber bands in the glove compartment were useful too. Around him, the other SUVs seemed ordinary and indistinguishable from each other. Kabos had yet to see another vehicle with the prowess of his current ride. He did have standards, after all.

◎   ◎   ◎

Just a few miles south in Memphis, the state police received a strange tip-off from an anonymous caller. The man suggested that the recent murder in Sligo of a pawnbroker was linked to the mess over on Union a few days prior. The caller gave an accurate description of the driver involved and claimed the same man was now driving a black Hummer. What was interesting about that is that while a Hummer had been reported, it was described as 'lost' rather than stolen. The owner couldn't actually confirm where he'd left the vehicle, or if it had been taken. He was having some sort of breakdown and was confused about events. He'd arrived back at his hotel without the vehicle, in a highly agitated state. Since then, the man was having frequent panic attacks and refused to leave the hotel room. His doctor had prescribed tranquilizers.

A BOLO, or be on the lookout, was broadcast to find the man who'd stolen the Hummer. The police expected to spot the guy quickly if he was still in the Memphis area; after all, it was a stinking vagrant driving a flashy car. The owner of the vehicle was a rapper in town for the music awards. It seems that the hip hop star had spent over $50,000 on extras for the vehicle. The Hummer was about as understated as Elvis Presley's jungle room.

◎　◎　◎

The atmosphere in Mitch's bar was slow and lazy. Jessie worked the lunchtime shift with Casey. He'd put on some U2 to remind him of Ireland. She served the few customers they had, while Casey counted stock behind the bars, talking non-stop about music, asking Jessie what she liked and who her influences were. Since leaving Ray's Records, Jessie hadn't really talked much about music and she'd missed that. They also argued over the relevance of TV shows like American Idol to music. Jessie thought that musicians should work their way up like she was doing but then Casey pointed out that talent contests were as old as the hills, and she'd be entering one herself in just over a week's time. Jessie could only grin and shrug. This brought them around to the topic they both really wanted to talk about—each other's band.

"So what was the name of your band again?" said Jessie as she polished glasses. "Holly and the Charlatans?"

"Oh, very funny missy," smiled Casey. "And for someone whose band doesn't actually have a name now, somewhat brave." Squatting down at the fridges, he began counting mixers.

"Fair point," conceded Jessie. "Actually we do have one we were using in Dorma, but it's really awful." She screwed up her face at the thought.

"Awww, come on now," said Casey. "Tell me…go on. Maybe it's not so bad."

"No chance."

"I won't laugh," he said. "Well, I'll do my best not to."

Jessie grimaced. "Okay, you'll hear anyway." She cringed. "How about…" She paused, not sure she could even say it. "Political Love…"

"What did you say?" Casey began to chuckle. "Jesus, Mary, and Joseph…Political *what*?"

From his crouched position, he kept on laughing and then completely lost it.

"Look, it wasn't my idea," she protested. "Our keyboard player Ed is a deep thinker…"

As she watched him collapse she knew it was pointless. Casey rolled onto his back and began howling, doubled over with tears spilling down his face. Under the shelves, Bear woke up and wandered over to him. Even the dog licking his face didn't calm Casey down. Jessie started to laugh, too. Casey was crying now, trying to say the name of the band and too weak to get up.

Mitch and Bella walked in to find their bar manager as helpless as a baby on the floor of the bar, and Jessie grinning over him with an ice bucket, about to empty its contents on his head.

"So, is one of you going to tell me what happened?" Mitch said gruffly. All Casey could do was hold his stomach with one hand and point helplessly at Jessie with the other. Jessie was pouting in an attempt not to laugh any more. Conceding defeat, she told Mitch and Bella the band's name, and her fate was sealed.

Mitch frowned.

"Political Love?" he said, and then started to smile.

From the floor, Casey's squeal was faint.

"Political Love..."

"Are they communists?" Bella said.

Casey began to get up and went down again. Within a few minutes they all lost it. It was a stupid, dumb thing that just got funnier, but none of them could explain why. Jessie laughed until her stomach hurt and hours later, she was still smiling.

Thirty-One

asey invited her to see his band. They were playing out on Poplar Avenue at a live music club that pulled in a regular crowd. Jessie got ready with a rush of excitement. She thought about calling Danny to tell him, but realized he'd be working his shift. After a long bath, she spiked her hair and applied dark eye makeup. Her outfit was selected with meticulous planning: a red plaid kilt, fishnet leggings and Doc Martens. She'd even shaved her legs. A white lace bodice she'd found in a thrift shop was worn under a black buttoned vest. Spinning around in front of the small bathroom mirror, she felt pleased with the result.

"Very rock 'n' roll," she said to no one in particular. From the doorway, Bear watched with his head to one side.

Jessie arrived at the Hi-Tone club around 11p.m. She'd told herself that being out in a crowded place was okay, but as she got out of the cab, the hairs on the back of her neck bristled. A line had formed and she began to walk to the back of it. Suddenly, she felt exposed. She was out in the open, and with Bear she was more conspicuous. Mitch had only let her go after she agreed to him making a call to the owner of the club.

"Hey, is your name Jessie?" The black bouncer put out an arm toward her as she passed.

"Yeah." She turned to frown at him. "Do you know me?"

"No, sweet pea," the big guy smiled. "But I've only got one 'lady plus dog' on my guest list here, and I'm guessing you're it."

He unhooked the chain from the metal post to let her pass.

"Tell Mr. Hanrahan that Tiny said hello." He winked.

"Aaah, right," she grinned, embarrassed for the second time that day. "Thanks for that."

A pasty faced guy at the front of the line lurched forward.

"You actually let dogs in here?"

He swayed before stepping back again.

"I do when the animal's better looking than anyone else in the line," the bouncer warned. As Bear walked by the bouncer nodded down at him. Jessie grinned, *Bear you did it again,* she thought.

With low ceilings, The Hi-Tone Club was a tight space, kind of moody and effortlessly cool. Jessie pushed her way through the crowd, and checked that Bear was close behind. In one corner, Casey and the band sat waiting for their slot. Casey spotted them both and waved Jessie over.

"Come on and meet the band," he said, standing to let her sit down. They were an all-male crew: long hair, black T-shirts, and bead bracelets. The contradiction was the guy in the white singlet over in the corner. He had the bone structure of a Roman emperor, huge brown eyes and his shaved head glistened. Dark tribal tattoos laced themselves up to his neck and no further. It made his features appear more flawless somehow.

"Guys, this is Jessie," Casey said. "Jessie this is Mark,

Goucho, Dave, and over on the end there, that's Holly." Casey couldn't resist a smile. "So the guys here have been asking me about your band…"

"Yeah, it's a band with no name – remember?" she said.

Casey fetched her a soda while the band asked about her own group and told her about the Memphis music scene. Holly smiled but didn't talk much. When he did speak, his voice was so soft that she struggled to hear him. Jessie wondered what he was going to be like onstage.

At midnight, they left her and Bear to begin their set. They launched with a cover of R.E.M's "What's the Frequency, Kenneth?" and the crowd jumped into action. Jessie was both thrilled and disappointed. Holly merely needed the stage to come to life, and his voice was as distinct as anything she'd ever heard live. First there was a mournful, soulful quality to it and then a raw, angry, hostile power. *They've got to have a weak spot*, she thought. *What's their flaw?* After a while she realized that their own songs didn't sound as good as their covers. In the contest, the finalists had to play an original number. *I need to work with Danny on our songs*, she decided.

Back at the apartment with Bear, it took a long time to come down. Seeing the band perform had made the competition seem thunderously close. She wondered about starting writing, but it was really late and she was working the next morning.

She finally stopped replaying the evening and went to sleep. *Danny will know what to do*, she decided.

Part Three: The Contest

Thirty-Two

It was Sunday afternoon and Danny and the others were due to arrive that day. Since watching Holly and his band Jessie had gone over their set in her head many times. In the end, her judgment was much the same as that night: they had more experience and they were great at covers, but their songwriting wasn't as good as hers and Danny's.

When she arrived downstairs for her shift, she found a telephone message from Danny, plus a request from Bella to clean the ornaments on display behind the bar. Jessie didn't mind; it would help pass the time. The bar was Bella's personal homage to the music industry. The collection of memorabilia stretched back to a napkin autographed by Buddy Holly and currently finished with a framed photo of Bella and Mitch with Kelly Clarkson. It was all pretty cool really. There was autographed baseball stuff, and a Cuban cigar box signed by Frank Sinatra that reminded her of the one her mother had sent. She opened it to find some old coins, some thread and a pencil; it gave her an idea. *No one would look for it in here*, she thought.

Of all the memorabilia, Jessie's favorite was the powder blue jacket in the glass case. Casey had told her that Elvis was supposed to have commissioned it himself, but the problem was that it looked way too small. Jessie couldn't help staring at it sometimes; its rhinestones danced in the light and the detail of the beadwork was exquisite.

Around four o'clock, the band arrived in a noisy clatter of bags and equipment. As usual Ed refused to leave his keyboards in the van. Casey welcomed them in. Jessie had told him the reunion might be awkward and was glad to have him there, but it was the thought of seeing Danny again that was weirding her out.

"Hey guys!" Casey shouted. "You must be Political Luurve."

He held open his arms and grinned. Danny smiled, Ed nodded, and Nico grimaced, but Sophie just stared at him. She watched as Sophie gave Casey her best lingering smile and shifted her suitcase awkwardly.

"Here, let me take that," he said and took the suitcase from her. "Guess you could all use a drink, maybe?"

"Fantastic..." Sophie purred and beamed at Jessie. "Hey Jess, how's life in Memphis? Danny tells us you've settled right in."

For once, Jessie was glad of Sophie's small talk; at least it broke the ice, but she hadn't really said hi to Danny and now the moment had been swept away. Within minutes, they were all settled in a booth chatting about anything that didn't really matter: their journey, the dull weather in Memphis, and what it was like to be on Beale. Casey delivered some drinks.

"So I'm guessing your shift just finished early then, amigo?" He gave Jessie a soft dig in the ribs as he lifted the beers onto the table.

"Yeah, well, if you're sure you can manage the late afternoon lull..." she smiled back. Danny frowned at Casey as he left. Danny's sharp tone surprised her.

"Okay, listen. We need to figure out a few things," he said, "first, we need a place to stay, plus a place to practice." He nodded at Nico. "Jess, we were hoping you'd have some ideas."

"Yeah I was talking to Case earlier..." Jessie said. "He knows someone with a condo near Riverview Park. The guy's away for a few weeks. He'd probably rent it if someone gave him a call." She looked at Danny for approval, but Danny just stared back at her.

"Well, that sounds promising, doesn't it?" said Ed, and looked at Danny, then Nico. "Are we going to call the guy then?" Finally, Sophie spoke.

"Sounds great. Let's do it." She nodded. "And how about a practice venue, Jess? Any thoughts?"

Jessie sighed. "Well, I'd really like to ask Mitch about this place, but I'm not sure." She grimaced. "You see, Casey is in direct competition with us. He's in a band too." She gave a shrug. "Maybe that doesn't make much difference..."

"Of course it makes a difference," Danny snapped. "We don't want anyone knowing our set list." He looked at the others for confirmation. Ed and Nico both nodded.

"I say we find somewhere else," Danny said flatly.

"Okay," Jessie said. "Well, I'll ask Case if he knows anywhere."

"Can't we just do something without asking Casey?"

It was Jessie's turn to look confused. *What's his problem?* she thought.

"Hey, what about naming the band?" she grinned. "We've always said we'd lose this dumbass name. Sorry, Ed…"

"Yeah, I've had it standing at the urinals in O'Neill's alongside guys howling at the band's poster on the wall," Nico said. "We change the name today."

"No, that's fine," Ed said cheerfully. "I've even had some thoughts."

Nico groaned, but Ed continued.

"What about…Shotgun Politics?"

"Ed, that's terrible," Jessie laughed. "You'll say Shotgun Love next."

Ed muttered, "Shotgun Love" and looked thoughtful.

From the back of the bar, a scraping noise drew nearer. Bear emerged from the kitchen with his new trophy. The chef had given him a beef bone and it was a monster. He slumped down next to Danny, who rubbed his head in welcome.

"Hey buddy," he said. "Whatcha do to the rest of the poor cow?"

Even Nico managed a smile as Bear dropped the bone with a thud.

"Look, does anyone have any better ideas?" Jessie wasn't sure where the conversation was going, but at least it was lightening the mood.

"What about Dog Kill Cow?" Sophie asked, watching Bear go to work on the bone.

"What about Dog Fight Ed?" said Nico, laughing at his own joke.

"Or Dog Fighter?" mused Sophie.

"Hey no, I kinda like that," said Danny. "Dog Fighter..." He looked over at the keyboard player. "Whaddya say, Ed?"

Ed scratched at his patchy stubble. "I'd say that we need to consider the political inference of the phrase..." he said.

Nico stared at Ed. "Is murder a felony in Tennessee?" he asked Jessie.

"Only if you get caught," Jessie grinned. "And even then, we'd all vouch for you."

The rest of the afternoon rolled on almost peacefully. The band loved the bar; Ed pored over every piece of Bella's memorabilia, while Sophie just wanted to know the price of the Elvis jacket. They began planning what Memphis sights they wanted to see first, and Jessie felt herself relaxing. The only potential dispute occurred as they passed too close to the topic of the set list. Jessie wanted to do lots of their own stuff, while Ed and Sophie wanted to do mostly covers. Danny wanted to hear some of Jessie's new material before deciding, and if Nico had an opinion he wasn't voicing it.

Up at Millington State Park, a team of police had been staking out the stolen Hummer for most of the day, until its driver returned at dusk. In the shadows, the man moved carefully toward the vehicle. The officer who spotted him questioned what he was seeing for a moment. It looked like a creeping dark shape and involuntarily, he shuddered. He gave the signal to the other officers to move and they slid into position. They were under strict instructions. Apparently this guy was violent and freakishly strong. Eyewitness accounts said he'd punched his way out of a car wreck. He must have been high as a kite. They'd brought air Tasers, which were strong enough to go through an armored vest. It was pointless negotiating with a drugged-up psycho. This guy needed to be brought down fast and hard.

As the criminal approached the vehicle, the first officer hit him square between the shoulder blades. Scarily, it took two other officers using Tasers before they finally brought him down. The officers then followed the rest of their instructions, chained his full body, blindfolded him, and called for backup. The three men trying to hold him down felt like they were sitting on a thousand-pound alligator. Even in chains he writhed and shook enough to keep throwing one of them off. When backup finally arrived, their shirts were drenched with sweat from the struggle.

Thirty-Three

The following night, the band now tagged as Dog Fighter sat in Jessie's apartment. Danny had agreed to using Mitch's bar on the condition that Casey wasn't around, which meant they were now waiting for the bar manager to lock up, so they could go downstairs and practice. Ed and Sophie were on the couch, Nico was on a stool, and Danny and Jessie paced around. Eventually they walked straight at each other. *Embarrassing,* thought Jessie.

Finally, they were interrupted by Casey's voice from downstairs.

"Okay Jess, I'm going..." he shouted. "And please, stay away from Dolly Parton's back catalog—you know we're currently working through that..."

"Yeah, right. Stand by your fan, Case," Jessie yelled back at him, chuckling. She picked up her guitar and song sheets.

"He's a funny guy," said Ed, smiling.

"Regular Bob Hope," said Nico and glared at Sophie, who stared back at him and raised her eyebrows.

"Irish 'charm' is the term they use for it," muttered Danny.

"More like Irish smarm..." countered Nico.

"Guys, can we lay off Casey?" said Jessie.

Sophie picked up a tambourine and jangled it noisily as she sashayed out.

Despite everyone's anxieties, the practice session went well. They ran through a few familiar numbers and the whole thing seemed to flow. Jessie had been experimenting with different styles of vocals and something had clicked. She'd realized she had been trying to sound like other vocalists she admired, but the mimicking was masking her own voice. She'd talked it over a little with Mitch. He said something about "being the song," which seemed to help. So now Jessie was focusing on the heart of the song, its sentiment, and meaning. In her mind, she was simply expressing emotion, which made her think less about how she sounded. After a blazing rendition of Janis Joplin's "Piece of My Heart," the band fell silent. Sophie clapped softly, nodding in satisfaction. Even Nico's mouth was agape.

"Okay, that's in," Nico said, and looked at Danny.

"Nice one, Jess, really cool," said Danny.

When Jessie at last fell asleep around five a.m., she was daring to hope that they might have a chance. She thought about Finch and wondered where he was and if she'd see him again. The feathers seemed to have stopped appearing and she missed them. *Maybe I'll see one tomorrow*, she thought.

In East Tennessee, wardens in the secure unit of Rushby State Correctional Unit were having a hard time processing a recent detainee. While state officers wanted very much to question him, the wardens refused to bring him around from sedation. So far he'd wrecked three cells and almost escaped when one of the wardens had some kind of brain failure and calmly opened the cell door for him. The prisoner had been stopped by a chemical restraint powerful enough to drop a buffalo. The decision had been made to move him down to Indian Bend and let those guys deal with him. Tough nuts were their specialty.

Thirty-Four

The final practice session arrived before anyone felt ready for it, least of all Jessie. The session had been awful, followed by the ongoing fight about the set list. Jessie suggested two originals and one cover, but everyone else seemed to want two covers. Jessie wanted to use their new rock punk number but Nico said it needed more work. When Nico proposed a Chili Peppers number with a big drum solo in the middle, Jessie rolled her eyes.

Sophie's suggestion was a compromise; their edgy version of the Johnny Cash classic "Ring of Fire." It was one of the first songs they'd worked on as a group. Danny loved it but he was worried that a parody of the famous local boy might actually sink them, even if they positioned it as a tribute.

By three a.m. they were yelling so loudly at each other that no one could hear anyone else. At his keyboards, Ed sat with his fingers in his ears, his face crumpled with emotion. After trying to calm Sophie, Jessie, and Nico down, Danny lost his temper, too.

They sat quietly while Danny shouted at them what was going to happen. As unpaid manager he had the final say. They'd go along with Jessie's suggestion. His logic was to avoid having a lead vocalist that wasn't behind her vocal. They practiced the numbers until dawn and no one mentioned the sequence. They parted in the early light, hardly speaking, Jessie watched Ed; he had an upset look, like he'd been in an earthquake, while Danny didn't even say goodnight.

Jessie knew that Danny had sided with her to avoid trouble. She went back upstairs and tried to catch a couple of hours' sleep, but sleep eluded her like a forgotten memory. She stared at the flaking plaster on her bedroom ceiling. The perfect set list was part of a bigger problem. Were they actually good enough? *Am I good enough?* she wondered.

Mitch had given her the first contest day off, along with the news that the psychopath vagrant had been caught with the stolen Hummer up in Millington Park a few days ago. It felt like one less thing to worry about, and she'd called Danny straight away to tell him.

Despite the fact she didn't need to get up early, by nine a.m. Jessie was downstairs sweeping up—anything to stay busy. She unbolted the front door to let in some air. Even now, the Southern heat was rising. Some Beatles fanatic was unlocking his bike from a nearby lamppost. His carrot orange military coat had white piping on the sleeves and across the front; in the early morning light, the suit glowed. The dark green baker's bike, complete with a bell and a basket, completed his outfit.

Jessie wondered why he was taking so long to undo the chain; his movements were gentle, considered. Finally she recognized the blue circular sunglasses. Finch.

"Man, are you even real?" she laughed. At her feet, Bear pushed past and trotted over; his tail wagged sharply.

"Greetings," he said and gave a theatrical salute. Bear reached him and sat down. Finch bent and stroked him as if he was silken, which made Bear rumble with pleasure.

"That's a stunning outfit," Jessie grinned.

Finch stood and looked down to admire his suit.

"Yes, I hear there's a music contest," he said, and ran his fingers down the rows of brass buttons on his front. "Thought this might help me fit in."

He looked back at her and smiled.

"Finch, it's fabulous," she laughed. *Be quick before he disappears.*

"Finch, can I ask you…just what is going on? I mean, my dreams—it's like you're in them, only a different you, if that makes sense…" As she heard her words she had the clear thought, *I sound like I'm going crazy.*

Finch bent back down to his bike and picked up the chain wrapped around the post.

"Jessie, sometimes things happen that we can't explain. It's not that they can't be explained, it's simply that we can't explain them. It's like a tapestry with a pattern," he said. "Stand too close, and you won't see it. Stand back, and the overall design is revealed."

"Right," she said. *Now he sounds crazy.* "Well, no… not right… I still don't understand… you see there's some weird stuff happening, and it's all started since I met you."

"Really?" he said, "or do your dreams simply draw your attention to current events?" Jessie tried to remember when the dreams had first started but couldn't. *I've been having them for ages*, she thought.

Finch tugged once at the chain and it fell away easily. He held it up and studied it. Jessie watched him. *Maybe there's something about the chain*, she thought. He dropped it into the basket on the front of the bike.

"It's just that there's a lot of things changing for me right now..." Jessie said.

"Well then, you must be changing on the inside. Jessie, are you changing on the inside?" She stared at him. *I do feel different, but isn't that because of what's been happening?* "The way to navigate is to ask yourself simple questions." He turned and looked at her. "Ask the simple question. Then wait for the answer. That's all."

"Ask the simple question."

"Then, in the quiet space that follows, the answer will surface."

He placed a thumb on the bell trigger and rang it, just once. "Aaah, that's for me. I must be going."

"I was hoping you might stay and talk..." she said.

"Jessie, what's the simplest question that you have right now?"

Yeah, like there's just one, she thought. She looked at him, opened her mouth, and then closed it. *Actually, there is just one*, she realized.

"What's our best song choice for tonight?"

"Perfect!" he said, and nodded. "Ask yourself that then." He kicked one leg over the saddle. The sign on the crossbar read: "Old times, new times—it's all just times."

At least that's what Jessie first thought, but then the word "times" also looked like "tunes"—odd. He pushed off from the curb and glided down the street. *Old tunes?*

He reached the junction, raised a hand, and called back, "Oh and hey, you might need to repeat the question a couple of times—you know, let it cook a while."

Jessie watched him go. She tried to piece it together. First he'd told her she could make things happen, and she could, sort of, but now there was this simple question idea. What was the point of asking yourself questions? *What's our best song choice for tonight?* She walked back inside the bar. *What's our best song choice for tonight?* Bear took a while to follow. *It's all just tunes.*

Back in the apartment, she found herself staring at Peggy's card. She tried to recall what Peggy had said to her as she was leaving. Then Peggy's words came back to her: "old tunes." Peggy had said "old tunes" too. The hairs on the back of her neck tingled. She needed to call Danny.

Thirty-Five

The band met in the Arcade restaurant pre-contest. The diner looked retro because it had stayed pretty much the same since Elvis and his buddies used to hang out there. A Formica bar with high stools stretched across most of the back wall and coffee sat in glass jugs behind the counter. When Sophie, Ed, and Nico arrived, Jessie and Danny were tucked into a corner table. Danny's guitar case was angled to hide Bear. Ed waved while alongside, in a black PVC dress that looked she'd sprayed it on, Sophie turned even more heads than usual.

For once, Sophie and Jessie had coordinated outfits; Jessie was wearing all white. It was a cool contrast that seemed to work. She'd found her dress in a thrift shop. It was a vintage 1920s straight cut with heavy fringing in tiers down the body. She'd loved it as soon as she'd found it, despite its vaguely musty smell. Bella had loaned her some white stiletto sandals, and once Jessie had learned to walk in them, they were a definite win.

By contrast, the guys had made their predictable subhuman effort with their clothes, but then jeans and T-shirts weren't going to offend anyone...except possibly the slogan on Ed's, which read "I see dumb people."

As the rest of the band drew near, Jessie wasted no time. "We've changed the set list," she announced.

"What?" Nico and Sophie shouted in unison.

"Jessie, can I handle this, please?" said Danny. Jessie stared back at him.

Danny turned back to the rest of the band.

"We've changed the set list," he repeated.

"Yeah, Danny, we got that," said Sophie. "Do you want to tell us what to, or should we save that for when we're all on stage?"

"No, look," said Jessie. "I realized you were right the whole time, Sophie." It was now Nico's turn to look shocked. "We need to cover the Cash number, 'Ring of Fire.' Johnny Cash is a local legend, plus it's fresh – it's a winner, I just know it."

Jessie took a breath and began building her argument, then stopped, as no one was listening, but they weren't disagreeing either. *They're thinking about it*, she thought.

"Well?" she said, looking at Sophie, then at Nico.

Nico chewed his thumb nail. "I always did like it."

Sophie smiled. "That's possibly because you get to go berserk on drums," she said. "Okay Jess. Let's do it. I like it too. That's great, I'm happy."

"Ed—you up for this?" Jessie said.

Ed woke from his daydream, and bit his lower lip, his expression serious.

"Yep, we're a band with a plan," he nodded. "Team tigers, let's get over there." He turned on his heel and pointed toward the door. "Here we go guys, from zeros to heroes…"

Sophie looked at Jessie and mouthed, "Team tigers…?"

They arrived at the venue for the first round; the Royal Theater, once grand and opulent, was now faded but still fabulous. No one was around the entrance, and the ticket booths and coat rooms were all unattended. They followed the familiar drone of a sound check: "Uh... one two, yeah... one two." Somewhere a sound technician strummed a guitar and chords clashed and reverberated around the auditorium.

Inside, bands and their equipment filled every corner as they jostled for space. Jessie stood and stared; everywhere people with huge hair and massive makeup, postured and positioned themselves for maximum impact. Near the stage, an undersized stage manager struggled to cope with the musicians circling him.

Jessie surveyed the scene and felt her panic rise. It was all getting a bit real. As usual, Danny took charge and after telling them all to stay put, he went over to the stage manager. The rest of the band fell silent. Sophie bent down to stroke Bear, who sniffed at the PVC dress.

"Okay, okay," the stage manager was almost shouting. "Look, one question at one time. Can you what?" As a Marilyn Manson look-alike edged closer, the stage manager jumped up on to the stage behind him.

"Okay, listen!" He waved his clip board. "This is how it's going to run."

Gradually, the circus calmed down.

"The full order is posted backstage. Basically the first three acts we need ready are Sacha and Teen, followed by Dog Fighter, then Rambling Rose," he said, nodding at a hippie-looking girl wearing mostly flowers.

Danny came back over and explained how it was all going to work. Basic gear was provided on stage, including amps and mikes, but they had to move other stuff on just before their set. All Jessie could think about was how much could go wrong. Danny scanned the stage as he spoke.

"It's fine; look, we can make that stuff work," Jessie said, but her stomach lurched. *Come on, just relax*, she thought.

As they walked toward the stage, the numbness in her legs got worse. They moved their gear backstage, found a place for Bear to sit and then stood in a huddle. No one wanted to state the obvious: only one band would go through. Fifteen bands would be culled to a single survivor and it could all end right here, tonight. In eight other venues across Memphis, seventy-five bands were going through exactly the same process.

"We're still up for this, right?" Jessie said. *Get it together.*

"Yeah, absolutely," Sophie said.

Danny and Ed nodded, while Nico glared at a member of Sacha and Teen. Their rivals looked pretty cool, pretty chic. The all-girl group walked on stage, and assembled themselves to start their set.

Jessie watched the lead singer Sacha, and watched for nerves. Danny said their website described them as an "eclectic Asian rock fusion." And from the sample download tracks, they were pretty slick. Sacha was the doe-eyed lead singer, a clash of East and West: black harem pants were matched with a crimson leather waistcoat and stilettos. Jessie looked at Sophie, who just shrugged. *Doesn't anything spook her?* Jessie thought.

Around them, the auditorium was far from a sellout; it seemed mostly family and friends plus a few music journalists with pads and pens at the ready. The stage manager appeared and ushered the three male judges to seats about five rows back.

One of the judges stood up.

"Right, okay girls," he smiled. "Just play the full set, back to back, no breaks." Then he nodded at the stage manager.

In the sudden silence, the four girls checked each other then launched into a familiar intro. They played two covers: "Lady Marmalade" and "Beautiful." The lead singer was flawless and carried the vocals effortlessly. Their original number had a strong rock rhythm, which was then blended with the evocative sounds of a sitar plus cymbals and flutes. Danny reckoned the set was a clunky contradiction, even if he grudgingly accepted that they actually could play. The judges watched with interest but no visible emotion. When the set had finished, the band walked off stage, flashing smiles and waving.

Jessie tried to focus. She bent down to Bear and made sure his collar was tied firmly to the rigging, even though she'd tested it twice already.

"Okay," she said, and turned to Nico and Ed. "Let's look tight walking on, remember?"

Jessie followed last, reached the mike and acknowledged the judges. *Show no fear,* she thought, and checked behind her. Sophie was in position. Nico squared his shoulders and nodded, while Ed just grinned back at her.

To her left, Danny threw his guitar lead to one side and cleared his hair back from his face. Jessie caught his eye and he nodded; she knew he meant encouragement, but she just felt responsibility—*it's up to me now*. She stared at the men in the fifth row, sensing her future was in their hands. *They think it's just a music contest*, she thought. The lead judge raised his hand...*let it begin*.

Thirty-Six

On stage, Jessie knew the band was waiting for her signal. They'd agreed on a sandwich: the Janis Joplin cover to show strong vocals, then a favorite original they'd been playing for a while, titled "Spirit Move You," followed by the thrash version of "Ring of Fire." She tilted her head back and on bass guitar, Danny launched in with the striking intro. As the introduction slowly wound down, she tipped the mike downward and began. Jessie took the vocal from a ragged yell to smoky sweet, but left the real power of her voice just below the surface. As she reached the home ground of their own song, Jessie felt her confidence strengthen.

When the band began the cover of "Ring of Fire" the crowd nodded and smiled at each other as they recognized the classic. At some point, Jessie relaxed and began to enjoy herself. By the crazy climax of Nico's big drum finish, the claps and cheers included whistles, too. *Whistles are good,* Jessie thought. When the crowd's applause faded and died, she was brought back by the distant sound of clapping and a dog barking.

"All riiight..."

She looked left to see the stage manager knelt down by Bear, grinning and holding both thumbs up. Automatically, she turned back to Danny; he was also smiling at her. *Maybe I did all right,* she thought. She looked at the judges but motionless, they simply stared back at her.

The band checked each other before realizing they needed to get off stage. In the wings, Rambling Rose waited to come on. Danny, Ed, and Nico moved their gear back to the van, while Sophie and Jessie watched the final throes of the Rose, who turned out to be more of a wailing wallflower.

They decided to return to Mitch's bar. The prospect of watching six more bands play three songs each was too much. Besides, Danny observed, by reputation they'd already seen the best of the rest. Sacha and Teen was the band they needed to defeat. The results wouldn't be out until everyone had played and the final scores were counted. It could be ages before the decision was announced.

Back at Mitch's Place, they gathered beers and went over the details of the set until everyone ran out of fresh viewpoints. No one was brave enough to be confident; they'd done okay, but was it enough? Then Danny and Ed decided to go back and hear the final results; it felt better to be walking than waiting.

In Mitch's bar, the rest of the band waited for Danny and Ed to get back. Over an hour later, they still hadn't returned, but a victorious Holly and the Italians had. Casey came straight over, eager to share their news.

"Hey guys," he said, and smiled at Sophie. "How d'ya do?"

Nico glared as Sophie beamed back.

"We're still waiting," Sophie said.

"So how did you do?" Jessie said. "Great from the look of those guys."

She nodded over to the jubilant band surrounding Holly.

"Aaah, terrific, we won our round." His eyes sparkled with excitement.

"Congratulations," said Jessie and Sophie in unison.

"Well thank-you ladies," said Casey. "And good luck with your results. I'd better get back, got some partying to do..."

Over at the bar the drummer dropped to his knees in front of Holly, and pretended to worship him like a god.

"Looks like it could be a fun session..." Sophie said.

"Yeah, we plan to hit Beale hard," said Casey. He grinned and returned to the revelry at the bar.

Two hours later Ed and Danny appeared. Danny scowled at them and Ed looked like a child who'd let go of a helium balloon outdoors.

"Guess that answers the question," said Jessie, *I feel sick,* she thought.

"I knew we shouldn't have played the stupid Cash track," said Nico. "That judge in the black shirt was probably his nephew or something."

"Shut up, okay?" snapped Sophie. "Let's just wait to hear..."

Suddenly Danny's face lit up. "We did it!" he shouted and grabbed hold of Ed.

"Yeah, they *loved* us," Ed shouted. "Especially the Cash cover…"

Sophie clapped her hands together. "Yeah, Nico was really confident about that one," she said.

Jessie grinned but felt confused. "So what took you so long?" she said.

"Rambling Rose demanded a recount and a judge's inquiry." Danny grinned.

"Seems like she couldn't believe she came in last," Ed said.

"So what happened to Sacha and Teen?" Jessie said.

"Oh yeah, that got really ugly," Ed sounded uneasy. "They stormed out muttering it was a fix." Then he hesitated. "One of them called your outfit tedious and dull—and said that you were pitchy during the Joplin cover…"

Jessie's mouth dropped as the band waited for her to detonate at the insult. *Have a nice day, remember?* she thought. Instead she raised both hands, and made peace signs.

"Political Love, guys, Political Love…"

Sophie howled and clapped her hands, Danny grinned, while Nico frowned at Jessie.

Jessie ran over to Mitch; he took one look at her face, shouted congratulations and reached over the bar and ruffled her hair. Then he made Jessie call Bella, whose squeal was so loud Jessie had to hold the phone away from her ear. She wondered about telling her mom and

Mary, but then checked herself. *Don't get carried away*, she thought.

They celebrated with another round of drinks, and then Sophie suggested they all go and join Casey and the band but Danny said no. He reasoned that they should all get a few hours' sleep before meeting up again at four a.m. for practice. The next round was the following evening, and they still didn't know who they were up against. They had gotten through one ring of fire, only to face another.

Thirty-Seven

After practicing until seven a.m., Jessie managed a few hours' sleep but was up and dressed by ten-thirty a.m. The original number they needed to play that night wasn't coming together and now she could think of nothing else. She wandered around the apartment, going over it in her mind and humming randomly, which sometimes helped. On the window ledge, she watched a gull's feather settle into place. *Maybe it's going to be all right,* she thought.

Tonight's contest was the second of three rounds, just them against two other bands. She knew that the odds were better, but the quality would be higher. Who were they up against? The thought of going up against Holly and the Italians made her stomach lurch.

Bear watched her pace around and took up a strategic position in a doorway. Eventually, she settled with her guitar and a pile of paper in the living room. As she began to play, Bear barked once: visitor alert. By the time Mitch had reached the door, Jessie was there to greet him.

"Well, I needed to come and say congratulations again. I hear that you did just great. The judges were all impressed."

"You heard from the judges?"

"Yeah, they loved the Cash cover. One of them is a

real fan. That was probably the clincher; too bad you can't use a cover twice."

"Well, actually it was a last-minute thing — look, come on in. Have coffee."

Mitch raised a hand.

"No I can't stay, Bella's got me running all over town looking for new drapes. Seems like she's given all ours away." He nodded at the living room window.

Jessie chuckled. "Yeah sorry 'bout that…"

They talked for a while about the contest and about what the judges were looking for. He walked toward the guitar and song sheets.

"You fixing up a storm for this evening then, Jessie?"
She grimaced.

"Me and Danny have been working on a number that will fly if I can get the chorus right," she said, thinking about the approaching deadline.

"You looking for words or music?" he asked.

"Both," she said. "Seems like neither's coming."

"So what's the song about?"

"It's about life working from the inside out," Jessie ventured. "Like a grown-up magic, kinda."

"Sounds like voodoo," he laughed.

"Ah yes, but it's voodoo that *you* do," Jessie said, thinking of the effect Mitch had on people. "It's voodoo that you do…" she repeated and stared at him.

"Sounds like you got your line…" he grinned and turned to leave. "You need anything else while I'm here?"

"Any idea who we're against tonight?" she said.

"Yup, you got Peeko and Mission Trivia. But just focus on what you're doing. Remember, don't get hooked by the competition."

Mitch gave Bear a farewell rub and descended into the black hole of Jessie's staircase.

Jessie was relieved that it wasn't Holly and the boys. *Maybe tomorrow*, she thought. For the rest of the morning she worked on the song, scribbling, humming, then singing out loud while she walked around. The band was coming later to practice the reworked number and a tension was beginning in her chest. *Nerves are good* she thought, as her stomach felt queasy again.

◎ ◎ ◎

Over in Rushby prison, the scheduled move of the detainee nicknamed "Godzilla" was going better than hoped. On hearing he was being moved to the Indian Bend facility, the crazy appeared to cool down. He swallowed sedative pills without a fuss before being put in leg irons and chains.

A small army of officers walked him out to an armored wagon. With his head bent, the prisoner shuffled along like a well-trained dog.

At the van driver's first sight of "Godzilla" he almost laughed. He'd heard the scary stories about this character, but as usual they were exaggerated. Sunken cheeks suggested the rapid weight loss that was common with new prisoners. The degenerate looked like he'd be brought down with a well-placed punch. The driver guessed that Rushby was sending him over to Indian Bend for some other reason, not that he cared. His job was just to drive.

After locking him behind bars in the secure compartment, some of the officers got in the wagon with him. There was only room for five guards, and the remaining wardens turned and walked back into the prison.

Inside, the prisoner lifted his head and watched the men leave. Then he turned to the nearest guard and smiled.

◎   ◎   ◎

By twelve, Jessie was still hunched over her guitar, trying to blend the sound with the new lyrics. In less than an hour, the band would arrive and she wasn't sure it was ready. *It has to be,* she thought. Bear began to whine and shambled toward the door. From the kitchen, sweet spicy cooking smells floated up toward them. Jessie's stomach lurched at the thought of food.

Over at the door, Bear sniffed around the gap at the floor. He looked back at her, his huge eyes pleading. By now, Bear was closely attuned to the bar's food preparation times and the new chef was a dog lover. Jessie sighed.

"Come on then," she said. Downstairs, she found a dish of cooked fish and vegetables waiting for him, in his own bowl. She left Bear and wandered into the bar to see who was working the shift, but there was no one around. *Who's supposed to be on today?* she thought.

At the end of the bar, a lone tourist waited to be served. Immaculate in a white linen suit and crisp Panama hat, the man emanated a calmness caused by all the patience in the world.

Finch.

"Now, aren't you just a sight for sore eyes?" Jessie said, and walked around to the serving side of the bar. "You know, I've given up trying to figure you out by now."

She grinned. *He's like sunshine,* she thought. He lifted the Panama off as a greeting and placed it on to the bar beside him.

"Jessie," he opened his arms wide, "how wonderful to see you in your place of work."

Looking around him, his gaze settled on the glittering Elvis jacket in the glass case behind her.

"That's an exquisite garment." His eyebrows raised.

"You're really into clothes, aren't you, Finch?"

"Well, some things are more special than others," he said. "The art is to know which ones."

Jessie laughed. "You know, I should have a pen and paper ready for when you show up," she said. "I never know what I should take note of."

She gestured at the shelves behind her.

"Can I buy you a drink?" she asked. "I never really said thank you for helping me and Bear. I mean, especially Bear." She held her breath as he considered the offer.

He put his head on one side, pouted and then nodded.

"Yes, I think I'd like a feathered fizz," he said. "Cranberry, grape juice, and lemonade." He paused. "Oh, and with a twist of lime," he said.

"That's a new one." Jessie grinned and searched for the juices in the coolers under the bar. "I guess there's no point in asking about the feathers, huh?" She glanced up at him, and then busied herself with his drink.

"They're a greeting," he said.

Jessie replied without looking at him. "Yeah? Where from?"

"Oh, another realm of perception, clearly," he said, "or just another realm." He rubbed his chin. "Maybe that's clearer."

She poured the cranberry and grape juice over ice. *Stay casual so he talks more,* she thought.

"Do you mean the place I've been going in my dreams?" She reached for the mixer hose and triggered a jet of lemonade into the glass. "Like another world or something?"

She popped in a mixing stick and pushed the drink over to him. He frowned at it and tutted softly. *And the scarecrow does the tutting thing too!* she thought. They both watched the drink.

"I forgot the lime," she said.

"Just a twist," he said, smiling again.

She retrieved the drink and fixed it.

"Aaah, perfect, thank you," he prodded the ice gently with the stick. "And yes, I'd say you've been going someplace. The dream dimension is another dimension. Like this dimension." He lifted the glass to his lips. "— only different."

"You mean different because it's just a dream world

or different 'cause I'm supposed to be figuring things out there, or learning things? Or — oh, I don't know..."

"Not really, because if you think about it, things that happen in dreams aren't so different; they're actually just resonant."

"Resonant?" she said.

"Like a chord is resonant...or...similar, yes, your dreams are similar to your life," he said, replacing the drink on the bar carefully. "No, the reason the dream dimension is different is that your ability to create there, to have things manifest, is stronger than here. Well, sometimes, not always." Jessie remembered how things had changed in the dreams when she'd thought of them, like the weather or the landscape.

"You mean that stuff works here, too?"

Finch looked directly at her. *Is that from the inside out?* she wondered. A calm feeling settled over her, like when she saw the feathers, only more so.

"That's what you meant by everyday magic," she said, "about life working from the inside out..."

He smiled and nodded. Bringing his hands together, he clapped softly three times. *I got it*, she thought. *It's like what happens on the inside of me happens on the outside of me.*

Suddenly, a cacophony erupted from the kitchen behind her. Men's voices shouted while Bear barked and Sophie's shrieking protests carried across all of it. Jessie smiled and shook her head.

"And now you're leaving," Jessie said.

Finch frowned at the unfinished drink. The raised voices of Danny, Nico and Ed got louder as Sophie led them all in and Bear trotted behind, barking non-stop.

"Hey Jess, are you working?" Sophie called over, click-clacking her way over in spiked heels. "What are you doing behind the bar?"

The guys were in an animated fight about nothing, which alternated with laughing, then arguing again. Finch stood, bowed and settled his hat into position.

Sophie's eyes widened as she watched the stranger in the white suit leave.

"So hey, Jess..." she purred. "Who's the Johnny Depp look-alike?" Her mouth was wide in admiration.

Jessie shook her head. "Soph, you wouldn't believe me if I told you."

Bear trotted past Jessie and as far as the entrance to the bar and looked out onto the street, his little tail wagging.

The band practiced the reworked number; Danny said it was fresh and current, while Sophie and Ed hotly debated the idea of manifestation. Later, as Jessie made her way upstairs, she saw Finch's drink still stood on the bar, his feathered fizz.

So − what if my life is working from the inside out? she wondered.

Thirty-Eight

That night the band was to play at the Orpheum Theater; where B.B. King and Louis Armstrong had played. On Main Street, they walked down the sidewalk of stars, with Ed reading out the names of the famous people who had trodden the boards at the Orpheum. Even Houdini had escaped from there.

Jessie wore the kilt and boots outfit that she'd worn to the Hi-Tone Club. She loved the boned bodice; it was like something a Wild West bar girl would wear. Under the black cropped vest, it was really cool. Sophie had produced grunge from glamour with Manolo spike-heeled boots, red stockings, and a black Chanel dress that she'd torn strategically to expose a useful amount of flesh.

They reached the grand lobby with its huge chandelier and imposing staircases. All around them, the buzz of the contest intensified. People lined up for tickets or read bios of the bands, while to one side, a local radio station interviewed a man wearing a vivid poncho: one of Peeko's members, Jessie guessed. Ed, Danny, and Nico had dropped the gear off a couple of hours before. Apparently the event was a sell-out and the crowd was going to be over 2,000 people. Danny led them to the back of the auditorium, where a female sound engineer greeted them.

"Hey guys, I'm Serena. You must be Dog Fighter. Is this Dog?" At the sight of Bear, she shuddered

"No, this is Bear," smiled Danny. "We're hoping someone will look after him during our set."

Danny smiled hopefully, but the sound engineer recoiled.

"Well, that won't be me," she said. "I can't stand dogs." She shook her head. "Maybe one of the guys backstage will oblige."

Her smile was apologetic, almost.

"Wuss," muttered Jessie.

Danny shot Jessie a warning glance.

"So, um, Serena, can you tell us how tonight will work?" Danny said.

"Sure, why don't you come and sit down, and I'll go over everything?"

Danny and the girl walked away.

"Hey, she's a babe," Ed said to Nico, who raised his eyebrows noncommittally.

"Look, can we just keep this real?" snapped Jessie, watching Danny and the sound engineer cozied over a clip board. Danny did the flicky thing with his hair. *Does he like her?* The idea felt odd. *Do I like him?* She knew she was scowling and tried to relax her face but it felt fake.

The first band began their set and the contest continued. Dog Fighter were on last, which meant they watched in the wings as Peeko and Mission Trivia played two strong sets. Peeko had a Peruvian jazz funk sound, which everyone admitted was kind of cool, but Mission Trivia sounded more current, with a screaming, thrashy rock sound designed to shock as well as entertain. On the upside, the average age of the judges was well above Mission Trivia's typical fan base, and Jessie hoped they'd just yelled their way out of favor. She knew the new number that they had planned was less edgy, with a bit more melody. It felt like a good compromise.

A feather floated down into the aisle in front of them. It settled close to Bear, who watched as Jessie picked it up. *It's a good omen,* she thought. As she turned it around in her fingers, a calm feeling crept over her, like quiet sunshine. *Where do you go, Finch?* She folded it inside Bear's neckerchief for good luck.

As the time for them to perform drew near, Jessie tied Bear, plus the feather, to the lighting rig at the side of the stage. Slumped and panting, he looked bad-tempered.

"Wait there buddy." She kissed the top of his head. "I'll get you some water when we're done."

To her right, the rest of the band walked out on stage and took position. She waited as agreed. *It's only two thousand people,* she told herself. Taking a deep breath, she marched out, head up, to face the biggest crowd of her life. *It looks like twenty thousand,* she thought.

Mitch had told them to kick off to a strong start and with no hesitation. Almost as soon as she reached the mike, Danny gave her the nod and they pitched into a Pink cover, "Don't Let Me Get Me." Its lyrics were perfect, and Jessie's bitter tone delivered the message:

"LA told me, 'You'll be a pop star,
All you have to change is everything you are.'"

She watched the faces of the judges and knew they'd
chosen well. They finished to solid applause, but Jessie
couldn't tell if it was any louder than for the previous
band. The band picked up pace with their next number,
Green Day's "Letterbomb." It was a risk, given that
they'd played Joplin and Cash last night. Jessie just hoped
the judges had heard of Green Day. Certainly their kids
had. The singsong start mimicked a nursery rhyme,
contradicting the profanity with which they were about
to explode.

Danny and Ed blasted in with keyboards and guitar
and Jessie held the mike tight. The delivery of the lyrics
needed to be sharp, fast and cutting. As Jessie caught a
sense of the crowd, she could see people moving to the
aisles. A quick look back at Sophie told her what she
already knew: the backup singer bounced like a pogo
stick, encouraging them out of their seats. The crowd
looked surprisingly young, school kids, some of them.
Jessie knew the verse was so fast that the adults couldn't
pick out the swearing, but the kids could and they loved
it.

When they finished, the applause included cheering
and whistles as the youngsters jumped up and down, still
clapping. The judges looked around them. The third
song was their own. It began with a basic guitar hook,

added a solid rock beat, then finally elegant keyboards
laid a path for the lyrics to walk through:

> "My mother told me Santa Claus
> Would come and fill all the drawers,
> But it turns out she was a liar;
> Her ass just set on fire.
>
> My father talked of Halloween:
> Goblins, witches, sights unseen,
> But he's so full of crap;
> I know what to think 'bout that."

Jessie sounded cheated, angry even. The words made
everyone listen to where this was going.

> "It's a mess of myth and magic,
> The death of which seems tragic.
> But the baby went out with the water,
> And Larry the lamb went to slaughter."

Jessie was yelling now at full volume:

> "'Cause the truth is more profound
> 'Bout a secret lost and found."

Sophie joined in; their voices melded into one.

> "It's like voodoo
> That you do;

When you do it clean,
Life's not what it seems."

In the aisles, they'd picked up the tempo and were dancing again. Jessie risked a quick look behind her; on drums, Nico was a Tasmanian devil, his arms a blur. On keyboards, Ed was playing fast and still grinning—*how does he do that?* The song climaxed with three clean guitar chords, and was met with silence, and then a riot of applause. *We nailed that*, she thought.

Jessie jumped up and down, unable to stay still. Sophie joined her, her arms over her head clapping with the audience. Nico and Ed came forward and they all ended up in a line across the stage. Grabbing Jessie's hand, Danny squeezed and whispered, "Nice one, Jess."

Looking out over the cheering crowd, the band dropped forward and bowed. *This feels incredible*, thought Jessie.

The stage manager signaled that they should stay on stage and quickly led the other two bands on behind them. This led to further applause and stamping of feet as the crowd realized that the judges' decision was already made. Peeko, Mission Trivia, and Dog Fighter stood shoulder to shoulder across the stage, all trying to look confident and disinterested at the same time. Jessie watched the sound engineer pass the lead judge a microphone. He stood up and held up a hand to try and quiet the audience.

"Ladies and gentlemen," he looked down at his card and smiled. "By unanimous decision, the winner of tonight's heat in the Memphis Newcomer Contest is... Dog Fighter!"

The crowd cheered and everything went crazy. Sophie and Ed jumped up and down hugging each other while Jessie laughed at them. She turned to Danny.

"We did it," she said. "We're through. Did we just do that?"

Danny grinned and was then hit by a catapulted Ed and Sophie. Sophie hugged Jessie and then bounced around again.

Eventually Jessie and the band walked offstage, smiling and waving at the audience. Even Nico did a jiggy-hoppy thing. Hearing the thunderous applause, Jessie felt more alive than she could ever remember. In the wings, she saw Bear pulling sharply against the rope with which he was moored. She ran over and knelt to release him. Nearby Danny was trying to calm Sophie and Ed down, reminding them that the final was actually tomorrow night. Nico watched them shrieking at each other and shook his head. Jessie untied the rope from Bear's collar and found the feather.

Danny walked over.

"What's that?" he asked, as she released Bear.

"Oh, not much." She held up the feather, and then smiled. "Just a bit of voodoo that we do."

Thirty-Nine

For the band, the next day was mostly about trying to keep calm. As usual, they couldn't decide what they should play in the final. Nico was firmly in favor of last night's track, saying that if it had worked once it would work again. It was original, and the rules said they could use it. The audience's response had been great, and the new hook was strong, but Jessie argued that the track worked last night because of the previous two numbers. It was a logical sequence. Tonight they needed a single song that would be strong enough to stand alone. She wanted to use her rock ballad. Jessie said it was ready to show them, but Nico didn't want to commit the day to a track he'd hardly heard.

Danny said that he was more interested in finding out what had won in the past, so he and Sophie went downstairs to find Mitch.

On the sofa, Nico played with his cell phone, while Jessie stared out of the window and Ed muttered to Bear.

"So are you going to live in Memphis after this?" asked Nico.

"Dunno. Maybe," said Jessie.

"Is your dad here?" he said.

Jessie looked at Nico, *how does he know about that?*

"I mean, wasn't he supposed to be some *amazing* musician or something?" he said.

Jessie scowled.

"Yeah Nico, something like that." She paused. "But then I guess you probably wouldn't notice a decent musician if one stood next to you."

"You mean like you?" he scoffed. "I knew it. You actually think you're better than all of us, Little Miss Musical Perfection. God help us if anyone else has an opinion."

Ed interrupted, "Oh no, hey, I don't think she meant that…"

Jessie's anger rose in a hot flash. She clenched her teeth and glared at Nico, but then a strange thing happened. As he glared back at her, Nico's face reminded Jessie of herself, *have a nice day,* she thought. He looked angry but there was also something else—a hurt maybe. *Make a choice.*

"Nico, you know what?" She leaned back against the window. "I think you're right. I can be an ass."

She knew he expected a clever twist, but pretending she had it all together when she didn't was exhausting. "I think I get so blinded by my obsession with winning that I just don't consider anyone else." Jessie walked over and sat alongside him. "Look, I know I don't listen enough to you."

Nico's mouth opened then closed.

"For what it's worth, I think you're an awesome drummer. Totally, Nico. You rock. Last night you blew them away." Jessie nodded and bent down to stroke Bear. Nico shrugged and rubbed the dog's head. "Look, the reason I've been so weird about the ballad is that it's about my father." Nico looked at her. "It's good, but I need help with the rhythms. It needs a big build on it…or something." Nico's eyes were so dark they made her hold her breath, but then his features softened, and he chewed his lip.

"Right, okay, well, why not run me through it then?"

"Cool," said Jessie, "I mean, thanks. Really."

Danny and Sophie followed the sounds of laughter up the stairs, and walked in to Jessie and Nico on the sofa reminiscing about the night before, while Ed laughed at their jokes. Sophie looked at Danny, as if expecting an explanation, and Ed just grinned and hunched his shoulders.

"I'm all loved up," he said.

"So guys," Danny sounded polite. "This song?"

Nico held up a hand.

"Yeah, it's settled," he said. "It's the rock ballad. The new number—we're going to work it through today. Give me and Jessie a couple of hours, and then be ready to rehearse."

Downstairs, Danny had confirmed the finalists: they were up against Holly and the Italians, plus the Mandevilles. Danny had found a website for the Mandevilles; apparently they were a sizable crew of seasoned performers from Nashville with an enviable following. Listening to Danny talk, the atmosphere grew tense.

Jessie needed to focus. "Look, forget those guys," she reasoned. "Let's not get hooked by the competition, huh?" She remembered Mitch's advice and how he seemed to really believe in her.

Their practice session didn't go well. Jessie couldn't think straight, which meant remembering lyrics was impossible. Plus, she knew the song really needed emotion to bring it to life, but she just felt numb. Nico kept forgetting his sequence of builds, and Sophie seemed more distracted than normal. By four o'clock they had it together, but it still didn't feel like a perfect performance.

Mitch arrived and tried to lighten the mood by reminding them that a rotten final run-through was a good sign. He also said the audience was expected to be the biggest ever because of the major stars performing later. Jessie had hoped that most people would hang back and not get there until after the newcomer contest, but Mitch said that was unlikely. Traditionally, the newcomer contest was a lot of fun, and the crowd applauded for the act they liked and the volume measured had a big impact on the final result.

Jessie knew the noisy crowd and chaos was no place for Bear so she asked Mitch if he'd look after Bear and wait for them backstage after the contest; Mitch agreed.

"So once again I don't get to see you perform," he chided. "Bella's starting to say you think I'm a jinx."

"No way, Mitch; you're my lucky star," she said. "Look, you'll get the first signed copy of the album," she said, hoping she sounded positive.

The driver of the armored prison wagon never reached the prison known as Indian Bend. He'd taken the back roads north, until the missing van was sighted by a chopper up in Kentucky. The driver had apparently smashed up his radio, destroyed the tracker device, and discarded his own weapon. When the officer walked freely from the vehicle, he was in no condition either to explain his own actions or the presence of the five dead guards in the back of the wagon. However, anyone still wearing a clean uniform hadn't been responsible for that bloodbath. The men inside looked like ragdolls, twisted and strewn in awkward poses. Their looks of horror were fixed on paralyzed faces. The escapee was assumed to be anywhere by now. A massive hunt was launched across five states, but news coverage was subdued. No one wanted this mess broadcast unless it was absolutely necessary.

Jessie spent forever agonizing over her contest outfit and wasn't happy with the result. White leggings under a pink micro-mini worked well, but the cream baggy sweater was too long. Bella's stilettos improved the look, but it still wasn't put together enough. Then a glance at the kitchen clock made Jessie jump.

"Bear, come on."

Bear jumped from the bed with a thud, and followed her downstairs.

Down in the bar, Mitch and Bella stood side by side waiting.

"Now, don't you look every inch the rock star!" called Bella. Beside her, Mitch beamed.

"Yeah, thanks. I'm not sure about the sweater," Jessie said.

Jessie trotted toward them, pulling at the waistband. Out of the apartment she was even less happy with it; the bright white leggings made the cream sweater look grubby.

"Maybe I'll just wear the T-shirt. We'll see."

Bella put her hands on her hips. "Well now, sugar, maybe we can fix that."

Bella moved around the bar, stood in front of the glass case, and lifted the combination lock.

"No way, Bella, I couldn't..." Jessie watched, as Bella quickly unpinned the powder-blue Elvis jacket from its backing. Even Mitch had never seen it handled before. As she marched across to Jessie, her face was fixed with determination.

Moments later, Jessie was actually wearing the Elvis jacket. Bella kept patting at it, touching its rhinestones and beads, and then tugging at the collar.

"But Bella, it was..." Jessie's voice was hushed.

"No love, it was mine," Bella whispered. "He had it made for *me*. And that's why it's so special."

At the end of the bar, Mitch shouted over.

"Well I've seen everything now," he said, then

chuckled. "Jessie, it's sure a dazzling sight. And it suits the occasion just perfectly."

Jessie still couldn't believe she had it on. Its heavy silk folded around her reassuringly. She moved her arms easily, watching its colored stones sparkle in the light. *This is so cool,* she thought. They filled the remaining minutes taking photos of Jessie in the jacket; then Bella and Jessie, Mitch and Jessie, and then Jessie and Bear. When the rest of the band arrived, Bella was trying to get the jacket on and cursing the size of her arms. As Jessie left Bear with Mitch, she grinned and couldn't stop. The jacket was special; even Finch had said so.

Kabos unearthed the ceremonial dagger from its hiding place in Millington State Park woods. As he unwrapped its cloth covering, Kabos sighed with satisfaction. At the edge of the woods, the stolen Lexus gleamed in the late afternoon sunshine. It was not as regal as the Hummer, but it was satisfactory, given the circumstances. Kabos glanced at the golden watch he'd taken from its owner. Killing the old man hadn't been required, but that wasn't a reason not to have the sport anyway. Besides, it was good practice for the evening ahead. He checked the watch again, and ran though his schedule; tonight was the night he'd make his father proud.

Forty

By the time they reached the Pyramid Arena, Jessie had run through the words to her song several times, but was still worried that she wouldn't remember them. Crammed in between her and Danny; Sophie fidgeted constantly.

"Hey, do we get a dressing room this time?" Sophie asked as they pulled around the back of the venue.

Her outfit was simple yet effective: a scorching pink Versace mini-dress, matching sandals, and little else. Her blonde curls were a heavy, unruly mass; up front and driving, Nico looked sullen.

"I mean, what if we needed to get changed?" Sophie chimed.

"No chance," said Danny. "That is, unless you want to tell Justin Timberlake or Michael Bublé to take a hike."

"Well, I wouldn't mind sharing with *either* of those guys," she said.

They pulled in at one of the loading bays, and Danny went off to find someone in charge. The rest of the band wandered after him like baby chicks. Around them, roadies ferried stage equipment, boxes, racks, and cabling. An MTV van with a mobile satellite dish had already begun its transmission. Stretched across the whole front entrance, a banner announced the Memphis Music Awards, each letter taller than the van. Jessie saw three hip hop artists she recognized, then watched a stretch limo pull up but didn't dare look to see who got out of it.

The Pyramid arena loomed above them as Jessie looked up at it her heart began to thump. *I'm just not ready*, she thought. It didn't help that Bear wasn't with her; she felt exposed, isolated. *Maybe I should have brought him.*

The band followed Danny down long corridors, but soon lost him in the crowd.

"Does anyone else feel like an impostor?" whispered Sophie. In spiked heels, she trotted to keep up. "Like we're just about to get thrown out or something?"

Ahead of them Danny re-appeared.

"Guys, I've found us a room to wait in for thirty minutes or so." Then he frowned. "And we're on last again. We follow Holly."

Jessie had no idea if that was a good thing or not, *it was OK last night*, she thought.

The room was actually a storeroom. They sat surrounded by bits of old stage gear, plus lost items from the cleaner's cupboard. Danny left them in the room to go and find the sound engineers. Jessie looked around for a feather. *Where's my lucky charm?* On a broken chair, Nico was in a stare-down contest with a set of stage lights. Even Sophie had gone quiet. Ed seemed the only one not struck dumb with nerves.

"Hey guys, just like the warehouse in Dorma, cool?" Ed lifted up an oversized spray can and sniffed it.

Jessie sighed. "Yeah, except for the fact that we're in the Pyramid arena in Memphis about to play before more people than I've ever seen at one time," she said. "Just the same, except for that."

"Maybe they'll let us play in here then," Sophie said.

The silence hung in the air.

"Or maybe we can just get out there and act like contenders," Nico said.

Sophie looked at him and nodded.

"Fair point, Nico. Good point, actually."

"So what are we doing in here?" asked Jessie.

"Well, Danny said it would help us stay calm..." Ed said, as he tried to fix the aerosol cap he'd just broken.

"No, she means we should be out there," Sophie stood up and smoothed down the dress so that it reached the category of indecent, rather than criminal. She grinned at Jessie. "Let's go and watch the losers."

As the band strode out, Jessie felt like they'd reclaimed some of their power. The feeling vanished instantly as she turned the first corner. Even this far from the stage, the roaring echo of ten thousand people under a fixed roof was like thunder. The Mandevilles had just walked out to a deafening welcome. *They're starting early*, realized Jessie and broke into a jog.

"They're playing country and Western!" Nico shouted up to Jessie. She turned back and nodded, but Nico wouldn't be dismissed. "They beat thirty-three other bands by playing country and Western?"

His tone was incredulous. Jessie stopped and waited for him.

"Nico, it's actually just called country these days," she said. "They're from Nashville. They've almost been signed twice. They've had loads of airplay."

Danny had given her the lowdown on the Mandevilles, plus their website had a blog.

"But they're *country and...!*"

But Jessie could no longer hear him. She'd just caught sight of the arena. From the backstage area they had a partial view of the masses beyond.

As the Mandevilles sidestepped around the vast stage, the crew behind was still in full operation. Guys and girl-guys rushed around in a uniform of jeans, black T-shirts, and work boots. Holly and the Italians were on next. She searched for Danny but couldn't see him. *Come back, Danny,* she wished silently.

As they drew nearer, Jessie could see through the lighting columns and stage dressing to front of house. The vast stage was flanked on both sides by steep walls of seating, all of which were taken. Up to the right, a penned-off VIP area was filled with beautiful people, plus the judges. In front of the stage, the temporary seating was also full, back to the three-quarter marker. Mitch had told her that the crowd wouldn't reach the arenas 20,000 capacity, and that had given her some comfort. Looking across the ocean of people, she realized it didn't actually make much difference. Once there were more people than your brain could handle, they all seemed to merge into one identity.

On the opposite side of the stage, she spotted Casey and the guys. Casey bounced up and down, shaking out his arms and legs. Alongside, Holly was motionless, his hands clasped in silent prayer. Jessie tried to guess what they'd play. Like all three finalists, they had just one song to win the crowd's vote, and therefore the contest. Again, Jessie wondered if they'd picked the right one. *Where's Danny?* she thought.

Then she spotted him over by a lighting rig, deeply engrossed with two of the stage crew. *Why's he so animated?* She thought.

On stage, the Mandevilles were a hefty bunch of three guitarists, a percussionist, two violins, a keyboard player, and a drummer. Their song was a good natured romp of stomping and chanting with an annoyingly catchy tune.

With a frenzy of fiddling, the band closed with a rocking big finish and the audience went wild. Jessie and the others watched as they sprinted to the front of the stage to take their applause. As the rules stated, no jumps, kicks, or pumping of applause were allowed. They were only allowed to smile and bow, which they did a lot.

Danny arrived back and explained there would be no sound check, no say over the sound levels, and both Ed and Nico would have to use the gear that was on stage. Danny had tried to give detailed instructions as to the equipment setup but the roadies would make no promises. The big concern was Ed's keyboards and his settings; he'd need to orient himself fast. Danny's plan was that Ed would run on first to try and give him a few seconds' head start. Jessie always walked on last, but would delay as much as possible. In the background, the Mandevilles were trotted off stage waving, as the MC dashed on from the opposite side of the stage.

"Ladies and Gentelllmennn...well, let's see if we can beat that crazy number, shall we?" The MC grinned. "And hey, these boys think they sure can...." He swung his arm to one side. "Give a massive Memphis welcome to...Holly and the Italians!"

The band ran on waving and grinning, and the cheers of the crowd were deafening. As the lead guitarist struck up the solid intro, Jessie recognized the track from their session at the Hi-Tone Club. It was rock with a pop-chart feel and a chorus that felt instantly familiar.

This is fine, she thought, *this is all fine.* She wiped her palms down the front of her leggings. As she looked up at the stage rigging, she took a deep breath, and blew it out again. Behind her, Danny put a hand on her shoulder.

"Just do what you do Jess, it's all we need."

She tried to smile but her mouth felt wonky. On stage, Holly's voice had an ethereal quality, like no voice she had ever heard before. Jessie knew that Holly had what every vocalist craves—an instantly recognizable voice. She watched him in his rapture, *it's just him and the song*, she thought.

Jessie turned to Danny, but he was already staring at her. To one side, Nico and Sophie stood close to each other.

"I just want to know, that's all," hissed Nico, holding two sets of sticks in one hand and gripped Sophie's arm with the other.

249

Sophie rolled her eyes upward. "Nico, can we not do this now?"

Sophie looked sideways at Danny.

"Nico—can you quit it?" Danny said. "We've got ten thousand people out there waiting to boo our sorry asses off stage if we screw up. Is that what you want?"

Nico's response was a sulky scowl.

Behind them the roar of the crowd for Holly and the Italians went from an initial cheer to thunderous. They watched as Holly and the band marched forward to the front lights. Nothing fancy, just smiles and a single bow to the crowd and the applause in the arena got even stronger. *That's so loud*, Jessie thought. After a signal from the MC, the band ran off stage toward them, and pushed past, laughing and cheering.

On stage, the roadies did a fast set-up of the equipment, swapping kit and setting levels. One of them removed a spare microphone stand and gave a thumbs up to Danny. Then the roadie picked up a plastic bottle from the stage, and ran off as the MC hurried on.

"Okay! You guys ready for a bit more entertainment?" he shouted.

The crowd's cheer swept back over him like a wave.

"Okay! Well, they're certainly the newcomers in town; let's hear it for them...Dog Fighter!"

Forty-One

The Pyramid crowd kicked off again, and screamed some more. Jessie watched Ed and Nico charge forward. Danny waited and then followed at a jog. Sophie sashayed on; her walk was confident but her smile looked rigid.

In the wings, Jessie stood and sucked in air as the thumping in her chest got stronger. She blew out and looked down at the jacket. Under the lights it sparkled and shimmered like liquid light. Its colors reminded her of the cobalt blue dragonfly. *Set a heart free*, she thought.

With a sharp nod of her head, she ran on stage, and raised a clenched fist to the crowd as she did so. For a lead singer, arrogance wasn't just helpful, it was essential. As she ran to the front of the stage, the white flash of lights blinded her for a moment. She lifted her hand to shield her eyes then changed the gesture to a wave. As she pulled the microphone from its stand, she held onto it tight.

"Well hello Memphis…" she grinned, strutted sideways, and then checked back at the band. All around her, the jacket glittered like a thousand stars. *Come on, Elvis.*

"You good people ready for a little rock with no roll?" she shouted.

The crowed screamed back at her.

Look like you're loving this, she told herself. A glance at Danny. Over his keyboards, Ed was poised ready. *Feel like you're loving this*. They were all set. She remembered Mitch's advice: replace the mike, keep the stand tall, and tilt the mike head down.

She swung the guitar around and got set. Her palms felt slippery, and her legs trembled and felt weak. She nodded her start signal back to Danny. *This is it*. A few weeks ago, this chaos had been just a dream. Then again, dreams and reality had been merging lately. *Maybe I'm dreaming now*, she thought.

The thump, thump, thump began from Nico, and on guitars, Danny and Jessie followed as Ed blended in to enrich the sound. Thrash with a melody, it projected a maturity that none of them felt. Pitched back, Sophie began her sulky sway, waiting to add layers to Jessie's vocals. *With the big start*, thought Jessie, *they won't see the shift to the ballad coming*. She stalked back to the mike, moved her guitar to one side, *slow things down, sing from nothing*. One hand kept the guitar at bay, while her other was on the top of the mike. The softness of her grasp was a hint of the style coming. *Half pace now, slow it down*. When she began, the lyric was harsh and raw. Her voice sounded ragged and torn.

"You left me and oh, so that's all gone;
Didn't leave me with strength to carry on.

Too many years I wasted my time,
Living a dream that's yours not mine.

Papier-mâché,
Hey, what do you say?"

Jessie stood motionless, and sung to her father.

"Take those years now; they're all gone.
I've burned in hell, I was so wrong
And you didn't tell me,
Let me carry on.

Papier-mâché,
Hey, what did I say?"

Danny, Nico, and Ed supported the vocal, cocooning the ebbs and flows, announcing the rises and falls. Sophie murmured the backing, sorrowful and soulful. Nico had judged the rhythms just right; the arrangement was a symphony. Jessie wasn't in the arena anymore; she was singing to a man she didn't even know. Her relationship with her father was done with, and this was a requiem.

"A life not lived is a life of faking;
The path less travelled is one I'm taking.
If there's regret then I didn't listen
To her just a little more…

Papier-mâché,
Hey, what does *she* say?"

Her voice was cracked now and breaking; the tears in her eyes made the dramatic delivery personal as she lived every word. A crescendo of bass and drums brought the number to its finish. With a sigh, Jessie looked down. *That's everything,* she thought. In the silent space that followed, the crowd exploded as one.

They ran to the front. They took their bows. Everything was so loud, but was it louder than last time? Jessie tried to take in the riotous noise and the ocean of delighted faces. *Is it enough?* she wondered.

The MC ran back on, followed by the first two bands. The arrival of the other two bands brought further cheers. The MC shouted into a dead microphone, but no one could hear him.

Jessie looked right and left. Nico was being barged and pushed into her. He looked shell-shocked.

"Nice one, Nico," Jessie said as she put a hand on his shoulder to steady him.

Nico nodded back.

Finally, someone turned the MC's microphone on.

"Ladies and gentlemen… we need to hear the decision from the judges!"

He looked down, pressed his earpiece and nodded.

As Jessie watched the MC, time slowed down. His head was still moving… he turned away, pressing onto his earpiece… he lifted his head. *What's happening?* The MC's face looked frozen. He held up his hand.

"Okaaay, well, let's hold it right there…it seems that

there's a little discussion going on with the judges." The MC wagged his finger at the audience.

"So, Memphis...we're going to have to wait just a *couple more minutes* to find out the result you've all been waiting for!"

He beamed at the crowd and a line of sweat shone as it trickled down from his temple. *What's stopping the decision?* Jessie thought.

She locked eyes with Danny. The crowd had started to boo and hiss and the MC held up a hand.

"Now yes, I know, nobody likes to wait..." he held a hand up. "Let's just calm ourselves and..."

The MC looked down again, and when he finally looked up at the waiting audience, he beamed at them.

"Laydeeeees and gentlemen...for a cash prize of $25,000, a week's worth of studio time and airplay all over the county, by a sliver and a shade, they made the grade... this year's winners of the Memphis Battle of the Newcomers *are*...Holly and the Italiaaaaans!"

The crowd erupted as Casey punched the air, Holly sank to his knees and the others in the band jumped up and down and yelled like banshees. Jessie went numb. *This is what shock feels like.* Her mind went blank. *Nothing, it feels like nothing.* She wanted to congratulate Holly and Casey, but they were surrounded by people. *We need to get out of their way.* Jessie pushed backwards; she met Casey's eyes for a second. He saw her and raised a hand, but then he was swept away into the chaos.

As the spotlights locked onto the winners, Jessie headed for the backstage shadows. Ahead of her Sophie followed Danny off into the wings and Nico went back to fetch his spare sticks.

Jessie walked off with Ed, *it didn't happen, it's all over,* she thought. If this was finished, what would she do now? As the numbness in her head subsided, Jessie realized that she'd made the mistake. It was her song, or maybe something about her delivery. The feeling washed over her, and she was suddenly seven years old again. Why would her father not want her? Why did he go away and never come back? The weight of the answer felt like a chasm had opened and she would be dragged down into it. *The real problem is me,* she decided.

Her tears blinded her and as she strode past Danny he put a hand out, but his fingertips didn't reach her. *I need to get away from here.*

Away from the stage area, Jessie broke into a jog. The long corridors behind the arena seemed to be there to taunt her. Reaching the end of one, she turned into the next that was even longer. When would the frustration ever go away? She wanted to find Bear. She wanted to have him with her. Mitch had promised to come and find them. *Where is he?*

As she turned into a third tunnel, the door at the end was open. The big guy's outline blocked the daylight beyond. At his side, Bear sat on the floor. Mitch had put a leash on him, *that looks so odd,* she thought. She slowed to a walk and wiped her eyes with the back of her hand, then faked a smile. As she got nearer, he did what she wanted him to do, and picking up pace again, she ran into his open arms. She cried for everything and all of it, especially herself.

Forty-Two

essie stayed with Mitch and went back to Mitch's bar. It was mostly empty, as a few people drifted in after the contest—regulars, hoping to talk through the results and share opinions. Mitch insisted on working and said he wanted to stay busy; Bella said she'd go home but told Jessie that she was to call her if she needed anything. Behind the bar, the powder-blue jacket hung in its case. The engraved sign at its base said *'Gone, but not forgotten.'*

Danny, Ed and Nico arrived and joined Jessie at a table near the stage. No one said much. Sophie ran in last, flushed, her eyes bright.

"Sorry."

Nico stared at the beer coaster he was destroying. Ed pulled her a chair. Sophie fidgeted into position before looking at Danny.

"What did I miss?"

Jessie stared into the distance thinking about what had happened: the numbers, the performance by Holly. Logic still told her that they should have won. She replayed what they'd done over and over again. Their own song was better, more credible musically. What Holly and the guys had done was predictable, mainstream even, but the injustice of it was irrelevant. They'd lost. One shot and they'd blown it, that's all.

From the bar, a server brought over a tray of bottled beers.

"On the house."

He nodded over to Mitch. The big guy touched his Stetson and kept serving customers. With the rest of the band older, Mitch turned a blind eye to Jessie being underage. Danny waved his thanks.

"That man's a giant," he said, to no one in particular.

Sophie voiced everyone's thoughts. "So what now?"

Ed spoke first.

"Well, shouldn't we try and figure out what happened?" Ed looked at Danny, then at the others, then back at Danny.

"We didn't win," came Nico's flat tone. "What else do you need?"

The beer coaster was in shreds. He reached for another.

"Look, we did okay." Danny picked up a Budweiser. "Think about it: we made it to the final three."

There was a pause before Sophie broke the silence.

"Final two…" she said, and then hesitated. "We came in second."

Jessie listened as Sophie explained that was why she'd hung back; she'd hung out with the stage crew for a while to see what they thought of the result.

"Apparently it was really close," she continued. "We just don't have the rep…"

"Rep?" Danny lost it. "It's a fucking newcomer contest, isn't it?"

Jessie turned to look at him. It was odd hearing him swear. His sudden anger gave him a wild look, like he'd enjoy hitting someone. That was new, too.

"Yeah well, seems like there's some different rules in play," Sophie said. "Holly and the guys, well, they're well-known around here, aren't they?"

Nico scowled at her. "And some of us know them better than others."

Nico tossed the mutilated coaster on the table. Her pout at Danny was petulant but Danny ignored her.

"Jess, are you ever going to speak?" he said.

She sighed, reached down to Bear, and stroked his head.

"You know, I think we just didn't know what we were getting into," she said. "I mean…I feel kinda stupid, like we missed the point."

Ed hesitated, "Yeah, but we still deserved to win…"

"So what are we going to do?" Danny said.

Finally, Nico picked up a beer and held it forward in a toast. "We get shitfaced, that's what."

Everyone nodded; the guys ordered more beers, and Sophie went onto Mojitos.

After going back through each music choice, sequence, timing, delivery, they all agreed that they should have won. After a while, Nico claimed what he said was a "moral victory." They all felt better until Danny pointed out that they hadn't been in a moral contest, they'd been in a musical one, and the prize money had just gone to Mr. Latin Charisma and his troubadours.

Jessie started mentally spending $25,000, and Ed mused over the tax implications. When Danny reminded them they still owed cash on the condo they'd rented, the mood went southward once more. Ed gave up halfway through his fourth beer, went to the restroom, and never came back.

"Lightweight," said Nico, and moved his beer bottle next to his own. "He'll be back at the condo by now."

◎ ◎ ◎

In the restroom, Ed stood in a stall and watched evil up close. His eyes were wide open, his whole body shook and yet he couldn't feel his limbs. Black eyes filled his field of vision, while the cloying odor of a swamp made him gag. Ed felt like he was having a nightmare that you hope you're going to wake up from. His back was jammed against the cold tiled wall, and he strained to move his head back still farther.

Ed tried to tell the whispering phantom anything that would make him go away. He'd already told him about Jessie and about the apartment, about the dog, about Mitch, and finally about the bar, but it still didn't seem enough. He didn't know about a ring. Ed loathed himself for not knowing about a ring. Ed knew that if he could tell the man in front of him about a ring, maybe he would go away. Maybe then Ed could wake up.

261

Hours later, the last few drinkers in the bar made a sluggish exit involving drunken goodbyes, lost keys, and cell phones. Sophie and Nico left to continue an argument that had hung in the air for most of the evening.

That left just Jessie and Danny. Bear lay under the table, his head rested on Jessie's foot. As the jukebox ran out of quarters, the bar fell quiet.

"Danny, that's it. Show's over," Jessie said. Danny had slumped over his beer.

Jessie bent her head to check his face. "Come on, Mitch will want to lock up."

Danny lurched back, swayed, and then seemed to register her.

"Not been smashed for a while..." he muttered.

Mitch began switching a few lights off as a polite signal.

"Yeah, I can tell." She put a hand on his shoulder to steady him. "And you need to make it back to your digs."

Looking at him, Jessie saw it would be easier to help him upstairs and give him the sofa. *That's if he doesn't throw up en route.* Mitch was showing a girls' night out to the door. One of them had fallen for the gentle giant and was trying to persuade him to give them all a ride home. He said he'd walk them to a taxi stand and followed them outside. *I wish Bella would show up.* She chuckled. *Now that would be live entertainment.*

Suddenly, the back of her neck felt bare and cold. Jessie felt chilly and shuddered. From the rear entrance to the bar, Kabos swept in like a shadow cast into a dark room. Bear growled and then began to snarl, *something's wrong.* Danny leaned back and checked under the table.

"Hey buddy..." he muttered. "Wassup? Have they gone?"

From the gloom near the restrooms, Jessie saw the knife flash.

"Danny, he's here!"

She jumped up and knocked over her stool then stumbled backward. The only other sound was Bear's snarl.

"Danny, get up!" Jessie screamed.

Danny leaned forward but the figure came at him as swift as a cobra. With a backhanded motion, Kabos knocked Danny sideways like a lion cuffing a kitten. He was flung twenty feet to the far side of the dance floor and lay motionless.

Jessie bolted for the bar, ran around behind it, and found the Sinatra cigar box where she'd hidden the ring. By the time she'd grabbed it and turned around, Kabos stood just a few feet away. He tilted his head down slightly, his eyes fixed on her. Bear stood between them, his bark loud and constant.

Forty-Three

J essie didn't move, couldn't move; as the sorcerer's muttering grew louder his eyes seemed to turn completely black. As the trance lay over her like a heavy blanket, she realized she could smell roses.

"You stand completely still now because your body can't hear you," he said.

She knew she should move, but she didn't know how. In the air rose scent mixed with the stench of rotted matter and filth, and for an instant, she thought she was back in the trailer. *I can smell the garbage rotting.*

Bear's rumbling snarl was a constant warning.

"You can only hear me now…and then tell me… where is my ring?" Kabos said.

Jessie uncurled her fingers to show the ring in the palm of her hand. In the half-light, it glinted.

"Bring it here," he said. She moved around the bar toward him and paused near Bear. A vague smell of roses again. *How is he doing this?* she thought. Kabos hissed as he moved toward her; his eyes held her like a rabbit before a snake. The ring was there; all he needed to do was take it.

"Stay very still…stand still." He nodded slowly. "I have to say hello to someone, don't I?" Again Jessie tried to move but her feet felt like lead. She watched as Kabos turned to Bear.

"Little pig, little pig…" he crooned, and crouched down, holding the dagger low. "Do you want to try and hurt me again?" Bear kept growling but retreated a step.

"Not so brave? Let's see how fierce you are now, little pig…now that I can bite you back…" Kabos sneered and looked back at Jessie. The ring sat in her open palm, she could feel its weight but could not lift her feet. Suddenly, from the entrance to the bar, Mitch ran toward them, and his Cuban heels rang loud the board floor. Kabos turned toward the sound.

Bear jumped at Kabos and bit down hard on Kabos' shoulder. This time the sorcerer was ready for him. With his free hand, he tore the dog from him, and Jessie heard flesh tear as Bear's jaws stayed locked. He tossed the dog across the room. Bear hit a stack of chalk boards, and they clattered to the floor. Jessie heard him yelp, and then nothing. Jessie stood with her arm outstretched, the ring in her open palm. *What just happened?* she thought.

Mitch launched himself at the intruder. Pitched at speed, Mitch was a juggernaut but as he crashed sideways into him, Kabos only staggered and then regained his balance. Mitch grabbed his knife arm with both hands. Kabos twisted and slammed Mitch hard to the floor. Mitch lay gasping, looking up into the sorcerer's eyes.

Kabos pointed the knife at Mitch's face.

"Another member of the band," he said. "So perfect that I am rewarded with a second trophy this night." He knelt down beside Mitch, holding the dagger high. "Let me show you how your friend Scuz died, holding the contents of his own stomach…"

Kabos' smile was a leer, his breath like an open sewer. Still the pungent aroma of roses encircled them all. *Who's muttering?* she thought.

Jessie watched as the knife was positioned above Mitch's stomach. He held his hand up to ward off the blow. As the smell of roses grew stronger, the muttering got louder. *He's chanting.*

"Just take the ring and go…" Mitch urged.

"What, and miss my greatest pleasure in all of life?" The sorcerer tilted his head. "I think not…"

The knife flashed and went down, but behind him, an autographed baseball bat swung low as Bella put her whole body weight behind it, and struck a blow to Kabos' temple that blasted him sideways. His head split open with the sound of an axe cleaving a log.

Mitch shouted at pain that didn't come. Bella strode past him to the attacker. Kabos' head lay at an awkward angle to his neck, his eyes shut. The dark, glutinous pool spreading around his skull looked more like oil than blood. Bella watched the body for a moment. Then she flung the baseball bat down and ran to Mitch.

Jessie came around to the sight of the two of them in each other's arms and the sound of Bella's choking sobs.

"S'all right, darling." Mitch made no effort to stand. "S'all right, darling. It's over."

"I had to come back; I don't know why, I just I had to," Bella said, her hands shook as she clasped his. Mitch pushed himself up.

The rose scent was still heady and from the corner of

her eye, Jessie's saw the corpse on the floor move. Slowly, the man's legs curled under him and his head lifted, and one side was plastered in dark blood. Kabos raised himself to a sitting position and regarded Mitch and Bella as they comforted each other. In her drugged-like state, Jessie fought to move, then as the feeling in her legs returned, she shook her head. *This doesn't look real,* she thought. *And who is muttering?*

She watched the wound on Kabos' head retreat, like a film played backward. Blood seeped toward his scalp as the white of his skull disappeared. Only the injury to his shoulder remained, where Bear had attacked him. He lifted his hand to the wound and frowned. *He'd fooled them,* Jessie thought. *This is just an illusion.* Truth flew at her like an arrow. A trickster! This man was a trickster. She could hear Finch at the bus stop, and she remembered his disgust: "Tricksters create illusions."

None of this is real! Jessie's head cleared. *I need to find what's real.* He'd said it twice. *"Only what's truly real is truly powerful."* She stepped forward. Kabos sensed the motion and turned to her. His dark eyes flashed all black in their sockets once more. Jessie searched for the knife. *If the knife is his, then it must be real to him.* There, by the stool, it glinted. She lunged clumsily toward it but in the same instant, Kabos scrambled forward. Bella's piercing scream woke Jessie completely. She reached the dagger before he did. With a hiss, Kabos pulled back.

Jessie held the dagger and her hand trembled. *Do it, do it, do it,* she willed herself to move. Gripping the jeweled handle more tightly didn't help; her head felt light, and then her neck and shoulders, *surely I'm not going to faint?*

From behind Kabos, Bear came at him a second time. With a short grunt, he leapt at the sorcerer's calf muscle. He bit down hard and shook, snarling as he worked to separate flesh from bone. Kabos' roar was a half scream as he struck down hard on Bear's back. Then he grabbed Bear and threw him the length of the bar. Bear landed with a heavy thud by the door.

Kabos turned back to Jessie.

"Look at me," he said. *Did he just hurt Bear?*

As Jessie looked into his eyes, they felt like dark pools waiting to drag her down. *It's not real.* She let the hand that held the dagger drop to her side. *Trick him back. Stand still like before and trick him back.*

"Jessie, move!" Mitch shouted.

Mitch strained to stand, while Bella held onto him. Jessie stared at Kabos. *He thinks he's got me.*

His move toward her was swift. Jessie lifted the dagger forwards and Kabos ran into it, plunging it deep into his own stomach. Jessie felt the blade dip and jerk upward with the force of him, and she held it steady until his belly hit her hand. As an arc of blood spewed from his abdomen, Jessie let go and sprang to one side. Kabos' shriek was incredulous and angry as he slumped to his knees, drew the dagger out, and stared at it for a moment before collapsing forward onto the floor.

Mitch reached him and turned his body over, but Kabos' lifeless eyes stared into oblivion.

Bella appeared behind them.

"I thought I'd killed him," she said, and picked up the knife. "Was this it?"

Her eyes searched Jessie's face, but Jessie was replaying what had just happened.

"Bear!" she shouted. "Mitch, where's the lights? Where's Bear? No Mitch, check Danny! He's there by the stage."

Jessie reached Bear and knelt down. As the lights blinked on, he tried to move, but didn't seem to be able to. His whimper confirmed her fears: his back was broken.

"Sssh, Bear. S'okay buddy... Mitch!" she screamed. "He's really hurt; we need to get him somewhere!"

By the stage, Danny came to. He shifted his legs, groaned, and felt his neck. Mitch bent down, and helped him to his feet.

"You okay, son?"

By the bar, Kabos lay in a spreading pool of blood. Bella stood over him, holding the knife. Danny saw that she was crying. Over by the entrance, Jessie knelt over a brown and white bundle that could only be Bear.

"I'm fine, Mitch; look after Bella." Danny stumbled over to Jessie, still holding his neck. As he reached them, he hung back.

Jessie crouched over Bear as his breathing became sharp, labored gasps. He lay in an awkward shape. She tried to straighten his body, but his yelp made her pull back. Then her face crumpled, and she began to weep. This time it was over. No reprieve. *Please, don't let this happen*. She started to sob. As she stroked his head gently, Bear's eyes never left hers.

"Come on buddy," she whispered. "Come on, little Bear, please don't leave me."

With shaking hands, she tried to heal him, tried to see him whole. Wasn't that how Finch had done it? Passing her trembling palms over his spine, she tried to imagine him well, but the panic of seeing him laying crooked like that was too strong.

Behind her, Danny took a step forward. From Bear's mouth, a thin line of blood confirmed the truth of it. His breathing became forced, coming in quick heaves, like he couldn't keep a breath. Jessie looked around at Danny; her eyes searched his. *Can't we do something?*

But it was already done. Bear's body tensed and then relaxed, his eyes lost focus and closed. Jessie's gasping sob marked it as the pain in her heart struck squarely. She fell forward onto him, and sobbed.

"Oh god no, Bear…"

She buried her face in his neck, wanting to feel his warmth, to be comforted by his familiar smell. Her stomach lurched and then ached with despair. Beneath her, Bear's body felt soft and still as all life left him.

Forty-Four

The senior police officer took initial statements from Mitch and Bella Hanrahan that told him everything he needed to hear. The intruder had hung back to rob the bar and caused mayhem in the process. The apartment upstairs was wrecked. A search of the restrooms had turned up a freaked-out geek who wasn't making much sense, but he looked like the type that would scare easily. A junior officer drove the young guy home and told him to call downtown in the morning.

The dead man was the exact description of the psycho they were looking for, and it was a relief that he'd finally turned up. The vagrant was wanted for murders in two other states. Outside, recovering the stolen Lexus was a bonus. It was a pity that they couldn't question the intruder about the killing of the five prison guards from Rushby, or the callous murder of a crippled war veteran at a pawn shop over in Sligo. However, Bella Hanrahan's description of what the man was about to do to her husband told them all they needed to know. This maniac liked to gut his victims.

The bar owner had tried to say he'd killed the guy, but it was obvious to anyone that his wife had struck the actual blow. When they'd arrived, she was still clutching the weapon, stood over the corpse like it might rise up and need killing all over again. It was a pity that the poor old soldier over in Sligo hadn't had such a gutsy lady to watch his back. The knife was interesting though; unfortunately it would end up in a state's evidence vault for the next twenty-five years.

The young girl hadn't been in a state to interview, but her boyfriend's experience seemed to corroborate the story. He'd been lucky that the intruder had chosen to simply knock him out. It was a shame about the dog; it was a handsome animal, a real powerhouse. The officer watched as the big guy wrapped the body in a blanket and carried it upstairs.

Once the police officer had satisfied his own assessment of the situation, he'd contacted his boss and gotten approval to suppress national news coverage. Tourism on Beale Street was something to protect, and the last thing they wanted was a story of carnage like this. Of course, the story would get out locally, but that wasn't going to do Mitch Hanrahan's trade any harm. More importantly, it wasn't going to do Beale Street any harm.

Upstairs, Danny helped Bella try and clear up the apartment. Somehow, keeping busy made sense. The intruder had thrown things about, emptied drawers. Most of it was just lifting things back into place, and the only real damage was the smashed Gibson and a table lamp. Danny watched Jessie walk past the guitar and not notice. Around four a.m. they gave up. Mitch rested Bear's body on the sofa, and stroked his head. Bella's eyes filled with tears again, and in the silence they both nodded their goodbyes.

Jessie and Danny slept in armchairs in the living room. Jessie wouldn't leave Bear, and Danny knew he couldn't leave Jessie. After a while, Jessie began talking, but she wasn't making much sense. She was talking about how they could fix Bear up, about "seeing him well." It was like she couldn't accept that he was dead, and he wasn't coming back. Danny had never heard her talk so much. He let her ramble on; he didn't understand a lot of it. Maybe she was still drunk, or in shock from the fight with the psychopath.

She seemed to be trying to piece events together, to make connections: feathers and coincidences and dreams she'd been having. She was talking about endings and beginnings, and life working from the inside out.

He tried to say the right things, but she wasn't actually responding to anything he said; in the end, Danny fell asleep while Jessie was still talking.

Forty-Five

The next day Ed and Nico left for Dorma. Danny said he'd stay for another day or so, until he was due back at work. Sophie said she was also going to stick around and that she'd taken a shine to Memphis. She planned to find a more permanent place to rent and see what turned up.

For Jessie, it felt like Mitch was never far away. He sat with her, tried to comfort her, and then sat with her some more. After that first night, Jessie stopped crying or actually feeling anything, just numbed to people and situations. She tried hard to act like she was functioning, but the whole thing felt cosmetic.

Mitch tried to tell her about the sudden interest in her as a vocalist. He explained that the contest had really marked her in Memphis, but she didn't want to see strangers and wouldn't think about talking to music journalists. Mitch made excuses to three A&R guys and a radio representative. He took their cards and promised she'd be in touch. Jessie refused to look at them. Everything about that night was something she wanted to forget.

On the third day, Mitch took her the ring. In the kitchen, it laid on the table between them, a reminder of everything.

"Jessie, I figure this is yours now. I guess you can do what you like with it."

They both stared at it. Just a ring, it seemed harmless now, but it was the object that had gotten Bear killed. Other people had died over it too; she picked it up and her eyes filled with tears.

"Mitch, it's more my father's than mine." Her voice was bitter. "He was the one who thought it was worth taking." She let it drop back onto the table.

"Then maybe you should return it to him."

Mitch reached into his shirt pocket and pulled out a folded piece of paper and pushed it across the table. It was an address in Nashville. His smile was an apology for the burden he'd carried since they met.

"Bella says I can't protect you from your past, and I shouldn't be trying to protect you from the future, either."

As Jessie's hand reached the note, he put his own over hers.

"And if the home you want isn't there, you know there's always one here with us." His tone was firm, but the tears in his eyes shone.

In Jessie's head she was already leaving. She'd been thinking about nothing else since Bear had gone.

They buried Bear in WC Handy Park. Danny, Mitch, and Jessie went in late at night and put him near one of the trees that he and Jessie had sat under. Jessie remembered him laying in the sunshine, gnawing on a snatched bagel. She told the story to Danny and Mitch, trying to sound happy. They all cried a little and pretended they weren't. Bella gave Jessie the photograph she'd taken of them just before the contest. She'd put it in a cheery frame, surrounded by glass beads. Jessie was knelt by Bear, trying to pull him close. Her hair was wild and she was grinning. The Elvis jacket shone in the sun. Alongside, Bear's sulky frown was one of his finest.

"Bella, it's great, really. It's perfect." Jessie's eyes shone with tears.

"And I hope it's okay," Bella said, "I had it copied and put behind the bar. A few of the regulars have been asking about him."

Jessie laughed and wiped her eyes. "Don't tell me—all men."

Bella tried to laugh but cried instead.

Soon after, Jessie told Danny she was leaving. In one of the booths near the bar, she'd tried to explain properly what she was thinking and feeling, but her reasons tumbled out like beads from a broken necklace. She told him she had unfinished business and needed to sort things out. Also about wanting to get away from Memphis for a while to think things through. She tried to explain about how being here with him, Mitch and Bella was too much for her to cope with right now, whatever that meant. When she said that she just needed to get away and get "some closure" she knew it sounded flaky. Jessie tried to make everything sound less like garbage by telling him that in the future she might want to come back again. In the end, she simply stopped talking. Most conversations felt pretty pointless right now.

Danny stayed quiet. She knew she wasn't making much sense, but he didn't push her.

Danny listened to Jessie's announcement, realizing what it really meant. It was fine if she needed to go and sort out whatever she needed to. Mitch had told him he'd given Jessie her father's address, and he could understand her need to know. But her conversation didn't mention Danny, certainly not in any future sense. He'd half-expected this, but had hoped for a better break.

Danny's realization of how strongly he felt for Jessie had come as more of a sinking, heavy dread. His feelings weren't actually confusing or complicated in any way. It was much more ordinary than that: he just loved her. He loved everything about her—the good, the bad, and everything in between. In the same moment, he knew his heart already was broken. It felt like he'd declared his feelings and she'd already rejected them. If she'd ever shown any signs of feeling something for him, it might have been different. In the end, she was a singer; he was the guitarist and amateur manager. Actually, he was the ex-guitarist and ex-amateur manager.

In the days after Bear, he'd waited to see what she'd do. Maybe there was some hope. It happened in films or songs. Then, of course, she was leaving again—running away probably, but that wasn't his problem. His problem was repairing the gaping chasm that had just opened up around his chest area. To make it worse, to put the last nail through his already torn, ragged and bleeding heart, she hugged him farewell like some casual friend. He stood in numb disbelief. Didn't she realize what he felt?

Jessie left for the bus station the next morning. She wanted to walk and to pretend Bear was still with her, trotting along and slowing her down, or trotting along and propping her up. She cried all the way down Beale Street.

By the time she reached the junction, she was blinded. *Stop crying, stupid*, she thought. Looking down, she wiped her eyes. At her feet, the feather was long, white and perfect. Jessie bent and picked it up, and then looked around her. She searched for Finch, but it was early and the street was empty.

Red-eyed, Jessie arrived at the bus station and bought a ticket for a Greyhound Bus. She tried to explain where she needed to get to, and then tears came again. The counter clerk nodded, and slowly explained the route. Kansas was a big trip, and Jessie knew she didn't look like she was in great shape to make it.

Jessie had made up her mind; her unfinished business was with her mother. She thought of the song she'd written for her father and the hollow shell of the dream she'd had. *My mom deserved more*, she thought.

On the bus, she looked again at the address in Colonna. She wondered what Pasturelands might be, and what sort of condition her mother would be in when she got there.

Maybe it was rehab, not that her mother could afford that kind of gig. She thought back to her last conversation with her mother. Whatever state she found her mother in, Jessie told herself she needed to try and help.

Forty-Six

essie reached Colonna by a journey of three buses and a local cab. She spotted the sign for Pasturelands, and asked the driver to drop her at the end of the long drive. It was going to take her a few hundred yards to try and figure out what she was going to say to her mom. The dirt track was framed on both sides by a white painted fence. Ahead of her, a young colt raced toward her and then turned and charged away. The horse kicked its heels up and ran back to the mare that stood watching. Jessie smiled. The sight of such energy eased some of fatigue she felt. Without Bear, she seemed to get tired more quickly somehow.

The long ranch-style house was positioned perfectly in the landscape with its panoramic views. Its lawns were glossy green under powerful sprinklers that shot water in random directions. Up ahead, a giant pickup gleamed next to a shabby Hyundai. Jessie recognized the wreck instantly: it was her mother's car.

Jessie walked up the slope to the porch, pressed the doorbell and felt her finger tremble against the button. She wished Bear was with her. Through the frosted glass, she could see a dark-haired woman walking toward her. Taking a deep breath, she pulled her shoulders back and prepared to meet her mother, but when the door opened, her sister stood in front of her; she was fourteen years old but looked more like twenty. Mary was tall and her chestnut hair was piled up in a messy knot. For a long moment, they stared at each other.

"Oh my god, oh my god!" squealed Mary, suddenly a child again. They were in each other's arms in a heartbeat.

"Mary, look at you!" Jessie pulled back, laughing. "You're taller than me!"

In the kitchen doorway, a man appeared and waited for the shrieking to stop.

"Well, Mary, you going to introduce us to your friend?" the man smiled.

Jessie recognized him from the newspaper clipping. He was the fourth member of the Braves, the one that stayed behind.

"That ain't her friend, Gabe." The voice behind him was dry, sour. "That's her sister."

Corinne wore shorts and a vest, still holding a hand spade, with earth on her knees and hands. Her features were fuller than Jessie remembered. She'd pictured her as gray and haggard, but the woman in front of her looked tanned and healthy. Mitch had called her beautiful, and for the first time Jessie could understand what he'd seen.

"Hello Mom." Jessie tried to read her mother's face.

"Hello Jessie." Corinne put the garden tool on the kitchen counter. "You found your father yet?"

"Kinda," Jessie said. "I mean, I know his address. I got it from Mitch."

She thought about showing them the piece of paper, but then realized that wouldn't help.

"Mitch Hanrahan?" Gabe smiled. He looked at Corinne and then back at Jessie. "You talked to Mitch Hanrahan?" he said.

It was Corinne who spoke first. "And what else did Mitch tell you?" Her expression was unreadable. "He say what a fine guy old Billy J. is?"

"Mom," said Jessie, sighing. "Look, what do you want me to say...that I've carried a stupid dream about finding out that my father was some kind of superhero, and it turns out he was just a flake after all?"

Her mother raised her eyebrows. "Well Jessie, that ain't everything—but at least it's a start."

Mary turned to her mother.

"So can she stay then, Mom?" she said, "Mom, please?"

Her mother looked at Gabe and sighed.

"Well, I ain't going to turn my own daughter back out onto the street, am I?"

Corrine turned and walked back outside. Mary hugged Jessie hard enough to hurt.

Jessie hadn't expected an easy ride and didn't get one. She was given the guest room, and Mary and Gabe tried to make her feel welcome. Mary was at school during the day, so Jessie read magazines or made offers of help that her mother refused. Jessie knew Corinne wasn't exactly being unfriendly; it was more confusing than that. After thinking she knew exactly what her mother was like, now it was like she didn't know her mother at all.

Her mother seemed to expect her to be the Jessie that had left in a storm. Corinne was guarded around her, and even Gabe noticed it. A late-night conversation between them on the patio had carried up to Jessie's open window.

"I'm only saying, darlin', that Jessie's not what I expected." Gabe's tone was soothing. "And Mary seems to think the world of her."

"That's just the point, Gabe," said Corinne, "Mary worships her, just like Jessie idolized her father. One word from Jessie, and I'll lose Mary as well. Don't think I can't see that coming."

Gabe hesitated. "So can't people change? Decide they've messed things up?"

"You mean like me?"

"Corinne, it sounds like she's had things pretty tough, too." Gabe's voice was sad. "She's brave, but you know?" He sighed. "Maybe everyone deserves a break one time."

In her bedroom, Jessie's eyes filled with tears.

"So like all this?" Corinne said. "OK yes, for certain I got a break."

"Look, we both got a break, darlin'," he said. "When you called me that night, it was like a piece of magic happening. I'd never forgotten how I'd felt around you." He chuckled. "I couldn't get in that truck fast enough."

Corinne laughed. "And there I was, only calling to ask if you remembered me," she said. "And you drive across the state to come knockin' on my door at four in the morning."

"Yeah well, sometimes you just know not to let a

chance go by," Gabe said, and then waited a while. "I can't help thinking that you've got a chance here with Jessie, and it's a good one."

As they went quiet, Jessie wondered what her mother was thinking. She fell asleep still wondering.

Jessie got up early and found her mother in the kitchen smoking a cigarette. The coffee beside her was strong and black. *She looks tired*, Jessie thought.

"Thought you'd given up," Jessie said.

"One won't do any harm."

Corinne gazed at the saucer she was using as an ashtray. "Should open a window. Gabe doesn't like the smell."

Jessie walked over and undid the French doors.

"Mom, he seems great." She paused. "I mean, I know you probably know that."

"Yeah, I reckon he saved my life." Jessie couldn't tell if her mom was joking or not.

Corinne stubbed out the unfinished cigarette.

"You got yourself a man, Jessie?"

Jessie thought of Danny.

"Um…no," she faltered. "Not really. I mean, I guess not."

It was a simple enough question; why couldn't she answer it?

"Well, when you do you better choose well." Corinne looked at her. "Choose someone who deserves you, not some damn fool who doesn't."

It was the nearest thing to a compliment she could remember getting from her mother.

"Mom, did I tell you about Danny?" Maybe her mom would know what was going on in her head. The slightest thing seemed to trigger an idea of him, like music, or other people's hair, or soap.

"No, but it sounds like you should have," she said. "Come on, let's go and sit on the patio; it'll be warm out there soon."

As the warmth of the sun grew, Jessie told her mom some things about Danny, like how smart he was, and how easy he was to be around. Later, when everyone had left the house for the day, Jessie felt like she missed him quite a bit.

Forty-Seven

After talking to her mom on the patio, the atmosphere in the house was definitely a few shades lighter. Sometimes Jessie found her mom actually agreeing with her, which was kind of freaky. That same night Mary had said she'd wanted a lower back tattoo, and Jessie and her mom had exploded in unison. Then Gabe had walked in on them all shouting and laughed just as loud. Things weren't perfect, just a little easier somehow.

But this morning, Jessie had woken up with the feeling it was time to go. She found Mary in her bedroom trying to put on eye makeup the way that Jessie did. Jessie watched her from the doorway a while; she kept getting the black kohl in her eye and having to stop. Jessie told her sister that she'd stay on another few days, maybe a week, max.

"Where will you go?" Mary pouted and picked at her nail polish.

"Not sure. Back to Dorma for a while," said Jessie, thinking of Danny. "Or maybe Memphis. It depends."

Jessie moved over to the bed and sat down next to her sister. She was still getting used to Mary being taller than she was. Jessie remembered hugging her a lot when she was tiny and wished it felt so easy now. She picked up the kohl pencil that Mary had taken from her own room earlier.

"You're putting this on the inside of your eye, but you need to keep it outside. Look."

She pulled on her own cheek and drew a thick line close under her bottom eyelash.

"Should I come with you?" Her sister sounded uncertain. "It's just maybe I should leave Mom and Gabe alone." She paused. "They seem so happy when it's just the two of them."

"Hey, don't even think that," said Jessie, "Mom's heart would break if you left her now."

Jessie wondered if she should say something, maybe to Gabe.

"You think?" said Mary. "Sometimes I'm not so sure."

"Look, take it from me, Mom's happy because she's got what she always wanted: a real family. So don't go having any dumb thoughts about taking that from her."

Jessie tugged her sister's hair lightly. She wondered again what things would be like if she stayed, but she knew she could not.

"Jess?" Mary sounded fearful again. "Will you be coming back anytime?"

Jessie hugged her sister.

"Of course I will, Dumbo," she chuckled. "Someone's got to fix your terrible fashion sense."

Later, Jessie called Danny's apartment using Gabe's cell. She paced around the patio and wondered what she was going to say to him. She decided that telling the truth seemed to be working out pretty good these days, even if it did sometimes feel awkward. When she finally dialed the number, she put on her best telephone smile, but the voice that answered was female. Apparently Danny had left Dorma with no forwarding address. She found the number of the supermarket where he worked, but it was the same news.

In desperation, she called Ed, who thought she'd rung to wish him good luck at music college, and then couldn't figure out how she knew he was going to music college. Maybe it was a sign she should let ideas of Danny go, she thought.

In the days at her mom's house she'd realized that she really liked him. For a while she had felt confused; feelings were difficult things to figure out clearly. So she'd gotten a piece of paper and written down what she liked about him but only got as far as the first few lines because after writing, "hair, face, eyes, teeth, mouth, mouth, mouth," she wound up staring out of the window thinking about him. So now she'd called him and Danny had vanished, so that was that. She was probably setting herself up to get knocked back anyway.

The next day she sent a postcard to Mitch and Bella, saying that she was staying with her mom and she'd be back in a week or so. She also sent one to Hank and Peggy, saying that she'd visit them when she was in town again. It would be better to tell them about Bear in person. Besides, once in a while she actually liked to talk about him. The photograph of him made her smile more often than cry. It felt like some kind of progress.

The last few days at Pasturelands came really close to enjoyable. Jessie was more comfortable around her mother as they seemed to reach an understanding—not that everything was roses, but at least they both wanted things to be different and so they were. One night on the patio, Jessie asked her why she'd sent her the old cigar box. Mary had gone to bed, Gabe had gone into town, and it seemed like a last chance to talk.

"Yeah, I bet that surprised you some." Her mother shook her head.

"That kinda describes it..." Jessie said. "But why then, Mom?"

Corrine looked at her daughter and sighed. "It was the day I gave up drinking." Her voice was flat. "I just got sick of the past spilling over into the present. You were gone, just like him. I thought you probably deserved each other." Corinne stared into the distance. "The weird thing was that Gabe's face on those photos really stuck out at me. His smile shone out as the one good thing about all of them."

Jessie remembered the wedding photo, the band of four plus bride and groom.

"And the day I mailed the box was the same day I called Gabe," Corinne grinned and poked Jessie's arm. "Which, you have to admit, is the smartest thing your mother's ever done."

Jessie shook her head at the wonder of it. If a domino had been knocked over that day, then it was her mother's finger that had pushed it. In the trailer park, she'd been desperate for things to change, to get better somehow. She'd longed for a break from trailer life, but the journey of the last few weeks had been as tough as all her time living on her own. *Maybe something's different though,* she thought. She felt more alive, for one thing.

"Mitch says you used to write songs," Jessie said.

"Sure did," her mother nodded, "and played a mean fiddle. Betcha didn't know that either," she said.

"Fiddle?" Jessie wasn't sure if that was cool or not. It kinda was.

"Aaaah, Jessie," Corinne sighed. "There you were, off looking for a musical parent, and here I was the whole time."

Jessie stared at her mother; a tiny fraction of the hurt her mom had buried had been uncovered. *I deserted her just like he did.* Her voice choked.

"Mom…I really screwed up, didn't I?" She wondered how much of her mother's sorrow she had not seen, or had rewritten in her head.

"You know what, Jessie? I think we both did. But then, you could have gone on to Nashville, and instead you wound up here." Corrine smiled, but the tears in her eyes gave her away and her voice became a whisper. "And that really tells me all I ever needed to know."

They hugged a real hug, a good hug, crying and then laughing at the stupidity of it.

That night, Jessie dreamed one last time of her friend the scarecrow.

The picnic wasn't even started and she'd just poured him a cup of English tea using the lovely china teapot, but the scarecrow said he needed to go and fix a fence somewhere 'cause someone else needed the help. That might have been sad but instead he asked her what the weather was like inside her chest, so she looked down and the sun's rays still radiated the golden warmth out all over the picnic and the meadow beyond. Then someone somewhere over a rainbow sang, *"Weather inside, weather outside…"* and it was probably the scarecrow 'cause after that he handed her a weather map that meant the forecast would be sunny with occasional light showers, but if the sun still shone that would make a rainbow appear. Jessie tried to say thanks but with cake in her mouth it came out a bit garbled and made her cough, then laugh and then cough again.

She woke up in the guest bedroom. *Weather inside, weather outside,* she thought.

Forty-Eight

Jessie spent a lot of the trip back to Memphis thinking about Danny. She couldn't make up her mind. She moved from launching a full-scale manhunt, involving missing persons, to simply accepting fate and moving forward. By the time she arrived at the bus station, she'd given up trying to decide. She thought of calling Mitch to come and pick her up, but then she wouldn't get to walk down Beale. Besides, it would be nice to surprise him. As she approached, she could hear jovial jazz being played somewhere and smiled. *I'm back on Beale,* she thought.

Her reflection in the windows still looked odd to her: a young girl by herself. Sometimes she could feel Bear trotting behind her. It was nice, a strange kind of comfort. Outside the old Schwab Building, a group of Hare Krishna students were handing out leaflets. They rattled tambourines, thumped drums, and smiled at everything. With their vivid orange kaftans, they reminded her of Peggy's sunflower card. Only one of them hadn't shaved his head; instead, he'd tied his long glossy hair in a pristine top knot. She grinned and then laughed out loud. Finch.

"Namaste," Finch said, and bowed, then offered her a leaflet. She took it from him; it appeared to be an advert for soft drinks.

"Good to see you," Jessie smiled broadly. "You've taken a liking to Memphis, I see?"

"Indeed I have. I'll have fond reflections of this mystical place," he sounded melancholy, "but regrettably, I'm moving on."

He looked over at the cluster of shaven-headed students.

"Are you always traveling, Finch?"

"Well, it's more that my journey never really ends," he said, then nodded behind her. "I see you lost your own traveling partner." His eyes were sad.

"Bear's gone…he died…it's been awful. Anyway, now it's just me."

"You know the best cure for a broken heart is to love some more," Finch said. *I wonder if I can*, she thought.

"Are you with these guys now?" she said, looking at the students.

"Yes, I think I need to spend some time among people for a change," he said. "I can be a bit solitary sometimes."

"That rings some bells," she said. Finch raised a finger.

"Ah yes, that reminds me…" He reached into the folds of his robe and took out a small pair of Buddhist cymbals. "These are for you."

The cymbals were dull brass, linked with leather. Very gently, he knocked them against each other. They sang out a rich chime that seemed to resonate around Jessie's head and chest, a vibrating, echoing sound that blended, then folded in on itself, until she couldn't tell if the noise had actually gone.

"Beautiful…" she said, and took them from him. "I love them, Finch, thanks."

He tilted his head.

"They're enchanted, of course," he said. "It's a complex process, actually, to do with helping your heart to resonate with the universe, very healing for it—you'll figure it out."

"I'll sure try." She paused. *He should have it*, she thought. "Look, I sort of have something for you too," she said and dug into her jacket. "Would you know what to do with this?" In her palm, the emerald ring glinted in the sun. From his robe, Finch produced a white piece of silk, wrapped the ring inside and put it into his pocket, sighed, and smiled a sad smile.

Finch held up his palm and instinctively she put her own hand onto his. His hand was cool and soft, pure gentleness.

Jessie watched as he continued down the street. She wondered again about telling someone about Finch, but she knew that everyday magic, and life working from the inside out would sound strange to most people.

Jessie walked into Mitch's bar, and as her eyes adjusted to the daytime gloom, she could see Mitch at the back, talking to a supplier. On the table in front of him was a line of brightly-colored bottles. Mitch spotted her and paused mid-sentence.

"Here's my girl!" he jumped up, and strode over. "Bella!" he bellowed over his shoulder. "Jessie's back!"

As she dropped her bags, Jessie wondered how she

had come to deserve that moment. Mitch picked her up and hugged her tight, while behind him the sales rep watched with a bemused expression. Mitch put her down eventually.

"And so now maybe you can take your own phone calls?" He pulled business cards out of his pocket. "I'm running out of excuses for where you are." Jessie took the cards from him.

"Mitch, are these…?" She read the first once twice.

"You've got A&R guys from three major labels, plus some independents. You've got the local radio station breathing down my neck for an interview and a live session, plus a whiny, pain-in-the-ass reporter wanting to do a piece…" but Jessie was still staring at the Sony logo on the first card. "Well, go over them yourself first," he said. "I'll run you through the details later."

Jessie looked up, but before she could reply, Bella marched out of the kitchen covered in white powder. In an apron and high heels, she looked like she'd been in a flour fight.

"Jessie!" she squealed. "Well, thank the Lord, you're back!"

Bella made a half-hearted attempt to get rid of the mess and then hugged her anyway.

"We need another woman around the place. All these men are driving me crazy!"

"You've been in the kitchen, Bella?"

Jessie's eyes were like saucers; she'd never seen Bella do any work in the bar.

"It's a long story. We lost another chef. I'm in there trying to show Danny how to make tortillas."

Jessie stared at her.

Danny stood in the kitchen doorway, waiting for her to see him. His shaggy hair was powdered white as well. Unlike everyone else, he didn't seem pleased to see her. His frown was watchful, wary, and his forced smile didn't reach his eyes.

"You kids just gonna stare at each other?" Bella put her hands on her hips.

"Come on, Bella." Mitch nodded at the beverage guy. "This fella here's got some new fruit mixers we might be interested in." He took Bella firmly by the elbow and maneuvered her over to the rep.

Jessie walked a few paces toward Danny.

"Hey stranger," she said. "You missed me?"

It sounded corny as soon as she said it, but it was out now.

"You mean like when you've been sick and you get better?" His response didn't make sense to either of them.

"What's that supposed to mean?" Jessie said.

"Nothing."

"Pretty dumb nothing."

"Look, well... sorry," he said. "Anyway, are you back for good?"

"Whatever that means."

"Want me to go?"

"Danny, why on Earth would I want you to go?" Jessie felt confused. "Did I miss something?" she said.

Danny frowned. "Well actually, Jessie, yes, you did." He advanced a few steps, and spoke quietly. "You missed the fact that I'm crazy about you and can't bear the thought of not being with you," he said. "But then, you're kind of self-obsessed, so that doesn't actually surprise me." He sighed and shook his head. "Look, you make me feel like a lunatic."

Jessie's smile broke into a grin. "Danny Brewer, if that was any kind of proposition, I almost missed it." She took a step closer. "Lucky for you, I could only ever be with someone who had a bit of a lunatic in him."

"Jess, you're not fooling, are you?" Danny said.

"Don't think so," she said, and took the final step forward.

They stood almost touching. She put her hand into his. *That feels pretty normal.* There were no fireworks, no sudden rush of feeling, just the gentle sense that this was all right. As Danny's fingers curled gently around hers, maybe it was even better than all right. *And maybe that's up to me,* she thought.

Jessie risked a glance over to Bella and the big man. Mitch grinned and raised one of the mixers in a toast; he checked the label.

"Hey guys," he called over, "Feathered Fizzes—will this stuff sell or not?"

Jessie got the feeling it would.

E N D

Acknowledgments

Someone once told me that it takes a community the size of a small village to bring a novel into production and for me that has become true. So many people have assisted this book's journey, in small ways, big ways and, frankly, 'sideways' ways. In particular, I am grateful for the help, guidance and support of the following; Hilary Achauer, Neil Clarke, Natalia Colman, Hannah Davis, Philipa Donovan, Roger Ellory, Jon Finch, Jo Fraser, Lucy Fryer, Leslie Gardner, Peggy Gibson, Hilary Johnson, Mayapriya Long, Kris Manvell, Trish Miller, Andrew Morris, Michael J Motley, Bill Murtha, Carol Smith, Cathryn Summer Hayes, Garry Prior, Holly Beth Vincent, Xanthe Wells, Frances White, Kathy Williams.

Royalties to charity

Proceeds from the sale of this book will support charities which provide food, shelter and education for street children and orphans, including:

Children of Mother Earth (COME International)

Ramana's Garden Children's Home (sayyesnow)

Food for Life Vrindavan (FFLVrindavan)

About the Author

A bit like Finch, Julie Starr shows up in different worlds in different guises. Wearing slippers as she works, she writes novels, short stories, verses and lyrics, because if she doesn't, her head fills up with the noise of them. In the world of business she turns up as an executive coach and mentor, wearing high heels and an appropriately serious expression. Julie has three books published on coaching and mentoring, and those have been translated into many languages.

Wellingtons are also favorite footwear of choice, to walk across muddy Cotswold fields and lanes, musing generally about stuff. During winter months, you might bump into to her wearing sandals, wandering around sacred sites in India, as part of an on-going quest towards enlightenment (or peace and quiet—either would be brilliant).

She has a husband, step son and two dogs—all of which have proved un-trainable.

For more writings and chat, speculation and debate, check out ruffdogbooks.com